INTO THE FLAMES

··

JENNIFER BERNARD

Publisher's Note: This is a work of fiction. Names, characters, places, and incidents are a product of the author's imagination. Locales and public names are sometimes used for atmospheric purposes. Any resemblance to actual people, living or dead, or to businesses, companies, events, institutions, or locales is completely coincidental.

Book Layout ©2017 BookDesignTemplates.com

Into the Flames/Jennifer Bernard. -- 1st ed.
ISBN 978-1-945944-15-4

For my wonderful readers. Thank you for all that you do.

CHAPTER 1

Brianna Gallagher anxiously adjusted her new blouse and scanned the cocktail-hour crowd gathered on the terrace at the Seaview Inn. Her date was waiting for her somewhere in that group, and once again she'd dressed all wrong. Why didn't they teach "dating basics" in school? What to wear, what to talk about. Apparently plant hybridization and the dangers of the lack of biodiversity didn't cut it.

Yup, she'd learned that the hard way, watching Denny Benson's eyes glaze over the last time she was here on a date at the Seaview.

Shake it off. New day, new date. A blind date, in this case. This was a new thing her friends were trying. The element of surprise supposedly added a special twist of fun, like a wrapped Christmas present. This particular date had been set up by her friend at the hardware store.

"He's perfect for you," Gretchen had insisted. "He's strong, he's kind, he's good-looking, he's outdoorsy, he's good with his hands. And he's new in town. He claims he's not looking for a relationship, but I talked him into drinks at the Seaview with my awesome friend. So just go! Give it a chance!"

Stay positive, she reminded herself. This was supposed to be *fun.* She was sick and tired of being everyone's adorable little friend. At twenty-eight, you really didn't qualify for the word "adorable" anymore.

As she took in the inn's sophisticated Chardonnay-at-sunset crowd, the men in suit jackets, the women in flirty cocktail dresses with pashminas against the November chill, her heart sank.

Overalls, even made from raw silk the color of sage leaves, were not a good choice. She probably looked like a wood elf. And why had she worn a billowing, puffy-sleeved blouse under the overalls? She probably looked like a *pirate* wood elf. A tiny pirate elf about to stab herself with a fork.

She could practically feel herself shrinking as she stood there amid the laughter and chatter. Desperate measures were called for. As a smallish person, she'd learned a few tips over the years. "Superman pose" was one of her favorites. It always made her feel bigger and more in command. After all, she was a strong person used to digging in the dirt and moving flagstones with her bare hands. Could any of these people here move as many wheelbarrows of mulch as she could? She didn't think so.

She spread her feet apart and planted her fists on her hips. Puffed out her chest. Lifted her chin. Silently roared. *I am a strong and confident woman. I deserve to be here.*

"Ahoy, matey," said a deep, rumbling voice from somewhere over her head. *Way* over her head. "Should we board first or fire a warning shot?"

She snapped her head up to see her friend Rollo gazing down at her, a grin splitting his bearded face. Rollo Wareham was one of the new Jupiter Point Hotshots, the wildfire fighters who had recently moved into the Fire and Rescue compound. They'd gotten to be close friends, and he was guaranteed to tease her about this.

"Excuse me?"

"You look like Peter Pan about to take on Captain Hook. Like you need a cutlass between your teeth."

Forlornly, Brianna relaxed her stance. So much for Superman pose. "You'd better be glad I don't have a cutlass right now," she muttered.

His expression shifted. The laughter drained from his blue eyes, which she'd always thought of as unusually kind and soulful. "I'm sorry. I didn't mean it as an insult. You want to board the Seaview, I'm right behind you. I got your back."

She waved off his apology. "Eh, don't worry about it. I'd rather be Peter Pan than Tinkerbell. And yes, believe it or not, I have been compared to Tinkerbell. Ridiculous, I know." Even though she'd grown into a normal-sized, if small, person, as a kid she'd been flat-out tiny. When she was eight, she'd given in to her mother's longing and dressed as Tinkerbell for Halloween. No one in Jupiter Point had ever let her forget that.

Rollo grinned, shaking his head. "Tinkerbell is always misrepresented. She's tiny but fierce. So, what brings you here tonight—" He broke off suddenly. "Wait a minute...are you here for..."

The same thought struck Brianna at exactly the same time. "You aren't here to meet..."

"...a blind date..."

"Are you?"

They stared at each other, then both burst out laughing. Rollo laughed until a tear came to his eye. It might have bothered Brianna if she hadn't been laughing just as hard.

"Third time this month," she finally gasped. "What is wrong with everyone in this town?" Twice before, friends had thrown them together in very obvious match-making attempts. Once at a party, once during a double-date. "Don't they know we're friends? Oh, and Gretchen said my date's name is Roscoe."

"That's closer than she usually gets with my name. Once she called me Rob Lowe." Rollo ran one hand through his shaggy hair, which he'd brushed back from his face, making him look like a brown-haired Viking. "She staked a case of kitchen tiles on us being a perfect match. I guess I can relax now. Wish I hadn't bothered with this freakin' tie."

She surveyed him with frank appreciation. "Honestly, you look great, Rollo. It's too bad it's just me, because no sane woman could resist you." Rollo was a towering, wide-shouldered guy, built from solid, hard-packed muscle, and with his charcoal gray dress shirt and black trousers, set off with a silver-blue patterned tie that matched his eyes, he looked amazing.

"Thanks, Bri. You look..." His gaze swept over her outfit and he seemed to choke a little before he continued. "Adorable."

She rolled her eyes. "Don't bother, big guy. I know I look ridiculous. I saw this in a catalogue and thought, well, I know I look good in overalls because I wear them all day long. Honestly, I've never been let down by overalls before."

"I like the color," he volunteered helpfully. "Green. My favorite. I see a lot of green in my line of work."

"So do I. I guess we have that in common."

They smiled at each other. Honestly, she felt a lot better now that Rollo was here. There was something about his huge size and his kind eyes that she really liked. Not *liked* liked, of course. No, she and Rollo were friends; they could talk for hours about just about anything. She loved hanging out with him but the truth was, she had a hopeless crush on a different firefighter. She'd been hoping a date with someone else would distract her from that obsession.

He presented his hand to her. It was huge, like the paw of a bear. "Are you hungry? I'm starving. And honestly, I wasn't looking forward to sipping on a glass of wine and chitchatting before I could stuff food down my gullet."

"Are you asking me out?" she teased. "Because we already did this. Twice."

"Please don't turn me down. You're my favorite non-date of all time."

"And isn't that the story of my life," she grumbled. But she put her hand in his, amused by the way it completely engulfed hers, and followed the hostess to a corner table on the terrace.

CHAPTER 2

Rollo felt a lot better after a huge serving of pork chops, potatoes and applesauce—not to mention the two dark ales he'd downed in pretty short order. Of all people to end up on a non-date with, Brianna was at the top of the list. He always got a kick out of her, and she was pretty, too. All that flaming ginger hair, her small but perky body.

He'd known Brianna ever since his friend and crew superintendent Sean Marcus had gotten together with her friend Evie. Over the past few months they'd clicked as friends. They'd gone to the midnight movie horror show, shared giant jalapeño burgers at the Milky Way, hiked in the hills around Jupiter Point. She definitely deserved a real date with someone who could properly appreciate her in all her uniqueness.

But he wasn't in a position to date anyone. He'd tried to tell Gretchen that, but she was having none of it. "Nope, sorry. You're too delicious to stay single. How about two cases of tile?"

He washed down his last bite of potato with a long slug of beer and pushed his plate aside. He didn't have to put on an act with Brianna, which was a huge plus to hanging out with her. Maybe it was all the time she spent with plants and flowers, but she had an amazing ability to accept people as they were. With her, he never got the feeling that he should shave his beard and quit being a firefighter and move back east and marry a debutante and...

Eh. No need to repeat the last thousand conversations with his parents.

"So, Bri. You might as well tell me."

"Tell you what?" She glanced up from her braised chicken and dumplings. Another thing the two of them had in common was a hearty appreciation of food. How she managed to eat so much with that tiny frame of hers, he had no idea. She could probably ride on his shoulders and he wouldn't feel a thing.

"Who your secret crush is."

"*What?* Who told you that?" Her green eyes were wide with dismay, a flush coming and going in her cheeks. With a light spray of golden freckles across her cheekbones, she really was pretty.

"No one. Like I said, secret." He smiled smugly when she wrinkled her nose at him. "You can tell Uncle Rollo. I'm a master of keeping secrets."

"Back up, back up. What makes you think I have this alleged hidden crush?" She put down her fork, the sleeve of her blouse dragging through the gravy on her plate. He grabbed a napkin and dipped it in water, then lifted her arm so he could dab the soiled spot.

"Well, this is our third sort-of date and you haven't fallen in love with me yet. The only explanation is that you're into someone else."

She rolled her eyes, which he totally deserved. He wasn't any kind of player—not like Josh, who'd flirted his way through several states before finally falling hard for Brianna's friend Suzanne. Rollo was very careful who he got involved with because it could never go anywhere. That was one of the reasons he kept Brianna firmly in the friend zone. She was a great girl but he couldn't get involved.

"Whoever he is, he probably doesn't know you're into him. Because if he did, he'd snap you up."

She stared at him for a long moment, a look of delight slowly taking over her face. "Wow, Rollo. That was pretty nice of you."

He dipped this head in acknowledgement of her compliment. "So? Might as well spill the beans. Maybe I know the guy. I can put in a good word."

A wave of red crept from her neck, up her cheeks, all the way to her forehead. It was fascinating to watch, actually, and by the time she was done, her entire face glowed with color. With that blush, combined with her fiery hair, she could light the way through a forest.

"Rollo, just drop it. There's no point. He doesn't even know I exist. Just pretend I never said anything. Oh wait, I never *did* say anything."

"You're right, you're right. You didn't bring it up, and I don't want to put you on the spot. But Brianna, don't sell yourself short. You're a little hottie, and if you like this guy, you ought to at least give it a shot. As long as he deserves you. If he doesn't, I'll kick his ass."

"You can't kick his ass."

"I can kick everyone's ass." He said it matter-of-factly, because it was true. Not only was he big and tall, but the hotshot training regimen had made him incredibly strong. Guys were always trying to pick fights with him just for the challenge of it. It was extremely annoying.

"I don't *want* you to kick his ass. Actually, it's more like *you* don't want to kick his ass. You wouldn't want to, if you knew... Ack! We should stop talking about this. Now. Before I—" She clapped her hand over her mouth.

Rollo wanted to laugh out loud, but he didn't want to hurt her feelings again. He knew what she was about to say. Brianna was infamous for simply blurting things out. All kinds of things. She always meant well because she was a sweetheart, but she had a bull-in-a-china-shop quality. He liked that about her, because he liked anything that went against the grain. Brianna was always real, always herself. Even when dressed in some kind of strange green clown outfit and puffy sleeves.

He rested his forearms on the table and cupped his hands around her elbows. "I promise you, on the grave of my dear departed Brunhilda, that I will never tell a single living soul about any of this. We're in a cone of silence here."

Her eyebrows flexed and drew together at a quizzical slant. "Who's Brunhilda?"

"My Newfie. I had her ever since she was a puppy. She died when I was thirteen and broke my heart. When I vow on her grave, you know I'm serious."

"Brunhilda? Who names a dog Brunhilda?"

"That just proves you didn't know her. It suited her. But let's not get distracted. Back to you."

She let out a long sigh and turned her attention to her chicken. "Why are you pushing this?"

He leaned back in his chair and folded his arms across his chest. "Because I want to help you out here. Do you want to keep ending up on dates with *me*?"

She made a face meant to indicate that *of course* she didn't. He tried not to let that sting. He and Brianna were friends. And he intended to keep it that way. He didn't have a choice.

"If it helps, I have a pretty good guess about who it is," he told her. "You can just nod once if I'm right and shake your head if I'm wrong."

"I can't believe you're turning my awkward hopeless crush into a game."

"But that's the thing. I don't see why it has to be hopeless. There's always hope."

She gave him a sly look from under her eyelashes. "*Always*? I'm not so sure about that. I don't think I'm the only one at this table with a crush."

His jaw flexed and he was suddenly grateful for the beard covering half of his face. That thing made his expressions so much easier to conceal.

"You're bluffing," he said calmly. "You know nothing."

"You keep telling yourself that." Smugly, she dragged a bit of roll through her chicken gravy, once again putting her sleeve at risk. He reached across the table and held it up, as if it were a train on a wedding gown.

He eyed her carefully, wondering how much she actually knew or if she was just trying to throw him off. He hadn't said a word to anyone—well, who would he talk to, anyway? The hotshot crew? Hell no. His little sister? She had her own train wreck going on, and besides, she was only fourteen. He didn't need to be confiding his broken heart to a troubled teenage drama queen. Maybe he could use a friendly ear, or a friendly shoulder to cry on.

The world would not miss those green overalls if they got tear-soaked.

"There was someone—keyword, *was*—but my situation actually *is* hopeless. But I'll tell you if you tell me. That way we have mutually assured secrecy."

"Mutually assured secrecy?"

"Yup." He sat back and folded his arms over his chest. "Take it or leave it."

For a long moment, her green eyes searched his face. They were so pretty, those eyes, kind of a woodsy green. Like moss lit by the sun. Anything that reminded him of the woods was good, in his book. He'd grown up in Manhattan, with summers spent in Maine, and ever since he was little he'd lived for the Maine part of the equation.

Finally, she nodded. "Okay. I'll tell you if you tell me. But I already know yours, so it's hardly fair."

"It's very fair, because I already know yours too."

They narrowed their eyes at each other, like two suspicious super-spies in a standoff. Then Brianna burst out laughing. She had one of the most infectious belly laughs he'd ever heard. It always spread a warm feeling through his entire body.

"Fine." She planted her elbows on the table and leaned forward. "You, Mr. Rollo Wareham the Third, have been pining after Merry Warren."

Pining was overstating it. Really, it was more that Merry represented everything Rollington Wareham III couldn't have. He put a hand over his heart. "Direct hit."

At first she looked triumphant, but then her expression faded to sympathy. "I don't know, Rollo. You could have picked someone more...I don't know."

"What?"

"Possible, I guess."

He winced. Well, that was Brianna for you. Blunt. Tactless, you might even say.

"Merry's very focused on her job," Brianna was explaining softly. "I really don't think she dates much, if ever. She's very particular. I wish I could say it wasn't hopeless, but it might be in this case."

"You're not telling me anything new," he grumbled. "I asked her out, she shot me down, we never spoke of it again."

"She was embedded with the hotshots for a little while, right?"

"Yeah."

Merry was a reporter with the *Mercury News-Gazette*, and she'd spent two weeks with the Jupiter Point Hotshots, observing as they battled a huge wildfire in Montana. He'd watched over her the entire time, kept her Thermos filled with coffee, sacrificed his favorite pillow when she kept getting neck cramps from camping out. He'd offered her the last of his bug dope, even though he wound up covered with welts because he was extra sensitive to mosquito bites.

And...nothing. All of Merry's fierce, focused intelligence stayed squarely on her job. She observed, she took notes, she asked questions, she never got in the way, she never complained. She was perfect. And gorgeous, with her light brown skin and dark curls. Her warm maple-brown eyes never looked on him with anything other than friendliness.

Brianna was watching him with sympathy. "The unrequited thing sucks, doesn't it?"

He shrugged. " So, you and...just guessing here...Finn."

Her face turned bright red instantly, as if she were choking on something. "You know?"

"I told you I knew."

It was hard to miss the way she clammed up and acted so awkward when Finn Abrams was around. He'd jumped to the obvious conclusion.

"Who else knows?" she managed.

He shrugged. "No idea. It's never come up. Everyone's exhausted at the end of the fire season. Sean and Josh are all sappy and in love. I wouldn't worry about it."

"Does he know?"

"Nah. I doubt it. Finn is...well, he's going through a rough time. He's got a lot on his mind."

"I know. It's so tragic, with the fire and his burns and all." She sighed, a long, wistful sound, and gazed off into the distance, over the terrace ironwork railings to the Pacific Ocean. The red glow from the tall propane heater on the terrace gave her a flushed look.

Or maybe the thought of Finn did that to her.

"He's so...he's so..." She set her chin on her cupped hand and sighed again. Her eyes went all dreamy and unfocused. And despite himself, he felt kind of jealous that someone as cool as Brianna was pining over his friend.

"Brianna?"

She didn't answer, completely lost in her Finn fantasy. It must be a good one, to make her blush like that...

CHAPTER 3

Brianna would never forget the first moment she ran into Finn Abrams. It was an accident—literally. She'd been doing her annual fall cleanup of the gardens at the Goodnight Moon B&B. She'd been trundling a wheelbarrow of wood chips down the path toward the bed of hydrangeas that needed an extra layer of mulch. The most handsome man in the world had stepped onto the winding brickwork path.

He was so romantic-looking, with dark curls tumbling over his forehead and his lean, brooding face, with those hollows under his cheekbones and shadowed, troubled eyes. Instantly, she wanted to brush his hair away from his face and pepper kisses on those full, unsmiling lips. Chase all the darkness from his expression.

She'd tripped over a brick, or maybe it was her own tongue, and lost control of the wheelbarrow. The next thing she knew, she was dumping wood chips all over his shoes. And his legs, which were bare below his khaki shorts. And then he lost his balance and she had to drop the wheelbarrow, which hit him in the bare shin. Then she rushed around to help him up, wading through the pile of wood chips to get to him.

When she reached him, he turned his face her way, and that was when *she* lost her balance and wound up on her butt in a pile of mulch. One side of his face was perfect, the other a red, angry, raised mass of burns.

"I…I'm so sorry," she'd stammered. "You surprised me. I mean, not because of your face…I mean, yes, because of your face but not *that* side of your face, I didn't even see it at first, and oh God, that's not even what I mean…" She buried her face in her hands and inhaled wood dust. Started coughing. Couldn't stop.

Finally the man extracted himself from the pile of wood chips and stood up. He was actually smiling—she thought, although the film of dust clogging her vision made it hard to tell.

"Thank you," he said sincerely. "Getting knocked over by a wheelbarrow is turning out to be the highlight of my day. Are you okay?"

"Yes." She coughed up some dust. "Are you? What about your shin?"

She watched with hopeless lust as he bent down to check out the red mark on his leg. He was movie-star handsome, even with the burn scars on his face.

"It's nothing," he told her, offering his hand to help her up. "Let me help you with your load here."

"No, no, I couldn't let you do that. You're staying here, right?"

"Yes, I'm Finn Abrams." He shook her hand once she'd made it to an upright position.

"Brianna Gallagher. I'm really sorry, again. I don't usually mow down the guests at the Goodnight Moon."

He brushed a wood chip off her shoulder and gave her a half-smile. "They don't know what they're missing."

Just then a woman sauntered toward them. At first Brianna thought she was Gwyneth Paltrow, she was so tall, her hair so blond and perfectly windblown. Later, she found out it was Annika Poole, actress and rising star. "Finn? Is everything okay?"

She reached the two of them and took Finn's arm and surveyed the scene with a vaguely perplexed expression. Brianna felt paralyzed under her distant scrutiny, as if she were a garden gnome. She wanted to explain, but had no idea where to start. *The sight of your boyfriend made me lose all muscle control and dump a load of mulch on his boots?*

No, definitely not.

"I'll…uh, clean this up," she said instead. "I just have to get my spade. Please don't worry about this mess, it'll be gone before you know it."

"It'd be a lot quicker with two of us." Finn frowned. But the willowy blond whispered something in his ear, and he made a face. "Sorry. I forgot we're already late for something."

"Really, I'm fine. Don't even worry about it."

The stunningly gorgeous pair turned to go, while she got busy picking wood chips out of her bra. Sadly, Finn chose the worst possible moment to turn back and caught her with her hand down her shirt. He pretended not to notice, but by the speed with which he steered the blond down the path, she knew he had.

Yeah, not the best first impression.

"Brianna!"

She jumped. Finally, Rollo's voice broke through her trance. "Sorry. What were you saying? I was a little...distracted."

"Look, Bri. The thing about Finn is—"

"I know I don't have a chance with Finn!" she cried. "I'm like..." She picked up a bit of potato from her plate. "A potato. And he's...I don't know...arugula."

"What?"

"Okay, maybe watercress."

He half-closed one eye and tilted his head. Then he scratched at his jaw, as if he was trying to mask a laugh. "This vegetable analogy is not really working for me. I have no idea what you're getting at."

"Okay, I'll spell it out. I'm *ordinary*. I don't have one ounce of glamour in me. But Finn is...romantic and tortured and brooding."

"Like watercress?"

She flounced back in her seat. That was the problem with spending all your time in the plant world. You thought of everything in botanical terms. "Fine, pick some other vegetable."

Finally he lost it and started laughing, the deep rumbles rolling from his huge chest, creases fanning from his eyes. "You're priceless, Brianna. If Finn had any sense, he'd be begging you to go out with him."

"Well, he's not. He's a little busy with his supermodel-movie star girlfriend."

Rollo made a face, shrugging that off with a flick of his endlessly broad shoulders. "Girlfriend is stretching it."

"Not helping."

"Will it help if I point out that everyone loves potatoes? What about French fries? Scalloped potatoes? Hash browns?"

"No." She looked at her hands, which she was twisting in her lap. Now she felt like crying. The whole thing with Finn was so hopeless. She'd tried to shake it off, but so far nothing had worked. None of these dates—blind or otherwise—made her forget about him. "I think the problem is me. I have no…game. No moves. No mojo. At least not when it comes to men. I'm always the friend. And that's fine, but…"

Once, just once, she'd like to be adored. She'd like a man to look at her the way Sean looked at Evie, the way Josh looked at Suzanne. As if she was beautiful and *essential*.

She lifted her eyes to meet Rollo's. Genuine kindness shone from their blue depths. She hoped to God it wasn't actually pity, because she didn't want that. Not for a second. She'd rather dive into a vat of wood chips than suffer through someone feeling sorry for her.

"Maybe…" Rollo paused, stroking his beard. Not all guys could pull off a beard like his, but it suited his bear-like build and thick head of walnut hair. "Maybe we can help each other."

"What do you mean?"

"I know Finn well. He's a good friend from our Fighting Scorpion days back in Colorado. He's actually staying with me for a few months. He's working on the screenplay for the Big Canyon movie. He claims he's going to help me fix up my house."

"Fix up your—oh, right. I forgot that you bought that house up on the cliffs. The Harringtons'."

"Yup. Escrow just closed and I'm moving in. Finn's taking over the guesthouse. The place doesn't need much, but he swears he's going to help out. Anyway, I think that if Finn spent time with you, he'd start to see what an outstanding person you are."

"Well, that's nice…" She actually felt her face heating from his compliment. Rollo was such a good guy. A really great friend.

"The one thing really missing at the house is some decent landscaping. I'm thinking about a koi pond."

"Are you really?"

"Fuck no. Never saw the point of koi. But I'll do it, if that helps you out. You need a reason to be around. Like I said, Finn's going through some heavy stuff. The burnover was tough on all of us, but it was the worst for him."

"Didn't you break your leg in three places?"

"Yes." He moved quickly past that, like someone who didn't like anyone feeling bad for him. "Point is, he's hurting right now. And he's under a lot of pressure. He could use a cute little Peter Pan-Tinkerbell type to make him smile. And I think if you were around, he'd start to see your true magnificence."

She snorted. Magnificence? Yeah right. "And what about *your* crush?"

"Eh, forget it." He scrubbed one big hand through his hair. "She doesn't want to get tangled up with me."

"Quid pro quo. If you're going to do a koi pond for me, I have to hold up my end."

"It's pointless. She's not interested and I have…a lot going on."

Somehow she got the impression he wasn't telling her everything.

"Once she knows you more, she'll love you just like the rest of us." Brianna couldn't actually remember a single time Merry had even mentioned Rollo. But Suzanne loved him, because he'd carried Josh out of a wildfire. And Evie loved him because he always, always had Sean's back. Everyone who *knew* Rollo loved him.

Why not Merry?

"We just have to figure out the way to her heart." She pondered, already relishing the challenge.

"How?"

She shrugged. "I'll just ask. Everyone knows how tactless I am. She grinned at the big man across the table from her. "Piece of cake."

"That easy, huh?"

23

"No, I was thinking we should have some cake. Have you ever tried their Chocolate Magma Cake?"

One great thing—among many—about Rollo was that she didn't have to hide her appetite around him. There was something to be said for a guy who was always up for dessert.

CHAPTER 4

A little over a year ago, Rollo and the rest of his team of hotshots had been trapped in a burnover in Big Canyon. A ferocious wildfire, moving faster than seemed possible, had simply run over them. For fifteen minutes the crew of nineteen hotshots—minus Finn, who'd taken off on his own instead of deploying his shelter—huddled inside their thin aluminum tents. The sounds of the firestorm outside—a tree exploding, the hiss of sap boiling, the fire-generated wind currents—warned Rollo there was a strong chance he'd die.

His life had done the proverbial flash-before-your-eyes routine. All of his twenty-nine years had unscrolled in his mind as if he was saying goodbye to it all. And in his heart, he was. Sean, the team leader, had tried some black humor to keep the panic at bay. It turned into a game of "if we make it out of this alive." Rollo had joked that if he survived, he'd get a job as a CPA. Safer, right? Funny, haha. Except that in those howling fiery winds, he heard his real doom.

If he made it out alive, his family would jump at the chance to make him quit firefighting. His days of freedom would be over. Goodbye hotshots, hello boardroom.

Members of the Wareham family didn't risk their lives in the wilderness. They didn't camp out on the fire lines until they stank of smoke and sweat. They didn't grow beards. No, they enjoyed their trust funds while they made more money for the Wareham Group. They attended top-tier social events and married other Mayflower descendants. That was his destiny, and he'd only managed to avoid that soul-crushing existence because he'd made an agreement.

He could live his own life until he turned thirty. Then the bill would come due.

Last month, he'd passed that landmark. He'd celebrated his thirtieth birthday getting drunk at Barstow's Brews with the guys. He told no one it was his birthday. He didn't tell anyone what it meant. He got wasted and told firefighting stories and soaked up every second of his last moments of freedom. He also wound up in a lengthy, fuzzy conversation with Craig Harrington, who was trying to unload his house.

Oops.

The next morning, the first email from his mother came.

When are you coming home, Rollington? Shall I have tickets booked for you?

Not yet. There's a hitch. I seem to have bought a house.

His phone rang immediately, but he stuck to email. *You can pull your matchmaker act long distance, can't you?*

You can't back out of this.

I'm not backing out. I'm quitting the hotshots. I'm giving you free rein to find someone eligible. But I'm staying in Jupiter Point. Nothing in the agreement says I can't.

She didn't like it, but she adapted pretty quickly. Ever since then, she'd been introducing him to likely candidates by email.

Lately, every morning he woke up to an email from Cornelia Nesmith. She was the first prospect who seemed halfway compatible with him.

On the morning after his non-date with Brianna, Rollo checked his email and saw that Cornelia had sent him a photo of herself jogging with her golden retriever in Central Park. She had a dog—that counted for a lot in his book. She also had thick honey-blond hair and a perky figure. A guy could do worse, he supposed.

He sent her back a quick note, then read an email from his brother, Brent. Lucky for Rollo, Brent had gone to business school and loved everything about the world of high finance. Rollo got copied on all the important board meetings and votes, but he was happy to leave the business side of things to his brother. The guy was a champ when it came to that stuff.

When he'd finished with his emails, he pulled on his running gear and ambled through his new house.

It still seemed strange that he owned a house. It was even stranger that a house he'd bought sight unseen while drunk on his thirtieth birthday would be so perfect for him. But it was.

It was an open, airy structure with vaulted ceilings, almost like a barn. With his height, he needed high ceilings, and these soared far over his head. The big picture windows looked out on a sloping lawn that dipped toward a retaining wall at the edge of a bluff. Just below, the ocean churned against a wall of rock.

Rollo got some coffee going and stared for a while out the window. This early in the morning, the sky over the Pacific glowed a gentle shade of lilac. He loved looking out over the ocean—possibly because it faced west, away from the Wareham clan.

A few minutes later, he knocked on the door of the guesthouse where Finn was staying. After a few curses and thumps, his friend cracked open the door. Rollo thrust a giant mug of coffee at him. The fragrant steam floated through the air, making Finn's bleary eyes brighten.

"Dude. You're a lifesaver."

"Late night?"

"Yeah. This screenwriting gig is for shit." He opened the door farther, letting Rollo come inside.

The guesthouse was so small he had to duck and turn sideways to enter. All the furniture had been left by the previous owners, who seemed to have had an obsession with flowery prints. He settled into a wingback armchair with an antique rose print and slung his feet onto the coffee table.

Finn, dressed in sweats and a t-shirt that read, "We find them hot and leave them wet," shoved aside the sleeping bag on the couch and sat down to put on his running shoes.

For a moment, Rollo wondered what about Finn got Brianna so dreamy. To him, Finn was just a guy. A good guy, hard worker and competent fireman. And sure, maybe better-looking than the average dude. Rumor had it he'd done a few commercials before he got into wildland firefighting. And before his face got scarred in the burnover.

Something had gone wrong during the burnover. He'd panicked and split. He'd survived on his own by taking shelter in a gravel streambed. No one really knew why he'd taken off, and some of the guys still hadn't forgiven him. Sean, for instance.

But Rollo didn't feel that way. In his view, no one was perfect, everyone fucked up once in a while, and everyone deserved another chance. The list of his own fuck-ups—that would take weeks to explain.

"How's it coming?" he asked Finn now, as his friend laced up his shoes.

"Oh, pretty damn fucking great. I wrote two pages."

That didn't sound like much to Rollo, but what did he know? "Um...way to go?"

"I ditched them. They were total crap." He drained half the mug of coffee, then sprang to his feet. "You ready to go?"

"Yup."

With Rollo taking the lead, they jogged along the narrow trail that hugged the cliffs. The morning light had a pearly, misty quality, with the sun still hidden behind the hills to the east. This footpath was one of the best things about the Harrington house. It went all the way down the cliffs into the valley, where a little subdivision nestled. In fact, Brianna lived down there somewhere in a log cabin.

The thought of her bright face made him smile. Maybe they should jog down to her place and surprise her. It could be step one in the process of getting her and Finn together.

Nah. He dismissed the thought as soon as it appeared. He glanced back at Finn, who was frowning at his feet with that dark look that came over him now and then. Brianna and Finn...he just couldn't see them together. Or maybe he just didn't want to.

His phone pinged. It had to be one of his family members. They were the only ones who called this early. When would they ever learn that the West Coast was three hours behind? Of course they *knew*. They just didn't care. As his mother said once, "Is it my fault you moved to a different time zone?"

He dug it out of his back pocket and checked the readout. The message was from Sidney, his little sister and the only member of his family who didn't piss him off every time they spoke.

Momster says you didn't go to clubs until you were 18 and I know that's BS why does she lie to me does she think I'm stupid?

He jammed his phone back in his pocket to focus on the grassy trail under his feet.

"Problem?" Finn asked from behind him.

"Sister. Nothing urgent. The teenage drama can wait until after my run."

Finn grunted, and they picked up the pace. "Thought it might be your date from last night."

"Nah."

"Bust?"

Rollo's turn to grunt. He wouldn't call it a "bust," exactly. The time always flew with Brianna. He got such a kick out of her. And then there was the deal they'd come up with. Speaking of which... "By the way, I hired a landscaper, so if you see a cute little redhead around, be nice."

"Cute little redhead? Single?"

"Yup. Word is she likes the dark and broody type."

"Not for me, dude. I'm talking about you. It's the off-season, you just bought a house, it's time you met the right girl."

Rollo picked up the pace even more. "If my mother paid you to say that, I'm fucking evicting you."

Finn laughed. "Anyone ever tell you you're an easy target? Damn, relax, Money."

Rollo ran even faster, until the margins of the trail slipped by in a soft green blur. The hotshots called him by two nicknames, Iron Man and Money. Iron Man because he had a knack for tech, and Money because of being a Wareham. He despised the nickname Money. At a bar in Montana, after too many beers, he'd nearly beaten up a guy on another crew for using that nickname. His guys had held him back.

"Whatever you say, *Hollywood*. So, about those two crappy pages you wrote..."

Finn snorted. "You know what I don't understand? Why everyone thinks you're so damn nice. Tell them to come talk to me, I'll straighten them out."

Rollo chuckled. Finn had a point there.

His phone buzzed again. This time, he ignored it. If Sidney wanted to vent, he'd listen, of course. But it would have to wait until he wasn't hurtling down a rocky slope alongside a steep drop-off. It was crazy to be running here. But to be a hotshot, you had to be a little bit crazy.

Back at the house, Finn retreated to the guesthouse to hammer at the screenplay some more, but Rollo felt the need for more exercise. He spent some time with his punching bag, which he'd set up in the lower-level den of the house. He needed to punch something. But it couldn't be a person. He was too big and powerful. Striking a blow that could hurt another human being...he'd done that once too often as a rebellious kid.

He was never going to let that happen again.

After his session with the punching bag, when he was dripping with sweat, he finally remembered Sidney's text. He checked his phone and saw that she'd sent a stream of emojis. He saw an animated turd, two crying eyeballs, a dancing hot pepper, a whole bunch of screaming faces.

Bad burrito? Fight with her best friend? Who knew?

He texted back an audio clip of happy birds chirping. Guaranteed to piss her off, but make her laugh at the same time.

All joking aside, he worried about Sidney. She'd gotten kicked out of two schools in the past two years. His parents kept sending her to new and different psychiatrists. But nothing seemed to help. His parents kept asking him to talk to her, but what could he say?

Yeah, I know your life is shit right now, but things will get better, so just hang on and don't do any kind of permanent damage like I did.

Yeah, maybe not.

CHAPTER 5

Brianna showed up mid-morning, while Rollo was trying to answer another email from Cornelia. He dropped it with deep relief.

As he opened the door, he grinned at Brianna so happily that she looked startled. "What's up with you?"

"Nothing. Ready for a break, that's all."

She glanced around the front yard, her eyes all lit up. A blue bandanna held back her bright hair and she had a smudge of dirt on her cheek. "I love this house, I can't believe I get to work on it. Seriously, you don't even have to pay me."

"Of course I'm going to pay you," he grumbled. "Don't be ridiculous."

As far as he knew, Brianna didn't know he was "Money" Wareham because he never talked about that part of his life. But he would never not pay someone for their work. His mother used to pull crap like that; if a jeweler or a tailor didn't produce something exactly to her specifications, she'd refuse to pay, no matter how unreasonable her demands. Rollo despised that attitude.

He let her in and quickly closed the door before Finn spotted her. They needed to prepare for this encounter.

"Are you thirsty? Want a drink?"

"Mostly I'm just nervous," she admitted. "I know it's silly but I can't help it. I'll take a drink, but really it's just a delaying tactic."

Smiling at her Brianna bluntness, he went to the fridge and they surveyed the options. "Red Bull, beer, Vitamin water?"

She bent to peer under his arm, then shook her head. "Never mind. I'm too nervous to drink anything."

He grabbed himself a Vitamin water and led her into the living room. She skipped to the window and stared in the direction of the guesthouse. Too bad he didn't have any herbal tea or maybe some tranquilizers. He'd never seen her so nervous.

"I know you're used to seeing me as a normal, semi-functional adult," she told him. "The only reason I'm letting you see this side of me is that I trust you."

He toasted her with the bottle of water. "I'm touched. I really am."

She exhaled a long breath, jittering back and forth from one foot to the other. "Neurotic question number one. Do I look okay?"

He scanned her, trying to see her through Finn's eyes. In her usual work clothes of grubby trousers and a blue checkered flannel shirt, she looked a lot more comfortable than she had last night. She looked great to him. But Finn had grown up in Hollywood and was used to models and actresses.

"You look great, for someone who's going to dig up my yard."

She frowned at him, pushing up her sleeves to reveal firm, freckled forearms. "This is what I always wear to work."

He looked her up and down. "Can you, I don't know," he gestured vaguely at her waist, "tie it up or something?"

A bit self-consciously, she undid the lower buttons of her shirt and tied the tails around her waist. Her very tidy, trim waist, he noticed. Despite the fact that they were just friends, he felt attraction tug at him.

Dammit. He couldn't be attracted to Brianna. Their friendship was a solid, bright light in his life. Besides, she had a crush on his friend. Also, he was supposed to be romancing Cornelia Nesmith. Jesus, how many more reasons did he need?

"Better." He cleared his throat. "What do you have on underneath?"

"Excuse me?"

"It looks like a, you know, a camisole type of thing. Can you ditch the shirt and just wear that?"

Her eyebrows lifted and she planted her hands on her hips. "It's November. You want me to go around in my undershirt? What about my bra, should I get rid of that too?"

Ugh, he really wished she hadn't mentioned the bra. Now he could actually picture her in just a bra, maybe a red one to match her hair.

What was going on? He'd never gotten turned on in Brianna's presence before. What was different now? Was it because he was paying closer attention to her than he ever had before—on Finn's behalf, of course?

Whatever. He had a job to do here. "Leave your bra on. Take the other shirt off. We won't be outside that long. You're just trying to get his attention, that's all. Men like skin, didn't you know that?"

Brianna cocked her head, looking thoughtful. "Men like skin," she repeated seriously, as if writing it down in a mental notebook. "Including goose bumps? Because there's a wind coming off the ocean right now."

Rollo felt a laugh welling up in his chest. "Just offering advice. Take it or leave it."

"Fine."

She untied her flannel shirt, unbuttoned it, and slid it off her body. Even though her manner was completely practical and not at all designed for seduction, his cock had the predictable reaction. Brianna's skin looked as if a fairy had scattered gold dust over her. Her arms were firm and muscled, her hands strong and capable. She was half pixie, half tomboy, and entirely, surprisingly delectable.

"Happy?"

Rollo nodded, not entirely trusting his voice. Yeah, no...attraction to Brianna was definitely not a good idea. He dug his phone out of his pocket, ready to dial Finn.

"What are you doing?" Brianna flew to his side and grabbed the phone out of his hand.

"Uh...calling Finn. That's the whole point, right?"

"No! I mean, it needs to look natural. Not like you're setting it up."

"It will. I'm going to ask for his advice about where to put the koi pond. He knows more about that shit than I do, he's from LA."

"Look, just...humor me. Let's go out there and we'll talk about the pond placement. Then if he sees us and wants to come out, he can."

"You're making this too complicated."

"Please. Come on." She stuffed his phone back in his pocket.

Oh hell. Her hand was so close to his package, and he was still half-aroused by the whole bra thing. He swallowed and held himself still.

She grabbed his hand and tugged him toward his front door. She might be small, but she was strong, and he found himself trailing after her. It amused him—no one pushed him around. He'd never lost a fistfight in his entire life. But petite, redheaded Brianna was now towing him toward his own front door like a tugboat steering an ocean liner.

He gave in and followed her outside. The ocean looked like a magic carpet of sparkles under the midmorning sun.

"How much does a place like this cost, anyway?" Brianna mused as they walked in the direction of the guesthouse. "Sorry, that's a rude question, isn't it? Forget I said that."

Rollo didn't answer. If she really wanted to know, the information was public. But he wasn't about to spill the beans.

Brianna kept going. "I keep forgetting you're like some kind of millionaire. You seem so normal. I mean, you have like, nothing in your refrigerator. Shouldn't a millionaire have more food than that? Or do you just order takeout all the time? Maybe you should keep a chef."

Rollo reached out and snagged her upper arm. "Hang on. You knew?"

She turned her open, pretty face toward him. "Knew what?"

"About the...well, the millionaire thing."

"Sure. Is it supposed to be secret? Everyone knows you have a big trust fund. How else would you be able to buy a house like this?"

Rollo grunted, annoyed at his own naïveté. As a hotshot, he mostly spent time with his crew, who knew him the way you know a well-broken-in pair of boots. He forgot about things like town gossip. "I could have saved up."

A smile quivered in the corners of her mouth. "This is prime real estate, bud. That's the Pacific Ocean right there, in case you hadn't noticed. I'm sure you hotshots get paid well, but not that well. It's okay, no one holds it against you that you're loaded. Well, Merry might."

"Really?"

"Yeah. I think her mom was someone's housekeeper. She has a grudge against wealthy people."

Great. It figured he'd go for the one woman for whom his trust fund was a black mark against him.

"But don't worry. I have some ideas, and I'm working on it." She gave him an encouraging smile.

"Could you please drop that whole thing? I'm begging you."

"No way! I want you to be happy, and you never look completely happy. You need the right woman in your life and that's where I come in."

He gave a double-take. Her cheeks flamed.

"I mean, to *find* the right woman. Not to *be* the right—oh, you know what I meant." She gave him a playful swat in the ribs and they both laughed.

Finn chose that moment to open the guesthouse door and step out.

He and Brianna froze. Rollo pictured the scene as if they were in a mannequin challenge. Brianna laughing up at him, her hand on his chest. Him grinning down at her.

He saw the exact moment that Finn came to the most logical conclusion. With mischief in his eyes, he came walking toward them.

"Hey there. You must be the new landscaper." He stopped short when Brianna looked his way. "Oh. It's you. I know you. Where have I seen you before?"

Brianna stared at Finn as if he was a vision from heaven. "I dumped mulch on you once."

Rollo felt his eyebrows climb up his forehead. Brianna had never bothered to mention that little detail. "You dumped mulch on Finn?"

She barely glanced at him. "It was an accident. I apologized."

"Repeatedly," Finn agreed. "Annika got a kick out of it, actually. I think it's the closest she's ever come to a shovel."

This got better and better. Finn had a habit of dating actresses Rollo couldn't stand. "Next time, dump the mulch on *her*," he told Brianna. "We'll all thank you."

"I don't plan to dump anything on anyone else. I'm a professional. Now can we get to work here?" She composed herself and offered Finn a bright smile. "Since you're here, maybe you can help us choose a good spot for a koi pond."

"A *koi pond*?" The incredulous tone of his voice suggested that she might as well be talking about digging a hole to China. "What the hell do you want a koi pond for, Rollo? Doesn't seem like your style."

"Maybe I want to meditate," he muttered. "With fish." Damn, he really hadn't thought this through. No one who knew him would believe the koi pond thing.

A smile was playing across Finn's face. He bent down and whispered something in Brianna's ear. A funny series of expressions crossed her face—humor, alarm, denial, confusion. She giggled, but didn't say anything. Rollo had the feeling she didn't know exactly what to say. If Finn was flirting with her, she probably wouldn't know how to respond. She wasn't a flirt, she was...herself. At all times. That was what he liked about her.

But then Brianna turned the tables and whispered something in Finn's ear, and Rollo experienced a strange, shocking bolt of jealousy. He hadn't actually thought Brianna had a chance with Finn. For one thing, they had nothing in common. Finn ought to stick with the starlets he usually dated. He had no business messing around with someone like Bri. But he was smiling at her as if he really liked her.

That was good. So why did he feel so unhappy about it?

"So...anyone going to clue me in on the secret?" God, even his voice sounded jealous. What was wrong with him?

Luckily, his cell buzzed at that moment, giving him a chance to regroup. He stepped away from the two of them—not too happy about that, actually—and answered the call from his mother.

As he listened to her rant about how secretive Sidney had gotten lately, and how she refused to do anything to help out with the upcoming Thanksgiving weekend charity event the Wareham Group sponsored every year, he watched Finn and Brianna talk.

Brianna didn't seem shy anymore, but sort of manic instead. She was gesturing toward various locations on the property, presumably potential homes for koi. Finn listened closely, shading his eyes and nodding earnestly at her various suggestions. That sense of envy returned. Brianna was a one-of-a-kind human being, and if she really cared that much about Finn Abrams...well, lucky guy, that was all.

"Will you *talk* to her?" His mother finally came to the point. "It's the least you could do. You abandon your family, ignore your responsibilities. At least keep your poor sister from heading down the same path you did."

"Mother, why don't you just lighten up on her? She's a kid."

"Lighten up? The way we did with you? That didn't end so well, did it, Rollington?"

God, she really knew how to needle him. "Stop throwing the past in my face. You should be glad I fucked up. Otherwise I'd be doing whatever I wanted right now."

"And now you're going to take your anger out on your own mother?"

"I'm hanging up, Mother. Goodbye."

"Talk to Sidney."

As he ended the call, he saw Brianna and Finn staring at him. "Everything okay?" Finn asked.

He didn't answer, since he wasn't one to lie. "You guys make a decision?"

Brianna nodded. He noticed that she was shivering. He ripped the cable-knit sweater off his back and passed it to her. "That would be a 'no' on the goose bumps, by the way," he told her.

She gave him a delighted smile before pulling it over her head. It hung nearly to her knees and the sleeves were about a foot longer than her arms.

He let his gaze rest on her as she showed him the spot she recommended. Her bright energy, her can-do spirit, her jaunty personality—it all washed away the aftertaste of that conversation with his mother like a drink of cool water after a run.

CHAPTER 6

As soon as they got back to the house, Rollo dragged Brianna into the kitchen for some hot tea so she'd stop shivering.

"This is a big mess," she told him as he put the kettle on to boil. "Finn now thinks I'm interested in you. When he first saw us, I was, I don't know, tickling you or something. When he whispered in my ear, you know what he said? 'Nice move. Nice outfit, too. Men like to see a little skin.'"

"See? Exactly what I said." He grinned at her.

"This isn't funny, Rollo. He thinks you like me because there's no way you'd ever want a koi pond. He thinks it was all a big scam to get me to come out here." She rolled her eyes. "Now what do we do?"

"Ah, shit." Rollo ran his hand across the back of his neck. He wondered once again why everyone seemed determined to pair him up with Brianna. "I can tell him I'm not interested. I can tell him I asked you out and you said no."

"Really?" She brightened. "Would that work?"

"No. Finn's pretty loyal. If he thinks you rejected me, he won't go near you. Also, if he thinks you *didn't* reject me, he won't go near you. It's a hotshot thing."

"Agghh." Brianna covered her face with her arms. "We totally screwed this up."

"I'm sorry, Bri. I still think the plan is good, we just hit a few roadblocks."

Strangely, he didn't care as much as he thought he would. She was still wearing his sweater and that did something to him. Made him feel...proprietary. Territorial, even. Which was damn confusing. And completely inappropriate, considering all the emails from Cornelia that were probably waiting for him.

He went into the kitchen and grabbed a bag of chips.

When he came back into the living room, she'd flopped onto the couch, rag doll style.

"You know, maybe you should just...look for someone else. What's so special about Finn?" Rollo sat next to her on the couch and ripped open the chips. He offered the bag to her and she plunged her hand in, coming out with a huge handful.

"Finn is..." She crunched on a potato chip, tilting her head to the side. "How can I explain this? I've lived in Jupiter Point my whole life. I was born here. My parents were born here. They met at Jupiter Point High, for goodness' sake. I love this place with all my heart. I know where the first wild strawberries grow, I know the tartest crabapple tree on the entire West coast. I know every plant that grows here, and which elevations are good for which varieties of roses. Did you know we have a wild thyme here that's just a little different from all other varieties in the entire world? Its flower has an edge of pink."

"I honestly didn't know that."

"That was kind of a rhetorical question."

"Right." He popped a barbecue chip in his mouth and let her continue. He was enjoying her rant.

"I would never leave Jupiter Point. I'm so rooted here, it's like I'm one with the soil. And I'm fine with that except for one thing. There aren't a lot of available men. And I *know* them all. And worse than that, they know me."

"Not understanding."

"They've known me since I had two little red braids and was called Pippi Longstocking. They know I'm a tomboy who tried out for cheerleading and fell on my ass while performing a jumping jack. They know that speaking in class always turned me into a babbling idiot. They know I put non-hybridized corn kernels in our time capsule project because I'm so worried about biodiversity. I'm not glamorous, Rollo. I told you. My only hope for romance is with someone new to town. Someone who doesn't know how non-sordid my past is."

He nodded his sympathy, even though he thought she was exaggerating her ordinariness. With all her gingery hair and that sunbeam smile, ordinary was not the right word at all. "So the town needs new blood."

"Yes. Enter the hotshots. Two of my friends have already fallen in love with hotshots."

"And now it's your turn."

"Yes." She let out a long breath. "I think it was love at first sight, Rollo. As soon as I saw Finn, I felt like I'd stepped into another world, you know? He's so glamorous and exciting, and the scars on his face actually make him *more* fascinating. And now he thinks we're into each other and this is a big mess."

Rollo munched more chips and pondered the situation. It seemed to him that there was one surefire way to clear up the misunderstanding. "We could be honest with him. Tell him how you feel. Reveal our evil mastermind plan."

"No! Don't you dare!" Brianna rolled over and launched herself on top of him. The bag of chips went flying, scattering chips everywhere. "I would die! Please promise you won't do that." She pinned his shoulders to the back of the couch and fixed him with a look that promised bloody revenge. "Promise right now, or I'll...I'll..."

"What?" He was laughing now, he couldn't help it. Their size discrepancy was so big it was comical, but she wasn't intimidated at all. "What do you weigh, like a hundred pounds?"

"See these fingers?" She lifted one hand and curled the fingers into menacing claws. "I dig in the dirt all day long, and these babies are *strong*. I can tickle you until you cry for mercy. Until you pee your pants. One word—just one word to Finn and I'll—"

Deep waves of laughter rolled out of him. "Now you have me curious," he managed through the chuckles. "Do it. I want to see what those hands are capable of."

She brandished the "claw" overhead. "You laugh now, big guy. But you don't know what you're asking. I can make you whimper like a baby. I can make you scream for your mama."

And then she pounced, digging her fingers into his side.

Maybe it was thanks to the long buildup, but his entire body lurched upwards. A laugh that was more like a spasm ripped through him. He let loose a full-throated roar, so loud he almost didn't hear Finn's voice.

"Oops, sorry man."

*

Brianna scrambled off Rollo's big, warm body and somehow landed on her butt on the floor. She jumped to her feet, desperately trying to regain some degree of dignity. Finn stood in the doorway, sporting a smile that said he knew exactly what was going on. But he didn't. He didn't!

"This isn't...I mean...we're just goofing around. It's not what it looks like," she told him, with all the composure she could summon.

He lifted one hand. "No need for explanations. You crazy kids have fun. Rollo, mind if I borrow your car? Last night I got pulled over for a broken taillight, I need to pick up some parts in town."

"Yeah, sure." Rollo sat up and dug in his pocket. Since she was wearing his sweater, he wore only a t-shirt, which made her realize she never saw him undressed to this degree. His muscles were spectacularly well-defined, bulging from the sleeves of his white t-shirt. He wore some kind of carved pendant on a chain around his neck. It rested against the hard bulges of his chest, rising and falling with his breaths. Kind of distracting, really.

For a moment, Brianna flashed on how it had felt to sit on his lap. It felt good. More than good—amazing. He was such a big guy, like a giant, gentle bear. But every so often she caught a flash of something else in his eyes. Something more fierce than gentle.

But she wasn't here for Rollo. This was about Finn.

As Rollo tossed Finn his car keys, Brianna realized this was a golden opportunity. "I can drive you, Finn. I'm heading back into town and I know exactly where the auto parts store is. I mean, I know where all the stores are. I'm from here, did you know that? Local girl all the way."

She cringed at the babble emerging from her mouth. Would she ever stop acting like a love-struck kid around this man?

Finn gave her an odd look, which her hormones interpreted as smoldering. "But how would I get back?"

"Oh." She hadn't thought of that.

Rollo stepped into the awkward moment. "I have to go in a little later, I can bring you back up."

Finn tossed his car keys back across the room. "Then I'll just wait for you, Rollo. No hurry. I can rewrite the scene I'm on again. Maybe number three hundred and five is the lucky charm." And he slipped out the door with one more knowing look at the two of them.

Brianna's shoulders slumped. This was so hopeless. Beyond hopeless, verging on pathetic. She glanced at Rollo, whose blue-gray eyes met hers with maybe a little too much sympathy.

"It just got worse, didn't it?"

"Probably. Don't worry about it, Bri. We'll try again. Next time you come up here to work, I'll leave so you can be alone with Finn."

"Doesn't matter. If he thinks I'm with you, he won't even look at me."

"Well..." Rollo rested his elbows on his knees and dug his hands through his hair. "Maybe it's better that way. Finn is used to girls falling at his feet. If he thinks you're off-limits, he can just get to know you. As a person. A friend. You can sneak in under his radar. Then at the right time, we tell him that we were never dating. That we've always been good friends—with *no* benefits. So there's no reason for him to hold back."

Brianna scrunched up her face. "I don't know, Rollo. Being friends with you, that's one thing. But whenever I'm with him, I act like a goofball. Not like myself at all. Ugh." She buried her face in her hands again. "I need some kind of brain transplant. Or a body transplant. Like, trade in my whole body and head and everything and get someone else's."

"Honey." Rollo stood up from the couch, which seemed to take forever because of his size. He came close to her and lifted her chin with his hand. "I want you to take that back. Right now. Some of us really dig the whole Brianna experience. Finn will too. Just give it a chance."

Brianna felt a little catch in her heart as she gazed up at the big bear of a man trying to reassure her. Looking into Rollo's eyes, feeling the kindness and affection pouring from him, made all her anxiety over Finn evaporate.

She threw her arms around him and pressed her cheek against his chest, where his heart kept a steady thumping rhythm. His beard brushed the top of her head. He smelled so good—like a tree fort in the forest, like autumn leaves and a walk through crisp mountain air. For a moment they stood like that, as if they'd surprised themselves by their sudden burst of mutual affection.

And then, once again, Finn's voice interrupted the moment. "Sorry! Sorry, guys. There's someone from the gas company asking for you, Rollo. I told her you were busy, but—"

They broke away from each other. Out of the corner of her eye, Brianna caught a glimpse of Finn's head disappearing out the half-open door.

OMG. Seriously? Again?

She turned to Rollo, whose face twisted into a look of apology so abject, all she could do was laugh.

"I promise I'll make it up to you," he muttered in a low voice. "Just come back later in the week. I'll do some fast talking in the meantime."

"You're a really nice guy, you know that?"

She had no idea why his expression shuttered when she said that. Oh well. She shrugged and hurried out the door, where Finn was chatting with Laurie from the gas company, who looked so dazzled she'd probably forgotten the difference between propane and Rogaine.

Completely discouraged—yet oddly happy—Brianna hopped in her old red Toyota pickup and headed to her next job. Having a friend like Rollo made all the difference when you were hopelessly in love.

CHAPTER 7

Brianna drove out to Melvin Turner's place, which was near the old farm currently being transformed into the Star Bright Shelter for Teens. Suzanne Finnegan was the driving force behind the project, but many people were helping out with it. Brianna had sweet-talked the old farmer into offering most of the property to the shelter in exchange for free labor from the teenagers who would be staying there. He couldn't handle the place on his own anymore, and she didn't have time to provide all the help he needed.

Since Old Man Turner was the grumpy hermit type, he'd kept one remote corner of the farm to himself. It contained a few acres, a small house, a vegetable garden and a shed, which was all he claimed he needed.

She found him in the garden, untangling worn-out tomato plants from their supports. The pile of dry stalks next to him reminded her of scarecrow marionettes.

"Are those the Brandywines?" She peered closer at the spent tomatoes. She and old Melvin shared a passion for heirloom varieties of tomatoes and other vegetables.

"A-yup. Biggest sellers, like always."

"Want me to take all this to the compost?"

"Why not? That's the way of life, ain't it? Straight to the compost we go."

She gathered an armful of stalks and walked over to the big pile of garden scraps corralled behind chicken wire. "You're in your usual cheerful mood, huh?"

"Don't get cheeky. Just cuz I let you come around here and pester me don't mean you can sass me."

His arthritis must be bothering him. Working outside in blustery weather was guaranteed to make it worse. "You got it. No sass for you, Gramps."

She stuck her tongue out at the older man, which wrung a thin smile from him. It was actually amazing that he was still working in his garden at the age of ninety. But in the past year, things had gotten much harder for him. She'd tried to help as much as she could, and hadn't charged him a dime for a couple of years.

"How about I finish this up and you make us some tea? I'll even drink some of that lemon verbena gunk you like."

He dropped the stalk he was working with and rubbed a knot out of one hand. "That's real medicine, girl. Don't let the doctors tell you different. You come in as soon as you're done, there's something I want to ask you."

"Sure. Be right in."

She finished pulling up the tomato plants and tidied up the compost pile. She gathered up the tomato supports, brushed the soil off them and stashed them in his garden shed. Melvin Turner had taught her so many of his garden-ing and farming techniques, but most of all, he'd taught her to take care of her tools and maintain an orderly space. Just walking into his shed gave her a sense of comfort. In this realm—nature, plants, growing things—she felt perfectly at ease.

So why did she turn into such an awkward disaster around Finn?

Maybe... A light bulb suddenly turned on. Maybe it was proof that this was true love! She'd never felt it before, after all. She'd had plenty of crushes, starting with Jimmy Crow-foot in second grade. She'd thrown spitballs at him until he'd finally looked at her with those beautiful black eyes.

Should she throw spitballs at Finn? That would definite-ly get his attention. She was willing to bet that Annika Poole hadn't lobbed a single spitball at the smolderingly handsome fireman.

She debated running her spitball idea past Rollo. He would definitely appreciate it. One thing she loved about Rollo was that he found her amusing. They laughed a lot while they were together. It was a relief, since often she felt at odds with the general population. As if everyone had been issued a set of instructions at birth, but she'd lost hers in the shuffle and was just winging it.

When she walked into Old Man Turner's kitchen, the tea kettle was whistling but he didn't seem to hear. He was hunched over the table, peering over his old half-moon glasses at a document. She crossed to the kettle and turned off the flame, then filled the rose patterned teapot with boiling water. He must have forgotten the whole project halfway through, because the crockery jar of dried lemon verbena sat open, the lid askew on the table.

Dementia was definitely setting in. She'd been noticing it for a while. Forgetfulness, confusion, even paranoia.

Melvin started when she brought the teapot to the table. "You're here."

"Yes, old man." She winked at him, though her heart ached at the confusion in his expression. "I'm here."

"Good. Take a look at this. Need you to sign off on it."

"Me?" She frowned and picked up the stapled pages. At the top she saw the typed words *Advance Directive.* "What is this?"

"You know me and doctors. I don't like 'em. I'm ninety and I'm ready to go. It's a damn miracle I lasted this long with all the folks that want me dead. When it's time, it's time."

"Oh, Melvin. No one wants you dead!" She reached over and squeezed his hand. Its knuckles were so swollen they felt like walnuts.

"It's happening if they do or if they don't. But I want it on my terms. No fuss, no special attention. It's all in there."

She scanned the rest of the document. Not only did it state that he didn't want any extraordinary measures taken to prolong his life, but it named her as a Health Care Power of Attorney. "But why, Melvin? Why me? The doctors will see this and they'll know what you want."

"It's not enough." He lifted his head and fixed her with a stern gaze. "I need someone to stand up for me. Someone who knows what I want. I don't trust anyone. Ninety years on this Earth and you're the only one I know who's straight and true. I pick you for this job. You can say no, and that'll be that. But I pick you."

Brianna stared at him, emotion welling inside her. Melvin Turner was the ultimate bachelor farmer. He'd never married, had no children. He'd devoted his life to this patch of land, to growing vegetables for the people of Jupiter Point. He wasn't from here, and her parents had hinted that there was some kind of mystery in his past. But he'd never said a word about any of that to her.

She turned to the last page where he'd signed his name. Looking closer, she noticed that it didn't say "Melvin Turner." It said something else, Markov Turk-something. Strange. It made her nervous, as if she was getting into something she didn't understand. "Why is someone else's name here?"

"Pour that tea, would you girl? It's getting cold."

She filled his favorite mug, the one with flying cranes around the rim, with fragrant liquid. The scent of lemon rose to her nostrils, bringing back so many visceral memories of this very kitchen.

"It's my name," he finally explained. "Name I was born with, but I gave it up long ago."

Simple explanation. What was the big deal? What was she afraid of, anyway? Melvin needed her. Of course she couldn't say no.

She took the copy on which he'd written her name and looked at it again. "This means you have to do what I say, right? If I tell you to relax while I finish your garden, you can't say no."

"Sure I can."

"Right here. *Power.* That means I'm in charge now." She rolled it up and stuck it in her overalls pocket. "This is going to be fun."

He picked up his tea and blew on it. "Don't get a big head or I'll rip that thing up."

"Big talk," she teased. "I'll be good, I promise."

"I don't need good. I need honest. Nothing but the truth. You get me?"

"You came to the right girl."

At least it made sense now that he'd chosen her. Brianna the Blunt. The one thing everyone always knew she'd deliver—the unvarnished truth.

"There's a red lockbox in the shed, it's got all my papers in it. It's not locked and you can look inside after I'm gone. All the instructions are in there about how I want to leave this world. Pretty simple, girl. If they could throw me in the compost, I wouldn't mind. Ain't legal, though. And I want to go out legal as I can."

Later, over margaritas at the Orbit with Evie, Suzanne, and Merry, she described the encounter, which made her even more sad after the fact.

"The way he was talking, it was like he'd already written his own obituary. And it's so sad that he doesn't have any family at all. How can I be the only one he can ask? Me, of all people?"

"What does that mean?" Evie, her best friend since childhood, bristled in her defense. "You're the perfect person for something like that. I'd choose you in a flash."

Brianna shook margarita droplets off the little plastic sword the Orbit had stuck in her drink. "Sean might have a problem with that."

Evie gave a dreamy sigh at the mention of her rugged fiancé. "I think I've finally talked him into getting a cat, by the way. I threatened him with getting pregnant if I can't get my cuddling needs otherwise satisfied."

"Thanks a lot," said Suzanne, who was drinking virgin daiquiris due to her own five-months-along pregnancy. "Nice to know I'm a living advance-warning system." With her long blond hair pulled back in a ponytail, she looked too young and cute for a soon-to-be mother. But Brianna knew she was going to be a great mom. She was phenomenally well organized, for one thing, and very compassionate. The teen shelter existed entirely thanks to her.

"Oh stop. You know I can't wait for your little guy. Or gal. I've already started planning the baby shower."

"No need." Suzanne signaled the waiter for another bowl of guacamole, since she'd inhaled the last one. "I already have it worked out. I'll email you the details."

They all laughed. Typical Suzanne.

"And I finally finished your wedding plans. I'll send that along too. Brianna, you need it too, since you're doing the flowers."

"Yes, ma'am." Brianna saluted her friend. She ignored the tug of jealousy brought on by all this talk of showers and weddings. She wanted those things too. But she wasn't gorgeous like Evie, or flirtatious like Suzanne. She was just...Brianna. It was hard on a girl's ego to grow up with the most beautiful best friends in the world.

Mercifully, Merry changed the subject. "I'm still curious about this old man," she told Brianna, her dark eyes gleaming with curiosity. "Sounds like there's a story there."

"I'm sure there is, but I don't know it." She lowered her voice. "He told me about a lockbox with his papers in it, and I'm halfway tempted to see what's in there. For one thing, Melvin Turner isn't his real name."

Merry's eyes sharpened. "What makes you say that?"

"Well, on the document I signed, a different name was listed. "It said Markov something or other, not Melvin Turner. He said it was the name he was born with. But why doesn't he use it? Why choose *Melvin* of all names?"

Merry sucked thoughtfully on her margarita. "I can do some digging through the archives if you want."

"No, that's okay. I'd feel terrible investigating a lonely old man. Forget I said anything about his name or any of this." Brianna could have kicked herself for being so indiscreet. What was her problem? Bluntness was one thing, but she shouldn't be blabbing about someone's personal information.

"Forgetting it right now," said Evie promptly.

The others agreed, causing Brianna to give thanks for such good friends. Merry signaled for another drink and once again jumped in to change the subject. "You girls who hooked up with hotshots, I need a favor from one of y'all."

Well, count her out, Brianna thought gloomily as Evie and Suzanne came to attention.

"Have you ever heard of Forest Service lookout towers?"

They all shook their heads. Merry's eyes lit up with the thrill only a newshound would experience over something as random as a tower. "Get this. There are people who sit all day long inside towers built deep in the wilderness, just looking for wildfires. Some of them even live there. They're kind of a throwback, but there are still a few here in California. I want to do a story on the people in those towers. I thought maybe Josh or Sean could get me some names."

"No!" Brianna nearly knocked over her margarita in her excitement. This was the perfect opportunity to deliver on her promise to Rollo. To *over*-deliver. A plan formed in her mind as quickly as one of her herb garden designs. "You know who's an expert on the history of the fire service? Rollo Wareham."

She'd have to send him a text right away instructing him to become an expert.

Merry's forehead wrinkled. "Yeah, but Sean's the leader of the crew, and—"

"And super-busy getting ready for the wedding and doing all the off-season management stuff, right Evie?"

She kicked Evie under the table. Her friend winced but nodded gamely. "He's definitely on the busy side."

"Rollo was just mentioning the other day that he wanted to do some hiking. Maybe even some camping. I bet he knows where the best towers are. And you know Rollo, everyone loves him. He's like, the most popular of the hotshots."

When Suzanne and Evie exchanged insulted glances, she backtracked. "I mean, the most popular *single* hotshot. Not that his marital status is at all relevant. We're just talking about his knowledge of weird towers in the wilderness, which I'm sure is extensive. And also how much time he has to check them out. Because he's neither engaged to be married or already married and about to have a baby. To the best of my knowledge..." She trailed off as her friends burst out laughing.

Suzanne folded her arms on the table and gave her a scolding look. "Brianna, are you trying to finagle a camping trip with Rollo Wareham? I'm sure he'd be happy to share a sleeping bag with you."

"No. No, that's not it at all." Her face was turning pink, she could tell. Which, of course, they'd all interpret in exactly the wrong way.

"Aw, look, she's blushing. Well, as far as I'm concerned, it's about time you two got together. You're perfect for each other," Suzanne announced. "Take it from the honeymoon queen."

"I really don't think so," Brianna stammered. But she couldn't figure out how to object to being "perfect for Rollo" without making him seem unappealing, which she didn't want to do in front of Merry.

Merry was tapping a finger on her chin. "This could work out perfectly. We'll all go hiking out to one of the towers. I'll do my reporter thing while you two get to know each other. And...you're welcome."

Brianna slumped against the padded back of the booth. She'd have to break this to Rollo right away. Not only did he have to bone up on fire service history, but Merry would now be trying to throw the two of them together.

So far, their plan was pretty much an utter failure.

CHAPTER 8

Every month, Rollo got a fat package of paperwork from the CEO of the Wareham Group. During the fire season, he didn't have time for Wareham affairs, so he usually spent the month of November catching up.

He brewed a big pot of coffee and spread the paperwork over the table in the breakfast nook. As soon as he sat down, his left leg, the one that had fractured in the burnover, began to ache. Damn it. The big hiking trip out to the Breton lookout tower was three days away. His leg better not give him trouble then. It always ached when the weather changed.

Or maybe it ached whenever he had to look at spreadsheets.

He had nothing against money—he liked it, and had a few personal investments and donations that meant a lot to him. But hedge funds and leveraged buyouts and all that stuff left him cold.

After about half an hour of frowning at an especially confusing report on a new kind of mortgage the Wareham Group was offering, he dialed his brother.

"Rollo-rollo-ding-dong," Brent answered on the first ring. "What's the word, turd?"

Rollo gritted his teeth. His brother still talked like a frat boy, probably always would. "I'm trying to figure out this new subprime thing. I thought we weren't doing those? We never used to."

"Oh no, dude, this is different. These are secured up the ass. *Muy* low risk, *muchacho*."

Rollo hated it when Brent pretended to speak Spanish as some kind of badge of coolness. Or something. He hadn't quite figured out what.

"Was there a vote about this?"

"Not everything goes to the board, dude. Why are you stressing about this? It's a good thing. Big cash cow. Third-quarter profits are insane. Bonuses for all. Well, not you. All you do is sit on your ass while I make all the money."

Brent laughed, a high, edgy sound that got Rollo's hackles rising.

"Well, you are good at it, the making money part. I just hope you're spending it wisely."

"Oooooh yeah. Wise is my middle name. Brent Wise-Ass Wareham." He whooped hyena-style. "I think the Warehams need a private jet, what do you think?"

In Rollo's opinion, the Warehams needed a private therapist, not a jet.

"You can fly all those bachelorettes out to your doorstep in Cali. Make them audition in person."

"I'm not auditioning anyone, idiot."

"Right, that's Mother's job."

Rollo clenched his jaw so tight it throbbed. "Tell you what, Brent. Why don't you come out to Jupiter Point? I'll show you around, we'll make a campfire on the beach, look at some stars."

Maybe some good old-fashioned stargazing would give his brother a little perspective. The incredible stargazing was one of the very best things about Jupiter Point. The way the wind currents swirled around the point made the air crystal clear. After the observatory had been built on one of the hills outside of town, the entire town had adopted a stargazing theme to appeal to honeymooners. They even had a motto: Remember to Look Up at the Stars.

Wise words.

But not to Brent, who could be heard yawning hugely on the other end of the phone. "You know what kind of stars I like, Rollington. Naked ones in my bed. Licking my—"

Rollo hung up. He wasn't in the mood for Brent's frat boy crudeness. It brought back too many painful memories. He'd been a lot like Brent back in the day. They'd both spent their childhoods being catered to and treated like spoiled kings. Maybe he'd still be like that, another version of Brent, if the incident that changed his life hadn't occurred.

He didn't regret the change at all. He'd left the old Rollo behind without a second thought. But he would always, always regret the damage done to everyone else. Especially Dougie Berkowitz.

Speaking of which...he flipped through the pages until he came to the quarterly report on the fund he'd set up for Doug as soon as he'd reached legal age. It was doing great. He noticed several withdrawals, which made him even happier. The fund was doing what it was intended to do.

Make up for his horrible past behavior, at least as much as he ever could.

His phone rang—Sean this time. "You busy? I need a favor."

"You got it." He shoved the entire pile of paperwork aside. Friends came first. Especially fellow hotshots.

*

Sean and Josh picked him up in one of the big Ford Super Duty's that belonged to the Jupiter Point Hotshots. Snowball, Josh's dog, sat alertly in the back, panting in Rollo's ear. Rollo was so happy to be away from those business reports that he didn't even mind. Maybe he'd get a dog himself now that he'd decided to stay in Jupiter Point.

"Where we going?"

"Back in time," answered Sean.

"Back in time" turned out to be the old airstrip that Sean had inherited when his parents were killed in a plane crash. It was located on a flat stretch of meadow not far from Stargazer Beach. The surrounding beach grass and gentle breezes, not to mention the vintage quality of the buildings, gave it a peaceful, out-of-time atmosphere.

They parked outside the rope that blocked the entrance to the tarmac. The whole thing consisted of two hangars, one runway, one tie-down area and one reception building—all of it about as ratty and rundown as could be.

"I have to do something with this place," Sean told them as he ducked under the rope. "I pay taxes on it every year, throw a little money into maintenance."

Rollo held the rope high for Josh, who was still using a cane. He'd broken his leg running after Tim Peavy when he'd lost it during the Yellowstone fire. The best thing Rollo had done all last season was carry the unconscious and injured Josh out of that burning forest.

"Might want to think about throwing a little more into maintenance." Josh pointed at the rusted tin roof of the reception building. "If a squirrel stepped in the wrong place, he'd be toast."

"I would, but I have a wedding to pay for. Evie gave Suzanne free rein." Sean glowered at Josh. "Which is your fault, by the way. Your little justice of the peace trick means they're doubling up on me and Evie's shindig."

Josh threw back his head and uttered an "evil mastermind" laugh. "You're dealing with a master here. Bow down."

Sean flipped him the bird instead. Rollo was listening to his friends' nonsense with only half an ear. The rest of his brain was sifting through ideas for this place. "Have you tried to sell it?"

"People have tried to buy it, but no one I'd sign any papers with. Remember that dipshit Brad White? The one running for office?"

"Hell yes." They'd all been present at the press conference when Evie finally revealed what Brad had done to her. That had been the end of Brad's political career, at least on a local level. "Asshole. He wanted to buy it?"

"Yes, he said something about condos. It's a great location."

Rollo and Josh were both aiming death glares at Sean, who threw up his hands. "I'd never sell to that guy. Relax. Look, I get an offer on the place every year. But it never felt right. Now I'm thinking, time to settle this thing. It's like a big piece of baggage hanging over me."

Josh stroked his chin. "And by the looks of this place, they would have lost that baggage here."

Rollo chuckled. Josh had a knack for lightening any situation. "So what'd you bring us here for, Sean? Got an idea?"

"Sort of. None of the offers I've gotten had anything to do with flying. Everyone wants to turn it into something else. But this town could use a flightseeing service. My dad did pretty well with the business. And we could use more air support for rescues. Think about all the wilderness around here, most of it inaccessible by road. If we had a couple of planes and rescue choppers based here, we could really save lives."

"Are you thinking the Forest Service would buy it?"

"Yeah. That's a possibility."

They all surveyed the windblown outpost with its tattered windsocks.

"Isn't that a tumbleweed?" Josh pointed at a tangle of dry brush bouncing down the runway. His dog, Snowball, chased after it, barking wildly. A gust of wind sent an old plastic bag skipping into the grass. Snowball decided to chase after that instead. Honestly, with the scraps of trash clogging the airstrip, Snowball could be here all week chasing stuff down.

"All right, so it might need some work," Sean admitted. "But you guys aren't doing anything, are you? Long winter ahead, nothing but time."

"Hey, I'm injured." Josh waved his cane in the air. "Broken leg, fire victim. Remember?"

"Rollo?"

"I just bought a house." At Sean's narrowed eyes, he threw up his hands in defeat. "Fine, whatever you need. Except the roof. Believe me, you don't want me on that roof."

"Excellent." With a big grin, Sean offered him a high-five. "I'm going to ask Brianna for some help too. She's good with tools, hard worker. At least she wouldn't make the roof cave in."

That gave Rollo an idea. If Brianna was going to be working on this project, maybe there was another potential set-up opportunity. "Brianna's always a good person to have around. Hey, can I bring Finn into this thing?"

Sean's smile dropped. Most of the hotshots who had lived through the burnover had made their peace with Finn. But not Sean. As the crew superintendent, he was responsible. He'd tried to run after Finn, but the fire was already on top of them, and it was Josh who made him stop and get into his own shelter.

Sometimes Rollo wondered if the effects of the burnover would be with them forever.

"Forget it," he said. "Finn's pretty wrapped up anyway. Count me in, though."

Sean nodded. "About Finn—look, I'll think about it."

"Everyone makes mistakes, you know." Rollo shoved his hands into the pockets of his jeans. "And with Finn...I don't know. There was something going on with him."

"Like what?" Josh asked.

"I don't know. He still won't talk about it. But tell me this, guys. During the burnover, didn't you both have some kind of...'come to Jesus' moment? Like, you're looking death in the eye and something big pops into your mind?"

Sean nodded. "Yep. That's when I decided to come back to Jupiter Point."

Rollo turned to Josh. "Josh? How about you?"

Snowball trotted back to Josh's side and he absentmindedly stroked her head. "Yeah, some shit went through my mind. I had trouble shaking it for a long while. But that's history now. What's your point?"

"Point is, something happened to Finn and he screwed up. Is there anyone here who hasn't screwed up?"

"Sure there is." Josh grinned. "My dog. Snowball is perfect in every way. Except for the time she ate Suzanne's rock collection. That was a fairly serious error in judgement."

Rollo threw up his hands and strode back toward the rope. As he ducked under, Sean caught up with him. Josh lagged behind, because Snowball had decided to gnaw on his cane. "Look man, I hear what you're saying. It's not the burnover, it's the damn movie. I hate that thing."

"Well, if it makes you feel better, Finn's hating it pretty hard right about now too."

"It does, a bit," Sean admitted with a grin. "I'm curious, though. What happened to *you* during the burnover? What'd you think about?"

Rollo crossed to the passenger-side door and opened it. Sean was still watching him steadily over the roof of the Super Duty. Once you'd cut line with a guy over weeks and months of back-breaking labor, you trusted him. Once you'd survived certain death with a guy, you trusted him. Rollo didn't trust many people, but Sean was definitely one of them.

"I thought we were toast. I was scared shitless. I knew everything was going to end."

"Everything? What do you mean?"

"Life as I knew it. The hotshots. My firefighting career." He got into the passenger seat, his jaw setting. He'd been putting off this conversation too long.

Sean slid into the driver's seat and stared at him. "What the hell are you talking about?"

"I have to quit. Promised my family. Last season was pushing it, but now I really have to. Family obligations, can't change it."

"You're serious, man?"

"I am. But we can get into this later." A lump had lodged in his chest. Leaving the hotshots. He'd said the words out loud, and damn, but they hurt. "I'm staying in Jupiter Point. I'll help you with this place if you decide to keep it."

"Thanks. I won't do anything until after the wedding. Maybe I'll hit you up in February."

Snowball chose that moment to clamber over him into the driver's seat. She wormed her way to the back as Josh stumped to their side.

"Is it unethical to feed your dog tranquilizers?" he grumbled.

"Old man," Rollo teased. "Was it just this summer you were young, single and footloose? Now look at you. Married, baby on the way, too decrepit to play with your dog."

Josh punched him in the shoulder as he heaved himself into the backseat, where he rubbed the muscles of his leg. "You're just jealous. Can't fool me."

Snowball curled up next to him and rested her chin on his knee. And Rollo had to admit—he really was jealous. No lie.

CHAPTER 9

"This is perfect," Brianna insisted as she and Rollo cruised the aisles of the Big Apple Supermarket. "There's no better way to get to know someone than during a campout. Ghost stories, singalongs, capture the flag, bug juice..." She sighed happily. "Some of my best memories are from camp."

"This isn't third grade," Rollo grumbled. "And it's November. Are you sure Merry's into camping? She doesn't seem like the type." He tossed a jumbo box of Triscuits into the shopping cart.

"What's that supposed to mean?"

"She's so plugged in. Computer, phone. Always thinking and working."

"That's why this is perfect. She won't have all those distractions. She can focus on big, strong, beautiful Rollo Wareham." Brianna's bright grin warmed his heart—it would probably warm a dead man's heart.

"You're kind of good for my ego, you know that?"

Brianna tugged the front of the shopping cart toward the dairy section. "Merry loves brie. Me, I'm more of a cheese platter girl, but she goes for the expensive stuff. Let's get tons of it."

"Can't we stick with hotdogs and marshmallows?"

With her arms full of wheels of cheese, Brianna fixed him with a stern look. "You have to accept that this is not one of your roughing-it camping trips. We're not fighting wildfires here. You're trying to impress a very hard-to-impress woman. Merry has sophisticated tastes. She likes brie and chocolate-covered strawberries and dipping biscotti in her cappuccino and you need to just go with that."

"So we're talking 'glamping,' not camping."

"Exactly. You need air mattresses and those cool camp chairs with cup holders." She dumped the cheese into the shopping cart. "Can you fit a cooler in your backpack?"

"Wait. Back up." A sense of panic flared inside him. "You said 'you.'"

"Yes. You. Something wrong with that?"

"You're coming with us, right?"

With a look of exasperation, Brianna reached for a container of French vanilla creamer on a top shelf. He watched the way her top rode up along her torso, revealing the sweet indentation of her waist. She wore low-rider jeans that snugly encased her ass, along with a collared plaid shirt that didn't quite reach her waistband. The exposed skin looked like silky cream. He had a random and totally inappropriate urge to lick it.

Goddamn. This was *Brianna*.

He dragged his gaze away and focused on the brie instead. Brianna seemed oblivious to his temporary brain freeze.

"Think, Rollo. This is your chance to be alone with Merry and win her over. I'm planning a gardening emergency so I can back out. "

"I thought it was a group kind of thing. That's a lot more relaxed."

Truth was, he didn't like the thought of being alone with Merry during the long hike out to the Breton tower and an entire night of camping. It sounded like a lot of pressure. He'd be wilderness guide and fake historical expert and brie provider all in one.

If Brianna came along, it would actually be fun.

Well, there was one way to get her to join them. "Finn's coming." Or he would be, if he wanted to keep occupying the guesthouse.

Brianna froze in mid-reach. Balanced precariously on the base of the cooler, she gazed back at him. "Really? He's going for sure?"

"Oh for Pete's sake." Rollo stepped around the shopping cart and grabbed Brianna by the waist. He lifted her up— good Lord, she was easy to hold, like a wedding-cake topper—so she could reach the creamer. As soon as she had it in her grasp, he swung her around and planted her back on the ground. She grabbed the cart, looking a little dizzy.

"Warn a girl before you spin her around, would you?" Her face was flushed, and she wouldn't quite meet his eyes.

Rollo's palms were still tingling from the feel of her compact body. "Sorry. I was afraid you were going to bring down the whole cooler. So what do you say, Bri? If Finn's coming, you don't want to miss out. This is your big chance to really connect with him."

She scrunched her face up. "I guess so. But Rollo, think of all the opportunities I'll have to get flustered and make a fool of myself."

"That won't happen. I'll be right there. You're comfortable with me, right?"

"Yes, of course. That's different. I don't have an awkward crush on you." She gave him a little swat on the arm. "But I guess you're right. If Finn's going, it's a golden opportunity. Fine. We'll make it a group trip. But you owe me."

"How do you figure?"

"I think glamping is ridiculous," she admitted. "And brie smells like when I wear the same socks for two weeks, which sometimes happens when I'm super-busy in the spring."

Rollo hid his laugh in his beard. He imagined Brianna sharing her opinion of brie with his mother. God, he'd pay good money to witness that. "Amen. The only thing worse than brie is gorgonzola."

Brianna made a face. "Merry likes that on celery."

"How about we stock up on chips and onion dip, just in case?"

"Yes!" They high-fived each other and went to raid the junk food aisles. Halfway there, Brianna put a hand on his arm, stood on tiptoe and whispered in his ear, "Please don't tell Finn about the socks, okay?"

Could she be any cuter?

*

Two days later, about a mile into the Sierra Nevada wilderness, Brianna had to face a hard truth. So far, getting ready for this trip had been a lot more fun than the actual trip. She and Rollo had done all the prep work together. They'd found the tower, planned the itinerary, bought the provisions.

Beer and snacks had been involved too. And of course they'd had to break off for a movie now and then.

Rollo was so much fun to hang around with. The minute she got near him and inhaled his pine-needle-and-wool-sweater scent, she got a little happier. She figured that meant they were really, *really* good friends.

Right now, he led the way down the trail, shouldering an enormous backpack as it if were a beach ball. He'd crammed as much as possible into his pack, with Finn carrying the rest.

Finn. God, he looked so handsome, with a wool beanie covering his dark, wavy hair and a tan sweater over loose corduroy pants. Every time she looked at him, she felt a stab of longing. He was just so perfect, as if he'd stepped out of an ad for Abercrombie and Fitch. Not even his burn scars took away from his good looks, at least in her opinion.

But nothing was working out the way it was supposed to. Finn and Merry had hit it off right away, since they were both writers. They'd been talking nonstop since the hike started—about computers and their favorite writing software and other stuff she had nothing to say about. And Rollo was way up ahead, his long legs eating up the trail. Brianna was left to bring up the rear. All she could do was gaze with hopeless longing at the sexy way Finn moved.

Both of the hotshots moved well, as a matter of fact. Rollo's bear-like build looked different out here in the woods—he walked with agility and purpose. He wore a red stocking cap that served as a beacon for the rest of them, along with a brown and green plaid woodman's jacket. His wide shoulders held the giant backpack easily; he didn't even flinch when he first slid it over his shoulders.

How could Merry not be impressed by Rollo's sheer strength and size?

Maybe because she was interested in other things, like Apple versus PC and who had won the most recent Pulitzer Prize for journalism.

Brianna kicked gloomily at a mossy log, which came apart under the blow. A mouse scurried out of it, which startled her so much she stumbled forward. Her Thermos of coffee flew out of her hand. As she watched in stunned disbelief, it winged through the air and thumped Finn on his right butt cheek.

He lurched forward, then spun around to face her. "Jesus. What was that?"

"Sorry." Brianna had landed on her hands and knees. She crawled forward to grab the Thermos, then pushed herself back into a standing position. "That was just me, throwing a Thermos around. Not intentionally, I mean. I tripped over something and I lost my grip on it. It went..." She made a sound like a bomb falling as she traced the arc of the Thermos through the air. "I mean, sorry."

Merry was folding her lips together to hold back her laugh. "I know what's going on here. Writers can be boring-ass conversationalists, right, Finn? I think we bored her so much she fell asleep on her feet."

"Our bad. Sorry about that, Bri. We can talk about something else." Finn rubbed the muscle of his butt with a grimace.

"I could...uh...want me to rub it?" Brianna offered. "I have really strong hands. Strong as a man's, really. I bet I can do that just as good as you, and it's easier for me to reach."

A smothered snort drew her attention to Rollo, who had walked back along the trail to see what was going on. He was making some kind of gesture at her, trying to communicate something. She had no idea what.

"That's all right," Finn said. "Some things a guy has to do for himself. I think this qualifies."

"Right. Of course it does." She nodded quickly, bopping her head like some kind of marionette. What was wrong with her? "It's okay if you change your mind. My offer will still be open. Later tonight, even, when we're done walking, it might start to stiffen up and..."

What was she saying? Her face was so hot by now, she was surprised it didn't burst into flames.

Merry came to her side and took her by the elbow. "Stop talking right now," she whispered in Brianna's ear.

Brianna snapped her mouth shut while Merry announced to everyone that she had to take a bathroom break and she needed Brianna to stand guard.

"What is wrong with you, girl?" Merry hissed as soon as they'd gone behind an ancient birch, out of earshot.

Brianna buried her face in her hands. "It's Finn. He makes me so nervous. He's so gorgeous. Every time he looks at me, I just...get stupid."

She felt an arm come around her shoulders. "Aw, honey. Are you telling me you have your eye on Finn, not the big guy?"

"The big guy? You mean Rollo?" At the very least, Merry ought to use his name.

"Yeah, Rollo. The big, quiet one."

"Rollo's not quiet."

"Really? Finn's already talked to me more than Rollo did the whole time I was embedded with the crew. Nothing against him, maybe we just don't have anything in common.

Doesn't matter right now. The point is, I thought the two of you were kind of circling each other. But you're into Finn instead? That changes everything."

Brianna stared at her in dismay. Poor Rollo. Clearly Merry wasn't considering him *at all*. She was so sharp and verbal, maybe she couldn't see the appeal of someone like Rollo. Rollo was more about actions than words. When he talked, he said things that mattered. Unlike someone like Finn, who could talk about anything and be charming in the process.

Hmm, was that a critical thought about Finn?

No. She'd called him charming. Nothing wrong with charming.

"Merry, please don't underestimate Rollo. He's a really good guy. Haven't you ever heard the phrase 'still waters run deep'? That's Rollo. There's a lot more to him than you realize. Also, you have to admit he's very attractive. It's just in a different way. He's not smooth like Finn. He's more...real."

Merry shook her head. She looked crisp and fresh in a bright yellow down jacket and fleece headband. "One minute you're pining over Finn, the next you're raving about Rollo. Make up your mind, Bri. Unless you want both. If they're going to fight over you, my money's on the big guy. Or if you want both, nothing wrong with a hotshot sandwich."

Brianna clapped her hand over her mouth to hide her shriek of laughter. "You. Are so. Bad."

Merry shrugged. "You know me. I'm all talk. You can have whichever one you want, girl. Just let me know so I can be wingman for you. Okay now, I need you to turn around so I can go pee."

Brianna obliged. She scanned the woods, absently identifying each plant in the understory while her heart ached for Rollo. Merry was never going to see him for the amazing person he truly was. She had a wall around her heart made of laptops and deadlines and other things Brianna knew nothing about. She'd have to find a way to break it to Rollo that this trip was pointless.

CHAPTER 10

It was a ten-mile hike to the Breton lookout, and much of that hike was uphill. Most lookout towers had fire roads for maintenance purposes. This one did too, but it took such a long and winding route that they'd decided to take a more direct scenic route through the forest instead.

The trail was a series of long switchbacks up the gentle slope of a hogback ridge. They walked through mixed woodlands of pine, aspen and birch, a terrain very familiar to Rollo from all his firefighting experience. The views that kept unfolding the higher they got were stunning. The deciduous trees looked almost garishly autumnal, a carpet of russet and persimmon and gold unfurling down the slopes.

His heart hurt for Brianna. What could he do to help build her resistance to Finn? As long as she kept babbling like a fool and throwing Thermoses at his ass, she'd never give Finn a chance to fall for her. He'd be too busy wondering what was wrong with her.

Merry jogged to catch up with him. "Listen, you don't have to talk to me. I just want to give Bri and Finn a moment alone. We got talking about the trees and plants and that's her area of expertise. She needs a moment to shine. If he sees her at her best, he'll fall for her in a flash."

Rollo grinned at her. "That's what I keep telling her too. She needs to relax and stop seeing him as some kind of god on Earth."

"True that." She craned her neck to listen in on the other two. "Bri's talkin' birch beetles. Perfect. Hey, do you mind if I ask you some questions about the lookout tower?"

Rollo hid a sigh. That was Merry, always on the job. "Sure, what do you want to know?"

"People just sit there all day and look for fires?"

"That's about it. They take readings, mark down temperature and barometric pressure and other conditions. Most of the towers are staffed by volunteers. Some work for the Forest Service. Their affectionate nickname is 'freaks on the peaks.'"

"I can see why. You're telling me people volunteer to sit all alone in a tower all day?" She rolled her dark eyes, the deep amber skin of her forehead creasing. "I gotta talk to one of these crazies. They must lose their minds from sheer boredom."

"Actually, they say the opposite. I heard one spotter talk about all the things she planned to do—like write, knit, draw, that sort of thing. She ended up spending all her time watching the weather. It changes all the time, every minute. A new cloud formation drifts across the sky, the wind changes, the angle of the sun changes. If you just sit back and watch, there's a lot more to see than it seems at first."

He glanced at Merry and saw that she was staring at him with an arrested expression. "Brianna was right about you."

"How do you mean?"

"She said there's a lot more to you than shows on the surface. Or something like that. She's a big fan of yours, you know that?"

"We're good friends," he said cautiously. He didn't want to give Merry the impression that anything more was going on between him and Brianna.

"Just a random question, but do you seriously think a man and a woman, both of them single and attractive, can be 'good friends'? You're telling me there isn't a single spark in there somewhere?" A moth flew past them and she swatted it away from her face. "I don't have the answers here; I'm just throwing it out there."

"Well." He thought it over carefully. "Yes, I think men and women can be friends. Sometimes that's the only thing you *can* be because of other circumstances."

Her gaze sharpened. "Now you got me intrigued. What sort of circumstances?"

Like...that you had to marry someone your family approved? But he couldn't say that. "All sorts of circumstances." He glanced back at Brianna and Finn. "Uh-oh. She's still talking about birch beetles."

"Oh hell no. What's he doing?"

"Listening. Nodding."

"Are his eyes glazed?"

"As a donut."

She sighed. "The plant nerd strikes again. Be right back."

*

About an hour before sunset, they spotted the lookout tower peeking from the canopy of the forest like a concrete periscope. Its big glass panes reflected the setting sun in a blaze of orange.

Merry took out her camera and snapped a photo. "How far away is it, do y'all know?"

"Maybe another hour," Rollo estimated. "Let's set up camp and hike the rest of the way in the morning.

She eased off her bag and dropped it to the ground. "Or—some of us could stay here and set up the tents, and some of us could check it out at sunset."

Finn slung off his pack and flexed his shoulders. "Let's go, Lois Lane."

No. Finn had completely misunderstood. Rollo opened his mouth to object, to say that he ought to be the one to take Merry to the top. That way Finn and Brianna could spend time together. But Merry was already smiling and zipping up her jacket against the evening breeze. It would look awkward to switch things up now.

"Take flashlights," he said instead, and crouched down to extract the tent bags from his pack.

Finn and Merry took off down the trail, already talking a mile a minute.

After a moment, Brianna knelt next to him. "I can handle this on my own," he told her. "You can go with them if you want."

"So I can bore Finn to death again? No, thank you." She reached for the tent he'd just pulled from his pack. "I'll set this one up."

She sounded so discouraged, so unlike her usual upbeat self. "It wasn't that bad," he told her. The lack of conviction in his own voice made him wince. "Here, we'll do it together."

He stood and searched for the most level spot for the tent, kicking stones and fallen branches aside.

"Not that bad?" Brianna wailed. "I told him about the reproductive cycle of the Bronze Birch Borer. In detail. He could probably write a thesis on it now."

"Well, birch beetles are a fascinating species." He shook out a piece of tarp he'd brought as a ground cover and settled it over the pine needles. "Don't be so hard on yourself."

"Birch beetles are only fascinating to geeks like me. He must have been laughing his ass off. You know, the ass I threw a Thermos at."

Rollo swallowed hard, trying to hold back his laugh. But she heard it and ducked her head.

"I'm such a disaster. You know what this is? This is nature's way of telling me that my genetic line should end here. I will never reproduce because I will never be able to talk to a man I'm attracted to. I'm an evolutionary dead end, that's what I am. Too awkward to duplicate. That's me." She flopped onto the ground and buried her head on her folded arms.

"Honey." He strode toward her and sat next to her, scooping her into his lap. She settled there as perfectly as a cat curled up in an armchair. "That's absurd. And I can prove it." Something glistened on the curve of her cheek, the only part of her face he could see. A tear?

He brushed it away, but she turned even farther away from him.

"How?" she muttered.

"Easy. Are you a virgin?"

She snapped her head up in astonishment. "That's kind of a personal question!"

"Yes. It is. Well, are you?" Their faces were so close that he could make out the faint trace of freckles on the delicate skin above her cheekbones. The fragrance of her shampoo—pear, maybe—rose to his nostrils.

"No, I'm not a virgin. Not since I took AP chemistry my senior year in high school."

"Uh...what?"

"Singh Dal, my lab partner. We liked each other and worked really well together. We decided to find out what all the fuss was about. I guess you could say it was kind of an experiment."

Rollo felt another laugh threaten, but he knew she'd take it the wrong way. So he kept his tone completely serious. "And? What were the results of the experiment?"

She cocked her head. "Some awkward moments, but overall, great. Sex is good, I like it. Touching, kissing, it's nice. And orgasms are the most amazing thing nature ever invented."

Oh God. Maybe this was a bad idea. She was cuddled in his lap talking about orgasms. No way his body was going to ignore that. His cock twitched hard. She smelled so good, like spicy pear tart and vanilla ice cream. "There you go." He hoped his voice sounded halfway normal. "If you can have sex and everything's working, you can reproduce. You're not an evolutionary dead end."

"That's not what I mean! I want to fall in love. I want my children to grow up in a happy family the way I did. My parents are still crazy about each other. My dad makes my mom banana pancakes every Sunday, my mom knits him socks. They're like a Hallmark movie."

That sounded so far from his family that he had to laugh. "I'm sure they have problems like anyone else."

"You don't know them," she said stubbornly. "I never saw any fights or conflict. I want *that* for my kids. I want them to grown up in a nice little nest of happiness the way I did."

He shifted her on his lap, surprised she hadn't climbed off yet. Pretty soon she was going to figure out that he was getting turned on by holding a warm bundle of sexy woman. Because Brianna *was* sexy. Cuddly and curvy and firm and fragrant. "Maybe your expectations are unrealistic, Bri. What's a relationship without conflict?"

She craned her neck to look up at him. "You're saying I should settle? Just be content with any old guy who wants to sleep with me? Call up Singh Dal?"

"God no." His arms tightened around her. Singh Dal could go fly a kite as far as he was concerned. "That's not what I mean at all. You deserve the man of your dreams."

He was just questioning her dreams, that was all. Finn wasn't a "nest of happiness" kind of guy. He had just as many demons as Rollo had, even though he didn't talk about them.

Brianna was scanning his face with those pretty moss-green eyes. "What about you? Don't you deserve the woman of your dreams?"

Ouch. She'd put her finger on his most sensitive sore spot without even realizing it. He'd never talked to her about the demands of his family. Would she even understand? "I'm a Wareham. I'll have to marry someone from a certain social circle. It's not about dreams, it's about duty."

"Really?" Her forehead wrinkled in a frown. "I never thought of you as a snob."

"I'm not. This is coming from my family. I have an obligation to them and that's just the way it is. Besides, I'd never inflict the coldhearted, backstabbing Wareham clan on someone who wasn't used to it. It wouldn't be fair to the poor woman. My mother would eat her alive."

"So...what about Merry? Do you think she could handle your family?"

He tilted his head and squinted, trying to picture Merry taking on his mother. Fact was—Merry wouldn't ever care about him enough to bother. "Luckily, that never has to happen because she thinks I'm just a big oaf."

"Don't worry, I set her straight. I told her you definitely weren't just an oaf." She gave him a mischievous wink.

"*Just* an oaf? You're living dangerously, girl." He bared his teeth at her. "You're playing with fire. Or the big bad wolf. Or both."

She raised one hand and curled her fingers into a claw. "Are you forgetting my secret weapon?"

"Like I could ever forget that." He gave a full-body shudder at the visceral memory. "And that's the difference between me and Finn. I get the claw. He gets an offer to massage his ass with your strong man-hands."

Brianna covered her mouth with both hands, eyes brimming with amusement. "I did that, didn't I?"

"Oh yes. I wouldn't have believed it if I didn't witness it." They were both laughing now, Brianna's charming little face lit up with joy. Her deep chortling snort rolled out of her, twining around his heart, brightening the fog inside. And without conscious thought, without any hesitation, he bent his head and brushed his lips against hers.

It wasn't necessarily a kiss; it was more of a sampling. He wanted to know what joy tasted like on his tongue.

Her lips were so soft, they sent shockwaves through him. Soft and warm and sweet, tasting of hazelnut and the raisins from the trail mix they'd shared.

She let out a gasp, her eyes opening wide. "You kissed me!"

"Yeah. I noticed." He did it again, more slowly, savoring the sweet drag of her slightly chapped lips. He pulled the lower one between his teeth, gently, just until he heard her release a soft sigh. Then he ran his tongue around the inside of her upper lip, tugging at it sweetly, deliberately, taking his time, feeling her melt in his arms. He still didn't allow himself to think about what he was doing and why. He was following an imperative that came from some risk-hungry, determined part of him.

He felt her heart rate speed up, but that could also have been the pounding of blood in his own veins. His ears rang with it. He ran his right hand along her torso, from her shoulder to her waist, then wrapped his hand around her hipbone. She was so small—and his hands so big—that his thumb was on her belly and his middle finger somewhere on her lower back. But she felt perfectly right in his grasp. As if everything made sense now, in a way it never had before.

"Rollo, what are we doing?" he heard her whisper against his mouth. "This is crazy."

"Want me to stop?" he growled in return.

When she shook her head quickly, he deepened the kiss, urging her mouth open with his tongue. She squirmed in his lap, nestling her rounded ass against his cock, which was about as hard as the tree trunk behind them.

And then a shriek pierced the air.

He pulled away, lifting his head to listen. The sound came from the trail that led to the lookout tower—the direction that Finn and Merry had gone.

He dumped Brianna on the ground and bolted to his feet. "Stay here," he commanded her, and took off down the trail.

CHAPTER 11

Brianna scrambled to her knees, rubbing her butt, which a branch had poked as she'd tumbled to the ground, a graceful move courtesy of the incredibly confusing Rollo Wareham.

First he'd kissed her with more passion than anyone ever had before, then he'd ditched her and started bossing her around. What the heck was wrong with him?

Or right with him?

She pressed her fingers against her lips, which still tingled and burned. She felt as if she'd been woken up from a trance. As if she'd suddenly been shown a new dimension. Hey, have you heard about this crazy 3D thing? Isn't it amazing that you can see depth as well as flatness?

Yup, that was what it felt like. Holy wow. She had no idea Rollo knew how to kiss like that. Or that he would want to kiss *her*. Where had that come from? What did it mean? What about Merry? And most of all, would they get a chance to do it again? Because she'd be counting the minutes until that happened.

Kissing Rollo...wow, that kiss changed things. Or did it?

This was extremely confusing.

But one thing was for sure. No matter how well he kissed, she had no intention of waiting for him to come back. Screw that. It sounded as if something bad had happened down the trail, and if Merry or Finn was in trouble, she couldn't just stay here and hope for the best.

She grabbed a tent stake and her Thermos. Both seemed like reasonable weapons, in case any were needed. Then she rose to her feet and set off down the path at a slow jog. When she heard tense voices up ahead, she sped up to a run. It was a male voice that didn't sound like either Finn or Rollo. And it sounded scary.

She slowed when she got closer, not wanting to reveal her presence. She tiptoed the last stretch, until she turned around a bend—and found a scene that made her draw in a gasp of horror.

A man was aiming a gun at Merry and Rollo. Finn was lying on the ground, on his side. Rollo had his hands in the air in a defensive gesture. The man wore a baseball cap from an Arco gas station and a greasy-looking denim jacket. His face showed several days' growth of beard. He looked young, probably about their age, and twitchy.

Too twitchy.

Brianna swallowed back her fear and tried to think of what to do. The guy was keeping Merry close with a hand on the shoulder of her down vest. Merry looked both freaked out and furious, as if she might kick the guy in the balls any second now. Which would *not* be good, even Brianna could see that. A user with a gun was much too unpredictable. Better to stay calm. Like Rollo.

Rollo was talking to him in his deep, rumbling voice, keeping his tone level and calm. Brianna couldn't make out what he was saying, but whatever it was, it seemed to be working. The guy hadn't shot anyone yet. She peered through the trees at Finn, her heart clenching. She saw no blood, and she hadn't heard a gunshot.

Since Merry looked more furious than terrified, hopefully nothing too dire had happened to Finn.

Brandishing her tent stake and Thermos, she crept closer. Should she go back to the campsite and call 9-1-1? The last time she'd checked, her phone had said "no service." And they were so far from the road, it would take forever for help to get here even if she could get through.

No. Best to stay and see if she could help.

The closer she got, the better she could hear what Rollo was saying. Incredibly, he didn't sound frightened by the gun being waved in his direction.

"Let her go, man. We're just out for a hike. Not looking for trouble."

"I'm supposed to get the girl," the man said. He looked at Merry and frowned. "They didn't say she was black, though."

"You must have the wrong girl, then. Let her go."

"Can't do that. Better make sure."

He tried to drag Merry down the trail, but she dug in her heels and didn't budge. "I'm not the one you're after, so let me go."

Merry flinched as the guy swung the gun toward her.

"Hey. Hey," Rollo said quickly. "Take it easy. We can figure this out. Is someone paying you to find someone? You won't get paid if it's the wrong girl. Look at me, dude. Look at me."

Brianna's heart was in her mouth, but slowly the man obeyed. The gun careened back toward Rollo. "What else did they say about this girl? Hair color? Eye color?"

"Dark hair, dark eyes. Supposed to be at the tower."

"I've never even been to the tower!" Merry snapped.

The attacker turned back to her, scowling. "I don't like your attitude. Hand me your pack. Might as well get something for my time."

Merry, looking absolutely furious, took off her backpack and handed it to the man. With his gun trained on Rollo, he rummaged through it.

Ah-ha. This was the perfect opportunity, when the jerk's attention was divided between Rollo and the backpack. Brianna crept through the trees until she stood in Rollo's line of sight. His eyes went wide, then he scowled and shook his head.

The attacker noticed, and swung around to scan the woods. Brianna froze. Would the cluster of bristle-brush pines be enough to hide her?

After a long, agonizing moment, the gunman went back to searching through Merry's backpack.

Brianna lifted up her Thermos and tent stake and waved them at Rollo. She had a plan, but no clue how to communicate it to him, especially when he couldn't react without tipping off the gunman. His eyes burned with fury. Was he angry at her or the gunman? She wasn't sure.

She shrugged it off. Time to take action. Her plan was to create a distraction with her Thermos. That would give Rollo a chance to disarm the gunman. It was a good plan, right? Sure it was.

She took a deep breath. Narrowing her eyes, she focused on the spot where she wanted the Thermos to land. In the woods, about thirty yards behind the gunman. Behind his back, so he'd have to turn around to check it out. But not too close, where it might freak him out. When she had the location firmly in her mind's eye, she hauled back and used all her strength to fling the Thermos that direction.

But this just wasn't her day, or maybe that Thermos was cursed. It went off-course, struck a tree trunk, and bounced back, right toward her.

She jumped out of the way and stumbled over a rock. The gunman spun in her direction, gun held straight out before him. The gun looked huge and black in his hand. She saw the exact moment he spotted her and decided to fire.

She dove behind the closest boulder. Covering her head with her hands, hoping her butt wasn't sticking out too far, she squeezed her eyes shut and braced herself.

No gunshot came. Instead she heard a series of thuds and grunts, a shout from Merry, then footsteps running her way.

When she opened her eyes, Rollo was crouching in front of her. His gray-blue eyes blazed with unholy fury. And she usually thought of them as so kind.

"What the fuck was that? Didn't I tell you to stay out of it?"

"What...what happened?"

He hauled her to her feet. "Are you okay?" Still holding her hand in his, he scanned her up and down, a quick, scorching survey that had her tingling.

"Yes, of course. What about Merry? And the man with the gun?"

"Out." He dropped her hand and folded his arms over his chest. "Damn it, Bri. When he pointed that gun at you..." He shook his head, fury tightening his expression again. Wheeling around, he stalked toward the others.

Brianna hauled a long breath into her lungs and followed after the large, angry man who vaguely resembled her gentle bear of a friend.

*

Rollo slung the unconscious gunman over his shoulder and headed for the lookout tower. Finn was still unconscious. Rollo instructed Merry and Brianna to keep him warm while he called dispatch from the tower.

She and Merry took off their jackets and tucked them around Finn, while Merry told her everything that had happened in a tone of pure awe. "I've never seen anything like it. When it looked like the bad guy was going to shoot at you, Rollo came charging forward. First he kicked the gun out of the dude's hand, then he just started punching him. I had no idea he could fight like that. It was just wham, bam, again, again, until he was just lying there on the ground. Not moving. Bleeding. I thought he killed him for a second there. Then he goes running into the woods to find you. My heart was racing so fast I thought it might jump out of my skin!"

"Wow." Brianna wished she'd seen it all go down. "All I saw was a bunch of pine needles in my face. And then Rollo glaring at me. I don't know why he's so mad. If I hadn't thrown my Thermos, the guy wouldn't have gotten distracted. I thought he was going to hurt you."

"Nah, it was more like he'd been hired to find someone. We need to tell the police. I wonder if it's a real gun."

"It's real, all right." Brianna sat on a pile of pine needles and hugged her arms around her knees. The aftermath of the adrenaline rush was making her shaky. The sun was behind the trees now, and the air was chilling quickly.

"How do you know?"

"Melvin Turner has a gun collection. He gave me a full tour once. Sometimes we do target practice together."

Merry sat on her knees next to her. "I swear, girl, you need to let me do a story on that man. There's something not right about him."

"Are you going to write a story about this? Hero hotshot takes down armed assailant with help of Thermos?"

"While screenwriter catches up on his beauty sleep?" They both started at the sound of Finn's raspy voice.

"Finn! Are you okay?" He was trying to get his arms out from under Merry's yellow down jacket, but Brianna tucked him in more tightly. "Don't move, Rollo said to keep you warm."

Looking irritated, he shoved the jacket aside and sat up, swaying a little. "I'm plenty warm. Jesus."

"But Rollo said—"

"He was worried about shock, but I'm conscious now and I'm not shivering, and I'm fine." He propelled himself to his feet. "Where's Rollo?"

Brianna and Merry exchanged a look of alarm. "He went to the tower."

"Then come on, let's go." He launched down the trail toward the lookout. "We have to help Rollo, for Christ's sake. He might need backup. That guy's dangerous, did you see how he went after me, Merry?"

Merry folded her lips together, but Brianna could guess what she was thinking. Finn and Rollo were both fit, strong, powerful firefighters.

But only one was a badass. Rollo.

CHAPTER 12

Rollo had been to the Breton tower before; luckily they hadn't changed the access code. He punched in the numbers and pushed open the door. Once inside, he propped the gunman in a corner and powered up the radio communications system. He called the forest ranger, who was based out of the same Fire and Rescue compound as the hotshots. He filled the dispatcher in on what had happened, and she called the state troopers, who immediately sent a car. He promised to wait until the deputies arrived. The last thing he wanted was to let the guy slip away.

His knuckles hurt. His shoulder hurt. His heart hurt.

He hadn't struck anyone that hard since the day he'd nearly killed Dougie Berkowitz. He'd vowed not to. Punching bags, sure. Walls, if he couldn't find something better. But not people. The crunch of the guy's jawbone, the fierce adrenaline surging through his system, the heady sense of overpowering someone weaker—it scared him down to his bones. He'd been there before. He knew what could happen.

Outside, night was descending like a dense purple blanket. He heard a sound at the lower door and figured it might be the deputies. Instead, he opened the door to Brianna, Merry and Finn.

"Come on in," he told them. "Cops are on their way. I got permission for us to stay here tonight if you guys want."

Merry came in first. He noticed that she was looking at him much differently than she had at the start of their trip. As if he were Superman instead of an oaf. "Thanks for dealing with that dude. I can't believe he had his slimy hands on me."

"He'll be going to jail for sure, if that's any comfort."

"It helps." She tilted her head, brown eyes glinting. "Not as much as seeing you whale on him, though. You were an animal."

He cringed at that description, knowing how accurate it was. He'd felt like an animal. A wolf or a grizzly bear or some other lethal predator.

Next came Finn, who wore a disgruntled expression.

"You okay?"

"I'm okay, yes, except for being left behind like a rotting log."

His friend gave him a little shoulder shove as he passed, but Rollo took no offense. "I wanted to get this guy locked up somewhere. I knew you'd be fine, tough guy."

Finn shot him a wry look. So much for that attempt to make him feel better. His gaze slid to Brianna, who was bringing up the rear. He was still furious with her. The sight of the gun veering toward the woods, the man sighting it on Brianna—God, he'd never forget that feeling.

He'd also never forget how he'd been kissing the day-lights out of her right before all hell broke loose.

Brianna sailed through the door, head held high. "Don't bother to yell at me anymore. I had a good plan, it just did-n't work out exactly as I intended."

"A good plan? You call getting him to shoot in your di-rection a good plan?"

"It wasn't supposed to be my direction," she hissed at him. "The Thermos was supposed to land *away* from me. What was I supposed to do, just wait and watch him wave that gun around?"

"Was that really too much to ask?" He lowered his voice to a growl in her ear. "I should have kissed you harder."

She felt her face flame. "What? Why?"

"So you'd stay put like I told you to."

"Oh my God. You're serious? Sorry, bud. I am not the 'staying put' type. I'm as strong as a lot of guys, and since I'm little, I can surprise them too."

"Oh yeah? With your strong man-hands? Were you go-ing to tickle the guy or give him an ass-rub?"

"Ha. Ha." She made a face at him. But when he caught the smile tugging at her pretty lips—delicious lips—he fig-ured they were okay. Thank God. If things got weird with Brianna over this, he might have to really hurt that loser with the gun.

*

The night improved a lot after that. The deputies arrived, took their statements, and hauled the bad guy away. They decided to stay in the tower overnight. The space was the shape of an octagon, with communications and testing equipment taking up most of the middle, and a small bedroom and kitchen area filling the rest. The big panes of glass on all sides looked out on the dark forest and a vast sky filled with the first evening stars. It felt as if they were floating over the forest in a glass bubble.

Before it got completely dark, Rollo and Finn jogged back down the trail to grab their gear. They left Brianna and Merry in charge of raiding the Forest Service's stores for dinner. By the time he and Finn returned, soup was heating on the stove and plates of crackers awaited their brie.

Maybe because he'd kicked the bad guy's ass—or maybe because of the brie—Merry showered him with attention. As they devoured the cheese and crackers, she asked him about fighting fires, about growing up in New York. It turned out they'd been to some of the same museums and parks when they were growing up. She was raised in Brooklyn, and he was Upper East Side, but they still had plenty of New York experiences in common.

Finally, Merry was taking him seriously, just as he'd wanted her to when she was embedded with the crew.

It felt damn good, he had to admit. But not nearly as good as he'd imagined. He didn't like the fact that it took a glimpse of his violent side to get her attention. He found that just a little fucked up, in fact. That was the side of himself he *didn't* like. The side he worked to conquer.

Brianna, on the other hand, was avoiding him. Every time he looked her way, she ignored him and focused on sipping her soup or chatting with Finn. Chatting *comfortably* with Finn. As if he no longer made her feel awkward. He wasn't sure how he felt about that.

That kiss in the woods had really knocked him off his game. Where had that come from? And what now? Brianna seemed determined not to make a big deal out of it, which was probably the right way to go. Why mess up an awesome friendship with kissing? Or more than kissing?

Problem was, he couldn't stop thinking about the "more."

But he couldn't have more.

"Hey, who's this?" Finn was peering at a photo tacked up on a corkboard in the kitchenette area. Rollo joined him and saw that the photo showed a young woman in a Forest Service uniform and green wool hat. She looked as if the photographer had caught her off guard. Her expression was...haunted. That was the best word for it. She was beautiful, even in a casual snapshot, with big dark eyes and a stubborn tilt to her jaw.

"I don't know. I've only been here once, and I didn't see her. Maybe a volunteer?"

Finn couldn't drag his eyes away from the photo. Even when Rollo mentioned the bottle of wine they'd brought, he barely reacted. "I'm going to find her," he murmured. "I want to meet her."

"Get a grip, Finn. Did that knock on the head hurt your brain? This photo could be twenty years old."

Finn rubbed the bump on his head and scowled. "I'm fine. Don't remind me. I'm never going to live this down."

"Bullshit. You did good. The man had a gun."

"Yeah, but the girls said you kicked it out of his hand and beat the crap out of him." Finn shot him a curious glance. "I never thought of you as a fighter."

"I'm not. At least not anymore."

"But you used to be?"

Rollo hesitated. He didn't talk about this kind of thing, but of all the hotshots, Finn would be the most likely to understand, being a black sheep himself. But before he could answer, he spied Brianna coming toward them with plastic glasses of wine.

Since he didn't want her to see Finn staring at the photo of the girl, he slung his arm around her shoulder and headed her off. He plucked one of the wine glasses from her hand and steered her toward the window the farthest away from Merry.

"You're avoiding me," he told her sternly.

She turned almost as red as the wine in her cup. "I'm not." At his skeptical look, she admitted, "Okay, I am. I'm just...confused. I thought you were head over heels in love with Merry, but if you're going to be kissing other people, I can't help you in your quest anymore."

"I didn't kiss 'other people.' I kissed you."

"Yes, but...why? You don't like me that way. How many times have people tried to set us up now? And every time, we just laughed it off."

All true. But things were different now. He could still feel her lips so soft and fresh against his. The spicy fragrance of her hair brought back the sensation of her warm, curvy body snuggled in his arms.

"We need to talk about this," he told her in a low voice. "We can't just pretend it didn't happen."

She nodded reluctantly as she sipped the wine. "Okay. But not here. After we get back to Jupiter Point."

"Deal. I'm not letting you off the hook, Bri. This changes things." She met his eyes. A vibrant kind of energy passed between them. Something intense and delirious, like the first hint of sunrise in a quiet forest.

"What are you two plotting over there?" Merry called to them from the easternmost window, where she'd been taking photos of the star scape outside. "And does it involve a glass of wine for me?"

They moved to the central island where the observation equipment was located and Rollo poured a glass for Merry. Finn finally tore himself away from the corkboard. They all crowded around the countertop.

"To quiet towers in the peaceful wilderness," said Merry wryly, raising her glass.

Rollo snorted as they all clicked glasses. They spent the rest of the evening telling stories, laughing, speculating about the guy with the gun, and watching the stars slowly shift across the night sky.

Merry and Brianna shared the tower's single bed, while Finn and Rollo slept on sleeping bags on the floor. Rollo didn't get much sleep. The incident with the gunman had shaken him right down to his core. When he finally drifted off, he dreamed about the fight with Dougie. Sharp, jumbled images: the look of shock and terror on the smaller boy's face, the way his head snapped back, the crumpled look of his body on the gym floor. The dark blood seeping into his hair.

Images he'd never forget. Images he didn't *want* to forget. Because as long as he remembered, he'd never do anything like that again.

Except that he just had. He'd knocked someone out with the power of his fists. He didn't even know how much damage he'd done. He wouldn't know until he called the hospital the next day.

It had to be done, he reminded himself. The guy was about to shoot, and Brianna was in the line of fire. He'd done the right thing.

The next day, he forgot all about the bad guy. He forgot about talking to Brianna about their kiss. Because halfway back to civilization, his cell service returned. He'd missed over twenty phone messages. His mother, his father, Brent, and members of various police departments had called.

Sidney, his fourteen-year-old sister, had run away from her school. After she set fire to the curtains in her dorm room.

Using their mother's credit card, she'd booked herself on a flight from New York to the West Coast. Destination—Jupiter Point.

CHAPTER 13

Brianna had left her truck at Rollo's house, so she got the honor of riding shotgun while Rollo drove twenty miles above the speed limit while trying to track down his sister by phone.

She wasn't hard to find, as it turned out. The minute they turned into his driveway, Brianna spotted a tall, brown-haired girl wearing horn-rimmed glasses, an over-sized black hoodie and dark blue leggings sitting cross-legged on the front lawn. She jumped up at the sound of Rollo's Jeep and ran toward them.

"Don't be mad, don't be mad, don't be mad," she chanted before flinging herself into Rollo's arms.

He caught her tight against him. "I'm not mad. I'm— okay, damn it, I'm mad. You scared the shit out of everyone. Why are you doing this?"

"I just need a break. No one has to freak out." She slid back down to the ground. Brianna scanned her outfit and noticed black ankle boots with chains on the sides, and a very expensive-looking black leather backpack. "It's practically Thanksgiving break anyway. Don't get all lecture-y on me." Pouting, she turned her attention to Brianna and Finn.

"This one's a fireman, I remember him," she waved her hand at Finn, "but I haven't met your friend the elf."

Brianna's face flamed. Would the phrase "I'm not an elf" be too ridiculous to utter?

"Run away all you want, but don't be rude to my friends," said Rollo sharply. "This is Brianna. Brianna, this is my sister Sidney. She's nothing but trouble and has no manners."

"Hi, Brianna. Elf was a compliment, by the way. I'd give anything to be an elf. But I'm stuck in giant territory."

Would the phrase "you're not a giant" be equally as absurd? "It's nice to meet you, Sidney. Welcome to Jupiter Point." Actually, that sounded kind of ridiculous too. The girl hadn't come for the scenery.

"Thank you! I'm glad someone's being welcoming." She screwed up her face at Rollo and slid her arm through Brianna's. Behind her glasses, she had big gray eyes a bit like Rollo's. "If Rollington decides to be a jerk, can I stay with you?"

Finn let out a snort. "Did you say *Rollington*?"

"Oops." Sidney clapped a hand over her mouth. "Was that a secret?"

Rollo scrubbed his hand through his hair, leaving the thick waves standing on end. "Of course not. Grow up, Finn. It's just a name, for Chrissake."

Finn, still laughing, gave them all a wave and went to unload Rollo's Jeep. "See ya later, Sidney. Welcome to the nuthouse, I think you'll fit right in."

Rollo rolled his eyes. "Come on, kiddo, get your stuff. Are you hungry? Tired? Do you need a shower?"

He strode to the overloaded messenger bag she'd left on the lawn and slung it over his shoulder.

"Yes, yes and yes. Then you can show me to my bedroom and I'll unpack."

"Sorry, sis. Not happening. After we get you straightened out, I'm booking you a plane ticket."

Sidney stopped in her tracks, then bolted behind Brianna. Brianna felt herself being gripped from behind like some kind of human shield. "I'm not going back, Rollo!"

Rollo swung around and marched toward them. Even though she wasn't the target of his hard stare, Brianna's heart jumped into her throat. He looked furious, worried, upset, concerned, and sexy as hell.

"You don't have a choice. Do you know how many messages they left on my phone?"

"Please! Not yet. I just need a little time. Please, Rollo! Work it out so I can stay with you just through the holidays. I'll homeschool. I'll do all my work online. I can live with you and cook for you and I won't get in your way, I promise."

He shook his head firmly. "I can't be responsible for a spoiled teenager who just ran away from her million-dollar boarding school. I'm still fixing up the damn house. It's a construction zone, in fact. I'm building a koi pond."

"I can help with that," Sidney said quickly. "I love fish."

"Brianna doesn't need any help. Right, Bri?"

Brianna opened and closed her mouth, probably looking a lot like a koi herself. "Um, sure? I mean, that's not really the point. Maybe you should sit down and talk before you make a decision." Behind her, she felt Sidney squeeze her hand gratefully.

Rollo's stormy gaze settled on her. "You know nothing about the situation."

"I know she's upset. Why else would she run away? And I know she trusts you, because she ran away *to you*. Geez, Rollo, would it kill you to just listen to her?"

Tension thrummed between the three of them. Finally Rollo turned to Sidney. "Did you set a fire at Bridewell?"

"Yes," Sidney said in a whisper that tickled Brianna's hair.

"Do you promise not to do anything like that here?"

Brianna felt the breeze from Sidney's frantic nodding.

"You won't run away again? You'll never turn off your phone? You'll behave yourself?"

More nodding. Rollo relaxed by slow degrees. "I don't know if they'll go for it."

"They will. They don't want me around anyway. That's why they sent me to Bridewell. If they know I'm with you, they can just stop worrying about me. That's all they want."

The wistful note in Sidney's voice made Brianna's heart ache for her. In her own family, everyone was always hugging and saying "I love you." She never doubted her parents' love for her. Or each other. But in Sidney's voice, she heard a very different story.

If Sidney stayed, Brianna vowed to take the girl under her wing and make her feel safe and loved while she was in Jupiter Point.

"Well, we'll see," Rollo grumbled. "Now come get some food into you."

Brianna nearly stumbled as Sidney gave her a tight hug from behind. "Thank you," the girl whispered in her ear. "Thanks for standing up for me."

Brianna turned and planted her hands on her hips. "Just so you know, I grew up here and I know everyone in Jupiter Point, so don't even think about finding trouble to get into. I will know."

"Cross my heart." The tall girl pushed her glasses up her nose, then made the sign of the cross. "I'd say 'hope to die' but that might freak out my overprotective brother."

Rollo growled at that phrase. "Don't push me, little sister. I'll have you on a plane so fast, you'll forget you were ever here."

"Sorry." Sidney stepped from behind Brianna and went to join her brother. He slung an arm around her shoulders and steered her toward the front door. After one last smoldering glance at Brianna, the two of them disappeared inside.

Brianna let out a long sigh and headed for her truck, which she'd left tucked away in the garage. Finn was still unloading the Jeep. In the midst of swinging Rollo's heavy backpack out of the rear, he gave her a goodbye salute as she passed by.

"That was fun," he called to her. "Let's plan another hike, except we'll leave out the dude with the gun."

"Good plan." She grinned at him, then stopped short. Wow. She was *cured*. She hadn't said or done anything awkward. She hadn't looked at Finn's butt, or thrown a Thermos at it.

One kiss from Rollo and everything had changed. Wow.

*

"Is that your new girlfriend?" Sidney asked as soon as they were through the door. "I like her."

"No. She's just a friend. Don't be such a brat." Rollo led her to his bedroom, since it was the only one with a bed. "You can have my room, and I'll stay on the couch."

"Don't be such an idiot."

"You don't want the bedroom?"

"Of course I do." She plopped herself onto his bed and bounced a few times. "I mean about Brianna. She's the kind of girl you should be with."

"Yeah? What makes you such an expert?"

A wicked grin spread across her face. "Because nothing would make Mother more insane than seeing you with a little redheaded elf with no fashion sense."

"Stay out of it," Rollo said firmly. "Brianna doesn't deserve to get dragged into the Wareham family shitshow. Just let her be. You promise?"

Sidney squinted and gazed into the middle distance. "I half promise."

"What the hell does that mean?"

"It means I want to hang out with her. Because she's nice. She can be my best friend while I'm here."

Rollo shook his head. Sidney always had a best friend of the moment. But she was fickle, and tended to change best friends as often as her contact lenses. Or glasses, at the moment. "She's twice your age."

"So? She's not all full of herself like you." Sidney stuck out her tongue at him.

He ground his teeth together. "First plane out of here. Don't forget."

"Yes sir," she said meekly.

He let her take an endless shower, then made her some tacos. But even though he grilled her over dinner, she refused to explain why she'd set her curtains on fire and run away from school. All she'd say was that she needed a break.

After some heavy phone lobbying, he got his mother to agree that Sidney could stay with him until the mandatory Wareham family Christmas, as long as she kept up with her schoolwork.

So suddenly, there he was, host to a fourteen-year-old runaway and a dropout firefighter. And occasionally a pretty redheaded landscaper.

He liked it. Sidney was his favorite family member, and he liked having Finn close by. He worried about the dude.

And when Brianna showed up to work on the pond, it turned into a sort of party. Sidney would sit cross-legged on the lawn and jabber away while Brianna dug in the rocky soil. She'd play songs on her iPod and show Brianna her sketches. Sometimes the two of them would dance to one of the songs. Rollo couldn't believe how quickly Sidney had latched on to Bri. But he was grateful for it, that was for sure. He trusted Bri with his sister—definitely more than he'd trust anyone in his own family.

Apparently gossip about Sidney had already spread through the Upper East Side. Cornelia emailed him. *Sorry about the family drama. If you need anything, please let me know. Teenagers are such a nightmare, aren't they?*

He didn't like that email at all. It reminded him that he had no business kissing Brianna, thinking about Brianna, or lusting after Brianna. None of the above. His future was Cornelia, or someone like her. He had to stop this attraction before it went anywhere.

But the sight of her digging up his lawn made him crazy. Brianna might be occasionally awkward in the rest of her life, but when she was working, she was pure grace, every movement confident and skillful. Sometimes she wore her usual overalls, but sometimes she wore cutoffs. He fixated on the sight of her firm, rounded calves with their healthy tan skin tone. Work boots and shorts were an incredibly sexy combination, especially when paired with a ribbed tank top that clung to her torso and waist.

At the end of the day, she always wound up with streaks of mud on her face, her arms and shoulders glowing with sweat. He wanted to strip it all off and bundle her into the shower. Run soap along her sleek curves, reignite the desire in her green eyes, that hazy amazement.

They still hadn't discussed the big kiss since Sidney had shown up. He wondered if she'd forgotten about it. It would be better that way. This thing between them, whatever it was, couldn't go anywhere. They should bury that one mistaken moment and never speak of it again.

But damn it, she kept showing up with her shovel and her shorts and her cuteness and her curves and...

Finally he couldn't take it anymore. He cornered her in the kitchen as she was filling her water canteen. "We need to talk." He took her elbow and steered her into the bathroom, the only place they could have some privacy. As soon as he closed the door, the room seemed to fill with tension. Or maybe it was lust—on his side, anyway.

"What's up?" she asked calmly. Little tendrils of sweat-damp red hair curled around her forehead. His hands itched to smooth them away.

How could she be so calm when his cock was already swelling just from being this close to her?

"I, uh, wondered if Sidney's told you why she ran away. She's been talking to you a lot."

She frowned at him. "Rollo, if she tells me anything I feel you need to know, I promise to tell you. But I'm her only friend here and I can't betray her trust."

"You were my friend first," he pointed out.

She lifted one eyebrow. "Are you jealous?"

"Don't be ridiculous." Maybe he *was* jealous, but only of her crush on Finn. "I'm just saying that I came first. Besides, she's just a kid."

"She's not really a kid. She's kind of in that in-between phase. It's a tough time."

"Believe me, I know," he muttered. "And my family doesn't make it easy. I know what Sidney's dealing with. She's a Wareham." He broke off before he revealed too much about the family dirty laundry.

She leaned against the sink and folded her arms across her chest. "What are you not telling me, Rollo? You and Sidney both. I know the Warehams are wealthy and privileged and upper class and blah blah blah. So what's the problem? Why do you get all gloomy anytime your family name comes up, and why does Sidney complain about them so much? And...she keeps referring to some bad thing you did in the past."

"She does?" Rollo felt his face tighten. Damn it, Sidney had no business telling Brianna his secrets.

But maybe *he* should. Part of him wanted to. But Brianna might not understand. She hadn't seen the dark side of life the way he had.

"Sidney likes to be dramatic," he finally said. "It's nothing you have to worry about."

"Rollington Wareham the Third." Brianna shoved a hand into his chest. "Aren't we friends? Don't friends tell each other the important stuff?"

He caught her hand against his chest. "Yes. It's just that some things..." He folded his lips together before he got carried away. She opened her hand against his chest. His heartbeat sped up in response to her touch.

He leaned closer as if a magnet was pulling him to her. Her eyes widened, her breathing quickened. A wash of pink spread across her cheeks. He saw her swallow, the muscles moving in her slender throat.

It was official; he wanted Brianna.

"What are we going to do about this?" he asked hoarsely. He held her hand tighter against his chest, wanting more than anything to slide it lower, across the bulge of his erection.

"This?" she whispered.

"Every time I get near you, I want you more. I don't know what's wrong with me."

CHAPTER 14

Every bit of her felt on fire. The way Rollo was looking at her, the feel of his broad chest under her palm, the excitement building between them...she'd never felt like this before. This time she didn't feel awkward at all—just wildly powerful.

Then his words sank in. "You don't know what's *wrong* with you? What's that supposed to mean?" she tried to snatch her hand away, but he held it tight.

"You know what I mean. We're supposed to be friends. I don't usually feel this level of lust for a friend. You're...Brianna. Same old Brianna."

This time she did manage to wrench her hand away. "Same old Brianna? Oh my God. I can't believe you just said that. You make me sound like an old jacket or something."

"You know what I mean." He dragged his hand through his hair, and for a moment she felt sorry for him. But just for a moment. Every feeling of inadequacy she'd ever experienced came rushing back. All the times guys had looked right past her at Evie. The billion times they'd asked her for Evie's number. The time Dylan invited her to the prom as a backup, then dumped her literally outside the gym door when his first-choice date showed up.

"No, I don't. You make it sound like I'm not worth lusting over. What about Merry? Would you ever call her 'same old Merry'?"

He didn't answer, which she figured was an answer in and of itself.

"No, you wouldn't. I'm tired of feeling like an old jacket. If you were really my friend, you wouldn't ever make me feel that way." She rushed to the door of the bathroom and pushed it open. As he went after her, it swung back and hit him smack in the nose, making him fall back a step. "Sorry. You know me. Same old awkward Brianna."

On the other side of the door, she stopped for a moment and turned back to confront him. His hand covered his nose, his blue-gray eyes watering.

"And honestly, this is just one of the things making me question our friendship. You need to start being honest with me."

"Okay. Okay. But you aren't going to like it." He dropped his hand. His poor nose looked a little swollen, but at least no blood was pouring out of it. "Come on. Let's get out of here."

She followed him out the door. Sidney sat cross-legged on a towel on the lawn. Earbuds in place, she bobbed her head to the music and mouthed the words to the song she was listening to. Her sketchbook was spread open on her lap. Sidney poured a lot of her emotions into her drawings.

Rollo put a hand on Brianna's lower back and steered her toward the running path that hugged the hillside. The thin winter light made everything look crystal clear, including Rollo's tall, broad-shouldered form. His jeans fit him so snugly, hugging his rear in a sexy, hypnotic way. His muscles bulged out of his t-shirt, his arms like thick tree trunks. She knew firsthand how strong he was, how physically powerful. Just watching him made her weak in the knees. How could she ever have found Finn attractive when *Rollo* was right there all along? She still didn't really understand it.

When they reached a quiet lookout, where the gray, gleaming ocean peeked through a grove of cypress trees, he stopped and drew in a long breath.

"You *are* worth lusting over. Believe me, I'm lusting up a storm. But it's not a good idea. I'm not the person you think I am."

She stared, totally confused. "You're not Rollo Wareham?"

"Of course I am. But I'm also Rollington Wareham the Third, and that guy's an asshole."

His blue-gray eyes, normally so kind, looked almost tormented.

"You think I'm a nice guy. The kind of guy you can always count on. I've heard you say that I have a good heart. That I'm kind. And I know you believe that."

"Of course I do." She frowned at him. "I know you, so I know it's true."

"It isn't. I've hurt people. Badly."

She shook her head, utterly confused. What people? Was he talking about girls? Had he broken someone's heart? "I don't understand."

He bent his head so he was staring at the ground. She saw his jaw flex under his beard. His shoulders hunched forward slightly.

"I was born into wealth, you know that. I was raised to think the world belonged to me. That I could do anything I wanted. That I would never pay a price."

He looked so pained that she wanted to wrap her arms around him and tell him to forget she'd ever said anything. "Look, Rollo, you don't have to do this."

"I do. I do. But don't say I didn't warn you."

She swallowed through a giant lump in her throat. All this time, she'd considered Rollo a friend—a big, gentle bear of a friend. Every once in a while she'd caught glimpses of other aspects of his personality. But she'd never seen him this serious. "Okay. Spit it out. I'm listening."

"As you've probably noticed, I'm also strong. Very physical. That's been true since the age of about ten. I shot up, I put on muscle, I was big and powerful and a spoiled, miserable kid. Every complaint Sidney makes about our family, it's true. My mother could never make up her mind about whether she actually wanted to be a mother, so she'd hire nannies, then fire them. Then hire a different one. My father believed in crushing the opposition, and that just about everyone qualified as opposition. Including his sons. Anyway, I'm not using that as an excuse. Just describing the territory. The result of all that was that I became a bully. A rich and powerful bully. I got into fights. I beat people up at school. And I never got punished because my father loved it when I came out on top."

Brianna felt her insides shrivel up at this description. It sounded nothing like the Rollo she knew. "But you're not like that now. The only time I've ever seen you hit anyone was on the trail."

"I know. Because when I was fourteen I put a kid in the hospital. I'd overheard him saying something about me, calling me a jerk. We were in the school gym, and I just slammed him. He dropped to the floor and started bleeding from the ears. I freaked out and carried him outside. Someone had called 9-1-1 and the paramedics showed up. I handed him over and watched them save his life. He missed a bunch of school and his parents ended up moving away. People said he wasn't ever the same after that. Even his face looked different because I'd broken his cheekbone. I went to the hospital to apologize. The fear on his face when he saw me...it just ripped my heart out."

Brianna touched his arm but he flinched away.

"I don't think you're hearing me. I'm not Mr. Nice Guy. I was a rich and spoiled asshole with a punch like a jackhammer."

"You *were*. I'm not arguing with that. But Rollo—you were fourteen. That was what, over fifteen years ago? What about the rest of high school?"

"My father sent me to a different school. I got into boxing at first, but as soon as I had to aim a blow at someone, I freaked out. I kept seeing Dougie's face. That blood. It was terrible. I dropped boxing. Switched to cross-country running and rock-climbing. That got me outdoors, and that changed everything for me. In the summers, I stopped going back to New York and started going on mountain-climbing trips. I got a better grip on myself, and being away from my family helped a lot. I went to college as far away as I could—Fairbanks, Alaska."

"You went to college in Alaska?"

"Yup. They have a great mountaineering program. That's where I first started volunteering with the Fire Service. I did that every summer and it was great. I need a way to channel my physicality. I know that much about myself."

Hearing him say the word "physicality" drew her gaze to the rippling muscles under his shirt, the way the material stretched so tight across his wide chest.

"As soon as I turned twenty-one and had access to my trust fund, I set up a fund for Dougie. I still felt so guilty and he wouldn't even see me. His family didn't want to talk to me, but I actually got a thank-you card from Dougie's mom. I was starting to feel okay about myself. I thought I was all better. A good guy. But then my dad started pressuring me to join the company, do my part for the Wareham tradition. I tried it for one month, and then I got into a shouting match with the CFO and nearly lost it. I knew I couldn't handle that life. So I quit and left New York. I thought about what I wanted my life to be. I didn't want to hurt people. I wanted to be a good guy. And I wanted to be outdoors working my ass off, the way I did in Alaska. So I got my red card and became a hotshot."

"Thereby saving lives and property and wild animals and trees," she pointed out. "So you *are* a good guy."

"Don't count on it." His low growl gave her the shivers. "You saw me on that trail. I could have killed that dude."

"He could have killed *us*. Geez, Rollo, I hate to say it because I'm pretty much a can't-we-all-get-along pacifist, but I'm really glad you were there and that you went after him."

He was shaking his head as if he didn't want her to defend him.

"Okay, fine, you're a big jerk for saving our lives. Damn you. Here's a question for you. What did you fight with the CFO about?"

"Excuse me?"

"When you were working in New York. You said you nearly lost it. Why?"

His mouth gave a wry twist, and a slow gleam lit his gaze. "He wanted to fire ten support staffers right before their pension became fully vested. Fucking asshole."

She poked him in the chest triumphantly. "See? You *are* a good guy. You're such a good guy that you've been beating yourself up all these years because of your bad behavior. If you were really bad to the bone, you wouldn't even care."

He stared at her for a long moment, then offered her such a sweet, genuine, affectionate smile that she nearly melted. "You're taking this better than I thought."

"Because I have faith in you. You're my friend."

His expression shifted, became just a little more closed off. "You really are a good friend, Bri. Thank you."

Yes. She was. The ultimate, eternal good friend. Same old Brianna.

But this moment wasn't about her. It was about Rollo finding a way to stop tormenting himself.

Summoning a bright smile, she said, "I'm such a good friend that I don't pick just anyone to grace with my friendship. Only the chosen few. You should really start appreciating it more. I don't like my friends beating up on themselves. Got it, big guy?"

His smile broadened to a grin flashing behind his beard. "There's something I've been wanting to do ever since we met. Now I'm thinking we've finally gotten to a place where I can get away with it."

"What?" She braced herself. Another kiss? Another hot, electric moment like the one in the bathroom?

Nope. Instead, he took her by the waist. Through some crazy feat of strength and power, he swung her through the air until she ended up straddling his shoulders like a kid. She dug her fingers into his hair. He grabbed her shins to hold her in place, and loped back toward the house.

"Are you crazy? What are you doing?"

"I just always wanted to do this." His laughing voice rumbled up from between her legs. His shoulders felt so phenomenally broad and strong and solid. Like a house. That moved. And that gave her a breathtaking view of the coast off to her right.

"Wow, so this is how things look to a tall person. Or someone riding an elephant."

"Did you just call me an elephant? Prepare to get car sick." And he picked up the pace to a jog. Laughing and shrieking, they made their way up the trail to Rollo's property, where Finn and Sidney came running to see what all the fuss was about. When they reached the half-dug hole of the koi pond, Rollo bent forward, as if he was about to drop her in.

When she finally slid safely onto the lawn, she collapsed onto her back, spread-eagle, laughing so hard she was breathless. Rollo was completely winded, grinning through big gulps of breath.

Finn stood above them, shaking his head. "Crazy kids. What are we going to do with them, Sid?"

Sidney narrowed her eyes, looking from one to the other. "I have a few ideas."

CHAPTER 15

After Rollo's revelation, Brianna didn't see him for a few days. According to Finn, he was helping the local Jupiter Point fire department with some off-season fire mitigation efforts. Brianna wondered if he was actually trying to avoid her. Maybe he was afraid of what she thought of him now. He shouldn't have worried. In some ways, her respect for him had gone up a notch. A strong person like him needed a strong conscience, and obviously his was extremely strong, even if he didn't feel that way.

Sidney was studying for her finals online, when she wasn't playing with Snapchat filters. Every day Brianna spent some time talking to her. She learned that Sidney had a bright, snarky side and a morose side. She loved post-apocalyptic books, songs about mental disorders, and silly memes on Instagram. She thought her parents were too obsessed with social status, but she also spent thousands of dollars a month on clothes. Her sketchbook was filled with scenes from a graphic novel she was writing. The plot involved a princess kidnapped and taken to another planet.

Even though Brianna had never met anyone like her, she adored her. And she worried about her. Once Sidney went back to Manhattan, would anyone spend time with her, beyond the hour a week she saw her therapist?

One day, she poked her head into Sidney's bedroom. The girl was flat on her stomach on the bed, poking at the laptop haphazardly askew on the floor. "Hey, want to help me out with some stuff?"

"What kind of stuff?"

"Fun stuff. Shopping stuff."

Sidney looked up at her, then back down at her laptop. "Pass. I'm from Manhattan. There's nothing to shop for here."

Hm. So it was a "morose Sidney" kind of day. "Really? Ice cream doesn't taste good outside of Manhattan?"

Sidney grumbled under her breath. "I'm not twelve. But fine. I'll humor your ice cream offer. But you better tell me what you really want."

"Fine. Bring some work boots."

Sidney's version of work books included two-inch heels, but Brianna said nothing. She was just glad to get her out of the house. In her opinion, Sidney spent too much time staring at her electronic devices.

Sidney settled into the passenger seat of her old truck and they rattled down the hill toward town. "Seen much of your brother lately?" Brianna asked her.

"He calls me every hour on the hour, it's annoying A.F."

"Can you blame him?"

Sidney heaved a sigh, as if all grown-ups were tragically the same. "Whatever."

In an effort to sweeten the teenager's mood, Brianna took her first to the Milky Way Ice Cream Parlor and treated her to a giant ice cream fudge sundae advertised as "best in the galaxy." Even though Sidney rolled her eyes at the cheesy line, the massive mound of ice cream worked its magic. No one on the planet could resist that amount of deliciousness.

They dove in with two spoons and didn't stop until Sidney was wiping out the bowl with her index finger. She groaned and sat back, resting her hands on her stomach.

"So, are you ever going to make a move on my brother?"

Brianna nearly choked on her maraschino cherry. "Um...no. Not planning on it. We're friends."

Sidney plucked at a rip in her black leggings. She was wearing her tortoiseshell-rimmed glasses today, along with thick dark eyeliner. "If you're really friends, then you should try to rescue him from a fate worse than death."

"Rescue Rollo? He's a firefighter, he's the one who does the rescuing."

"He won't be a firefighter for long. And he won't be single for long."

Brianna's stomach gave a little dip, as if she was on a roller coaster. "Wh...what do you mean?"

"Pretty soon he's going to marry some Park Avenue debutante bitch that my mother picks out from a lineup. And he'll be miserable for the rest of his life. So yes, he does need rescuing."

Brianna stared at the girl. Was she being overdramatic? Rollo had mentioned something about marrying to please his family, but she hadn't really believed him. "Rollo's his own man. I'm sure he'll choose his own partner."

"He can't. He made a deal with my parents."

"A *deal?*"

"Sure. They're big on deals. Everything's a negotiation and they usually have all the cards." She picked at a scab under her ripped jeans. "Rollo didn't want to work with my dad and Brent. He wanted out. But he didn't want to lose his trust fund, because he does all kinds of good things with it. He gives away money like it's candy. They told him he could do what he wanted until he was thirty, but they'd have a say in who he brings into the family. They probably have their eyes on the next generation, knowing them." She pretended to gag.

A sour taste gathered in Brianna's throat. Where would she rate in Rollo's world? Probably somewhere at the servant level. He was the privileged prince; she was the peasant girl.

What did it matter, anyway? They were friends. Friends who'd kissed exactly once. Never to be repeated.

She suddenly remembered that the Star Bright Shelter for Teens had received a huge anonymous donation that helped launch it. Had Rollo contributed that?

He *was* a prince, in the ways that really counted. And princes had family obligations.

"Well, it'll probably work out," she managed. "Maybe Rollo likes debutantes."

"Rollo hates everything to do with Manhattan. Including the debutante scene. He turns into a stiff, scowling statue in a tux. Never smiles. That time he was carrying you on his shoulders and laughing? That was the happiest I've ever seen him. Can't do that on Park Avenue."

"I wouldn't know. I've never been to New York."

"*What?*"

"Nope." Brianna put money on the table to cover their bill and rose to her feet. She needed to get moving, breathe some fresh air and get her hands in the soil. "I have a project I could use an extra hand with. Want to come?"

"Were you bribing me with that ice cream?"

"Absolutely."

Sidney grinned, back to her happier self. "Well, it worked."

In the truck, heading toward Melvin Turner's place, Sidney returned to the topic of New York.

"It's crazy that you've never been to the center of the world. How is that even possible?"

Brianna laughed. "It might be the center of your world, but mine is right here. I have this landscaping business, you know. From March to November I'm slammed. I'm also the caretaker for a lot of the vacation homes around here. I just built a greenhouse to grow flowers for local businesses. I'm always busy."

"But...but...this is New York we're talking about."

"Someday I'll come visit you. You can show me all the sights. How's that?"

Sidney clapped her hands in glee. "We'd have so much fun."

Brianna had to wonder—would Rollo be there too? Married to a debutante?

She shook off the thought as they drove onto Old Man Turner's property. "Have you ever built a fence before, Sidney?"

"*Built* a fence? Don't you just buy them and stick them in the ground?"

"I'll take that as a no."

Brianna wanted Melvin to have a hand railing around his garden, something he could hold on to now that his balance wasn't as good. So Sidney helped her dig post holes while Brianna cut the lumber to size. Her carpentry skills were limited to simple things a garden might need, but she always enjoyed that sort of work. It required figuring and designing, some physical labor, and the results were so satisfying.

Even Old Man Turner seemed happy, when he wasn't grumbling. Sidney's holes were lopsided; Brianna's cuts weren't perfectly square. Brianna was used to his complaining, and barely noticed, but Sidney found it hilarious. She kept teasing him right back, which really got him riled up. When Melvin shifted into a confused rant about leaving the country to escape from some bad guy, Brianna figured it was time to go. She just hoped he never acted on any of his delusions.

Sidney fell asleep on the ride home, which Brianna saw as a victory. She'd worn the girl out, but at least she'd gotten her off her electronics for an entire afternoon.

When they got to Rollo's house, the sun was setting over the ocean in a pool of liquid gold. Sidney woke and rubbed her eyes.

"Nice job today, Sidney. You worked hard and you helped out an old man. Well done." She dug a twenty-dollar bill out of her pocket and handed it to her. "This is just a bonus."

"Dude, I'm like, a millionaire. You don't have to do that."

Brianna tucked it into her hand. "You earned it. Unlike the rest of your money." She winked at the younger girl.

"Good point." Sidney took the twenty and waved it high in the air. "Feels kind of nice, actually."

"Please don't buy anything inappropriate with it," Brianna added. "Your brother might toss me in the koi pond again."

"What'd you do this time?" Rollo's deep voice slid over her nerve endings like a caress. He was at the driver's side window, one hand braced on the roof of her truck, six feet plus of hard muscle packed into t-shirt and jeans.

Sidney made a face at her brother. "She made me slave all day and all I got was a big fat twenty-dollar bill."

"And the best ice cream sundae in the galaxy," Brianna pointed out.

"True." Sidney grinned and tucked the twenty into her bag. She got out of the truck and did a little dance. "Pizza slices on me?"

"Sure." Rollo bent his head so he could look in the window. His face was so close, she could turn her head and their lips would touch. Tingles swept across her skin. "Brianna, you in?"

Brianna snapped herself back to reality. Rollo was even more off-limits now. They were friends *and* he was going to marry a debutante.

"Sorry. I have a pie-baking date with my mother. It's our pre-Thanksgiving tradition." Rollo looked at her blankly, as if she was speaking a foreign language. "You know Thanksgiving's coming up, right? And it often involves pies? That you bake?"

Rollo exchanged a glance with Sidney, who'd skipped around the truck to link her arm with his. "Did you grow up in a Norman Rockwell painting? Believe me, our mother never made pies, and I'm pretty sure our usual Thanksgiving dessert was pot de crème. Do I have that right, Sid?"

Sidney ignored him. "We're invited, right, Brianna? To Thanksgiving?"

"Um..." Brianna stalled for a moment. "It won't be glamorous, like what you're used to." What would the two Warehams think of her absurdly ordinary family? She shook her head, ashamed of her hesitation. "Of course you're invited. Just don't expect anything very exciting. Prepare for an overdose of niceness."

"Can't wait." Rollo grinned. "What should we bring?"

"Um...extremely low expectations?"

CHAPTER 16

The Gallaghers lived on a farm and kept chickens and goats. They raised their own turkeys for Thanksgiving. John Gallagher proudly showed off the mighty golden-brown birds in their roasting pans. They'd also grown the pumpkins for the pie, gathered the eggs for the popovers, and picked the last of the currants for a red currant chutney.

Norman Rockwell would have been in heaven.

Actually, Rollo was too.

Brianna's parents were short, freckled and redheaded. If they hadn't been married, he would have assumed they were related. They were just as adorable as Brianna was. They hugged every guest who arrived, whether friend or stranger. Mr. Gallagher kept pecking kisses onto his wife's cheek. Mrs. Gallagher proudly told stories about all the baby goats Brianna had raised and the gardens she'd created around Jupiter Point. Rollo and Sidney had brought a bottle of Harveys Bristol Cream Sherry as their contribution. His own father would have barely noticed the gesture, but John Gallagher's eyes lit up.

Rollo loved the Gallaghers on sight—and their farmhouse.

The entire place was a throwback, with its wood stove and plank floors, wide window seats and claw-foot bathtub.

The dining room was filled with a long trestle table set with squat yellow candles and centerpieces made from autumn leaves. The old wooden chair squeaked under Rollo's weight.

Any time a bunch of firefighters got together, things got raucous. The three Jupiter Point Hotshots—Sean, Josh and Rollo—kept the group entertained with stories from the fire lines. Suzanne talked about the great name hunt for her baby. She and Josh had bought every baby name book in existence and still couldn't decide.

Evie's parents gave the gathering a touch of class. Molly McGraw, who had an advanced case of Parkinson's, sat in her wheelchair at the end of the table, her white hair parted elegantly to one side. Her husband, the Dean, carefully cut her food into bite-sized pieces.

Rollo tried to imagine his father hand-feeding his mother. Yeah, right. If his mother had Parkinson's, she'd be tended to by a rotating staff of caretakers, not her husband. Then again, his parents never seemed to like each other much. Their marriage was all about mutual benefit, about advancing the Wareham family name.

Which was exactly what they wanted for him, too. A marriage that was the opposite of the Gallaghers'.

He shoved the thought aside. Not yet. *Not yet.*

For now, he was here, with Brianna, her family and some of his best friends, and he soaked in every minute. He couldn't take his eyes off Bri. She wore one of her typical cringe-worthy outfits, a felted wool mini-dress in russet over forest-green tights. Maybe she was channeling Robin Hood, but he didn't care. Her vivid hair glowed in the candlelight, her smile so bright it could have lit the candles if they went out.

He loved the way she occasionally rested her cheek on her mother's shoulder, like some kind of affectionate cat. He loved the way she translated her father's rambling account of the year they tried to raise lambs. He loved the way her hearty chuckle lifted everyone's spirits, the way she refilled drinks, offered seconds, and put everyone at ease, even the strangers at the table, such as the new neighbors who'd just immigrated from the Philippines.

Rollo couldn't work out what role she played in his life. She didn't fit into any of the usual categories. Not just a friend. Not just someone he was attracted to. Not just the landscaper digging up his lawn.

No, it was something beyond all of those, something more encompassing.

Brianna, he realized, was the one who made things okay.

When she was around, the big dark knot that lived inside of him dissipated. Brianna's warmth and sheer *realness* made everything feel different. Normal.

Which was funny, because he knew that she considered her "ordinariness" to be a flaw. He didn't see her as either ordinary or flawed.

It was, by a long stretch, the best Thanksgiving he'd ever experienced. He knew Sidney felt the same way. She sat next to him the entire time and didn't utter a single snarky comment.

And the pies! As Bri had mentioned, she and her mother always got together two days before Thanksgiving and went on a pie-baking frenzy. They made fifty in all. Some went to local food kitchens, some went to neighbors and friends. By the time Thanksgiving rolled around, only ten pies remained for the Gallaghers' guests.

It seemed like a lot until he tasted them. And then he had to try each type of pie, as did everyone else, and ten pies seemed like barely enough.

After dinner, he offered to help with dishes—hotshots were used to kitchen duty—but Mrs. Gallagher waved him away.

"Show him the farm, Brianna. Cleanup can wait."

Brianna's gaze slid away from his. "If he's interested."

"Very," Rollo assured her. Mostly, he wanted to steal a moment alone with her.

He checked on Sidney, who was comparing apps with the kid from the Philippines. She was completely wrapped up, so he followed Brianna out the door of the mud room into the farmyard.

The night was crisp and black, filled with chill starlight and the warm illumination spilling from the back of the house.

"Your parents are like a dream," he told her as she pulled a beanie over her curls. "They're amazing. This whole place is."

"It's your basic farm," she muttered. "Seen one, seen them all."

"Oh come on. This is the first time I've seen a farm where Brianna Gallagher grew up."

"Exciting stuff." She batted her eyelashes at him. "Want to see the well I fell into when I was little? Or my kitty cemetery? My tire swing? The fairy houses Evie and I used to make? So many landmarks, I hardly know where to start."

He stared at her, feeling something kindle inside him, something that needed to be said. "Why do you do that?"

"Do what? Oh wait!" She pointed across the yard toward a chicken coop. "I almost forgot my first shop project. Did you know my parents had to fight to get me into the class? It was supposed to be just for boys. Sometimes I've wondered if that was when it all went wrong for me."

"Wrong? What do you mean?"

"After I aced shop, all the boys figured I was one of them. I completely lost my air of mystery." She twinkled at him. "Such as it was."

"See?" He caught her wrist. "*That.* Why do you do that? You downplay yourself." He tugged on her arm until they were nearly chest to chest. He took her chin in his hands and tilted her face so he could watch the starlight illuminate her skin. "You make yourself out to be some kind of run-of-the-mill person. Nothing special. I don't like it."

She ran her tongue across her lips. It was probably a nervous gesture, not a seductive one, but it had a striking effect on his cock. "I know what I am. Who I am."

"Yeah? Who are you, then?"

She shrugged. "I'm...nobody. Nobody spectacular. I'm a hard worker with a green thumb. My whole life has been completely normal. Nothing special at any point along the way. Want to know the most special thing about me?"

"Sure. Shoot."

"I was best friends with the most beautiful girl in town."

He shook his head, not putting it together.

"Evie," she said impatiently. "Evie McGraw. About to marry Sean Marcus, remember her?"

"Of course I know Evie. Jesus. Yes, she's very attractive." Evie, with her long brown hair and sage-green, silver eyes, her quiet smile and slim poise, was definitely a looker.

"Did you know there's graffiti written about her on the wall of the police station? An epic poem about how beautiful she is. Her pearly teeth and other stuff. No one would ever write graffiti about me."

He tried not to laugh. "But—she's no Brianna. Around you, I wouldn't notice her."

To his surprise, her eyes filled with tears. "Don't do that," she whispered.

"Do what? Did I offend you?"

"Don't pretend I'm something I'm not. Don't try to make me feel better. I am who I am and I'm fine with that. Mostly."

It was that last word that did him in. He cradled her head between his palms and made sure her eyes met his. "I won't have it, Bri. I won't. If you're so ordinary, why couldn't I take my eyes off you all night? Why is the first thought I have in the morning whether you'll be coming by to work on my damn pond? Why do I want to throttle Finn when I see him chatting you up?"

Her eyes were wide as her apple pies. "You do?"

"Hell yes, I do. Finn's my friend, but he doesn't deserve you, Brianna Gallagher. He doesn't appreciate you. I know I promised to help you catch his eye, but I'm not doing that anymore. Screw Finn."

Her throat muscles rippled as she swallowed hard a few times. "The thing is...I think I'm over that silly crush."

"You are? What makes you think that?"

"Well...it seems that...you're the one I keep thinking about. Not Finn. But I know I shouldn't because you—" She broke off, biting her lip as if holding something back.

"Because you think I have a thing for Merry?" Rollo brushed his thumbs across her cheekbones. "I never really did, you know. Maybe during the fire season, but it was long over by that night at the Seaview."

"It was? Then why did you want me to set you up with her?"

"I didn't. That was your idea. Remember? I was kind of humoring you." He grinned at her. It felt so good just to be with her alone like this in the moonlight.

She gave him a playful swat on the chest, then took his hand to lead him across the yard to the shadowy outbuildings. "*Humoring* me? You're going to pay for that."

He paced next to her. Her hand in his gave him such a feeling of rightness. "I already paid. I had to watch you flirting with Finn."

"And I had to watch you mooning over Merry!"

"Mooning? I never *mooned*."

"You mooned." She reached around him and slapped him on the rear. "Holy crap, Rollo. You're all muscle. You're like iron."

Hot, sweet lust shot through him. Suddenly none of the reasons to stay away from Brianna made any sense. He wanted her. Plain and simple. "You touched my butt. You know what that means."

"No idea."

Keeping her hand in his, he swung her so they were face to face. Then he drew her closer, so their fronts brushed against each other. Her eyes met his, filled with light and fire. "Trouble. Big, big trouble."

Fire seemed to ripple between them, the kind of flame it was impossible to resist. He sure couldn't. He didn't stand a chance. Into the flames he went, into the heat and light and joy.

She met him there, and all of a sudden they were all over each other, running their hands up and down each other's bodies. Inhaling, nuzzling, nibbling. He drew up her mini-dress, found the waistband of her tights. Felt her skin jump in response to his touch. He wanted to reach inside and touch her right there in her family's backyard.

Luckily, she drew back before he totally lost his cool. "Come on," she whispered. "I'll show you the barn."

The barn. Sounded good to him. Any enclosed space would do. He followed her across the yard toward a vaulted structure that looked too tidy to be a barn.

"My mother uses it as a studio," she whispered as they slipped inside. Without a light on, he couldn't see much, just empty space with a few easels set up in the corners. "Honestly, she's terrible at painting, but she has fun and I actually find that quite inspiring. She doesn't care what other people think about her painting, all that matters is that she enjoys it. Don't you think that's pretty cool, really?"

"Are you babbling?"

"Of course I'm babbling. I'm nervous. I don't know what's going on here."

"I don't know either," he admitted. "I just know I want you like crazy. I can't seem to stop."

She stared at him in the dimness. Then she surprised him by leaping into his arms, which he managed to fling open just in time to catch her. She wrapped her legs around his waist and tilted her face up for a kiss. He consumed her mouth with a hunger that shocked him. Her body writhed against his. Her strength outpaced her size, so she no longer seemed tiny to him. She seemed fierce and determined and just as lusty as he was.

"I was wondering if you'd ever kiss me again," she whispered between rapid pants. "I thought you decided it was a mistake. I thought we were never going to talk about it again."

"I don't know, it might be a mistake," he muttered. "I can't lose you. You're too important to me."

"Why would you lose me because of a kiss?"

"If I have my way, this will go way past kissing," he growled. To prove his point, he cupped her breasts through her dress, brushing his thumbs across the hard points already pressing against the fabric. "Oh man. You're driving me crazy here."

She arched her back, hanging on to him with her legs, sheer pleasure lighting up her face as he teased her nipples. "That feels so good," she said in a crooning voice. "Your whole body feels incredible. I want to see you naked."

His cock jumped. She reacted with a full-body tremor. "You're playing with fire, Bri." He ground his erection against the sweet, hot space between her thighs and watched another shudder travel through her. He couldn't wait to see her come, to see her skin turn pink, her body shake with ecstasy. He wanted her in his bed, naked, all night, all week, all month, all—

Voices sounded from outside. "I'm so flattered, my dear. You know I'm not a real artist. It's only a hobby and I never pretend otherwise. But I do love my dabble time, as I call it. There's nothing quite so relaxing."

Brianna jumped out of his arms and landed like a cat several feet away. She straightened her dress, then leaned against the wall and folded her arms, the picture of innocence.

Rollo reacted more slowly; lust still rampaged through him. He shoved his hands in his pockets to hide his raging erection and sent up a little prayer that it would work.

The light flashed on. He blinked in the sudden brightness.

"My goodness, I didn't know anyone was in here!" Mrs. Gallagher swept in, followed by Evie and Suzanne. The two younger women caught on immediately.

Suzanne bit her lip, her blue eyes brimming with mischief. "Enjoying a little dabble time, Bri? Wouldn't it be easier with the lights on?"

Evie took in Rollo's painful situation with one quick glance and stepped between him and Mrs. Gallagher, blocking her line of sight. "Oh, but it's such a peaceful space. Even better in starlight, I imagine."

He cleared his throat. "We...uh...couldn't find the light switch."

"Totally understandable," Suzanne teased. "Since it's on the *wall*, not on Bri's—"

"Oh my gosh, look at that landscape!" Evie interrupted. She crossed to the big easel in the corner. "I should mount it in my gallery."

"Really?" Mrs. Gallagher frowned at the very rudimentary painting of the promontory called Jupiter Point. "I just started that one yesterday."

"Is that right? You'd never guess," Evie said. "Suzanne, come look at this use of color." She reached back for Suzanne's wrist and yanked her along with them.

"You mean green?" Suzanne rolled her eyes.

As soon as everyone's backs were turned, Brianna and Rollo rushed to fix themselves up. Rollo turned toward the wall and visualized buckets of ice cubes falling on his head. Brianna adjusted her dress, patted her hair, fixed the angle of her beanie.

"This isn't over," he mouthed to her when he was presentable.

"What?" she mouthed back. God, her mouth...all pink and plump from his kiss. He dragged his gaze away so he didn't get hard all over again.

"You don't have to whisper." They spun around to see Mrs. Gallagher shaking her head at them. "We busted you fair and square."

Brianna turned red. Back at the easel, Suzanne quaked with silent laughter, until Evie flicked her on the arm to make her stop.

Mrs. Gallagher gave the two of them a conspiratorial wink. "Your secret's safe with us. Right, girls?"

"Well..." Suzanne began.

"Completely safe," the older woman repeated firmly.

Reason number two hundred and five why Brianna was so cool. Her mother.

CHAPTER 17

Brianna stayed to help with the cleanup. By the time it was done, she was too exhausted to drive back to her little cabin in the valley. Curled up in the window seat of her childhood bedroom, she watched the moon rise over the Gallagher farm. Like many native Jupiter Pointers, she knew her way around the night sky. She recognized Castor and Pollux, the two bright stars holding up one end of the Gemini constellation. Sirius sparkled with particular intensity just above the tree line. She'd always loved watching the stars because of their purity and stillness. Change came slowly to the night sky, unlike the world of plants.

And unlike her personal life.

What the heck was going on with Rollo? First they were friends, then they were mutual matchmakers, then he was completely off-limits...and now they were making out in her mother's studio? Her head was spinning.

Kissing Rollo was beyond anything she'd experienced. It was fireworks and starlight. It was like a dream. But now she was awake. Wide awake, staring up at the open patch of moonlit yard and remembering everything Sidney had told her.

Rollo had a duty to his family. He wasn't destined for someone like her. He had a different life to live and it couldn't possibly include a tomboy gardener who liked to cross-pollinate tomato varieties. He'd mentioned his family situation before, but she hadn't really paid attention. She hadn't understood what it really meant until Sidney had explained it.

Now that she knew, there was no question in her mind. No matter how much she wanted Rollo, she had to stay away.

So when he called her the next day, she told him she had a meeting with a new client. The next day, she informed him that she was spending the day in her sadly neglected greenhouse.

The day after that, Rollo texted her that he was going hunting for a few days with Sean Marcus and that Sidney was tagging along for the experience. Brianna breathed a big sigh of relief and used the opportunity to finish digging the koi pond.

If Rollo was around, she'd want to make out with him some more. This way, she could just think about him every few minutes.

After the hole was completed, she ordered some specialized plumbing parts and the rubber liner. Since they were going to take a few days to arrive, she fired off a text to Rollo updating him on the status of the pond. She included links for some koi vendors so he could start picking his favorite varieties. Quite possibly he didn't care and would just roll his eyes. But she was a professional and she always gave her clients a chance to state their preferences.

She went to work on other projects, congratulating herself on her quick recovery from her attraction to someone off-limits.

Then Rollo texted that he was back from his hunting trip. *Come over for venison stew and we'll talk koi. And other stuff.*

Just seeing his name on her phone screen gave her a rush of excitement.

Face it, she was nowhere near recovered from this attraction. But she could still be professional. *Koi. Koi. Just focus on the koi.*

She spent a ridiculous amount of time sorting through outfits before reminding herself that this was Rollo and he knew exactly how pathetic her wardrobe was. So she stuck with a clean pair of jeans and a turtleneck sweater in nubby oatmeal cotton. In the catalogue it had looked cute, but on her body it looked a little like upholstery.

It's just Rollo, she reminded herself. She had no business getting nervous about seeing Rollo. *Just be cool, like everything's normal. Like you're the great friends that you always have been. Focus on the koi.*

She brought a bottle of red wine and some late Brussels sprouts she'd harvested from her parents' farm. When he opened the door and she got a full dose of the man, butterflies flew right into her throat and she could barely say "hi." He wore a hand-knit sweater in a deep forest green that set off the clear blue-gray of his eyes. His skin had the kind of color that meant he'd been spending time outside. Her hands itched to feel the soft bushiness of his beard. He smelled like he'd been tromping through the woods. Like autumn leaves and open air and...

"You smell like mulch," she blurted. Then turned red. Oh no. Was the awkwardness with Finn now transferring to Rollo? "I mean, in a good way. Rotted leaves make great mulch. Pine needles are too acidic, so they aren't great mulch, but you smell like them too."

He regarded her kindly, with no hint of laughter. "I'm really happy to see you too, Bri," he said gravely. "I missed you."

"I missed you too." She longed to hurl herself at him and feel his big broad chest against hers. *Get a grip, girl. Focus on the koi.* "Of course, I've been really busy with the koi pond so I haven't had a lot of time to think about you or what happened at Thanksgiving. You know, how we almost..."

Cringing, she raised the grocery bag so it blocked her face.

"Do you think you could erase the last few minutes?" she begged from behind the bag. "I don't know what's wrong with me. I brought Brussels sprouts. And wine. Do you think maybe we could—"

"Say no more." Rollo plucked the bag from her grasp and pulled out the bottle. "I'll open this up. You take charge of the Brussels sprouts because I have absolutely no clue how to cook little green balls. I'll pour you a glass of wine."

She nearly collapsed with relief as he disappeared into the kitchen. It was nerves, that was all. Because she hadn't seen him since their make-out session. He brought her a glass of wine and they sat next to each other on his couch. Brianna with one knee bent under her, Rollo with his long legs askew. "Where's Sidney?"

"At the movies with Finn. She says hi."

"Oh." And just like that, all the tension came back. She was alone in Rollo's house with him. On his couch. And he smelled so good. And there was wine. She took a long swallow.

"Focus on the koi," she muttered to herself.

"Excuse me?"

"Koi. We should talk about the koi."

"Yes, we'll get to that. But there's something else I wanted to talk about."

Oh no. He probably wanted to rehash what had happened at Thanksgiving. If they started talking about kissing, she'd want to do it all over again. Already the flame of desire was sparking in her lower belly. Just his nearness did that to her.

"I should get the Brussels sprouts into a pan," she said quickly. "Be right back." She jumped up and fled to the kitchen. "I don't know why these little guys have such a bad rep," she called to him. "They're best on a grill, but even sautéed in butter they're amazing. Just wait, you'll take back your 'little green ball' dig."

"Oh really?"

She jumped. He was right behind her. How could such a big guy move so quietly? "Geez, Rollo. Surprise a girl, why don't you?"

"Sorry. Just checking the stew." He lifted the lid on the big cast iron pot on the back burner. Rich, fragrant steam wafted into the air. "And wondering what just happened."

"What do you mean? I came to check on the little green balls." She gave the sizzling Brussels sprouts another poke.

He ground pepper into the stew, then added a splash of his wine. "I don't believe you. You were running away."

"That's silly. Why would I run away after coming over for dinner?"

"That's what I'm trying to figure out." His curious blue-gray gaze was too much for her. He looked so attentive and focused, as if he was seeing her for the first time and she deserved careful study.

She poured herself another glass of wine and hurried back to the couch.

He followed her more slowly. The cushions sank from the weight of his big body. His big, powerful, well-muscled, gorgeous... Oh my God. What was she supposed to focus on? Whatever it was, she'd forgotten it completely.

"Do you like this wine?" she asked desperately. "I googled what kind of wine goes best with venison stew.

That's why I got this Cabernet. I'm not really a wine expert because I'm such a lightweight. I never have a chance to enjoy the taste because I get buzzed so quickly."

He leaned closer and lifted her wine glass from her hand and set it on a box of books he still hadn't unpacked. "Okay, that's it. What's going on? You have something on your mind."

"Of course I do." She scooted a little farther away from him on the couch. "I have lots of things on my mind. For instance, I'm anxious to hear about your hunting trip. What'd you bag? Three point? Six point? Where'd you guys go? Who got the first deer? Is it hard to kill a deer? I don't think I could do it, their eyes are too soulful. I'd be haunted for the rest of my life."

Roll's eyes gleamed with amusement. "This is about Thanksgiving, isn't it?"

"Oh, don't be silly. That was over a week ago." She gave an airy wave of her hand, managing to hit the frame of the couch. Ow, that hurt.

He picked up her hand and pressed his lips to it. His mouth felt warm and firm against her skin. Amazing. Her insides went liquid. Her brain turned to mush.

"Yeah, a week, and that's the only thing I've thought about since then. That night was the best thing that's happened to me since...I don't know when. I want more of it. Much more. But there's something I have to tell you about and I can't quite figure out how."

"Tell me...?" Delicious tingles were running from her hand all the way up her arm. Her entire body felt as if it was waking up. He ran his thumb across her palm and even that light touch sent streaks of pleasure flowing through her.

"Yes. It might mean nothing to you. But I tell everyone I get close to."

"We've been close friends for a while now," she managed.

"Not that kind of close. The kind of close where you get naked."

"Naked..." The image of Rollo naked burned into her mind. Hot lust burst into flames inside her. She wanted him naked, right now. Right this minute. Nothing else mattered, not his family, not her peasant-girl status, nothing. All her worries went right up in smoke, as if they never existed.

"I have to tell you something about my family and what's expected of me," he was saying. His expression was so grave, so worried.

"I know, I know," she said impatiently. Before, she'd been determined to stay away from Rollo. Now she wanted to hurry this along and get to the naked part. "You have to marry someone who gets your parents' stamp of approval. Which would never be me in a million years. Your mother has a list of debutantes and you made a deal with your parents, I get it. You can't marry me. Don't worry about it. Just...what you were saying, about getting naked?"

He frowned at her in surprise. "You know about all that?"

"Sidney told me the whole story. I get it. You're from a fancy family and of course they only want certain people to join the Wareham club. Don't worry, Rollo. I know I'm not the right type. I'm okay with that."

He groaned. "God, that just sounds so godawful. I swear, Bri, to me, you're perfect. This has nothing to do with who you are. It's about who *they* are."

Geez, why were they even talking about all this when she was about to combust from sheer lust? "Rollo, I don't care about any of that. I'll probably never meet your parents and they'll never have to decide if I'd be better off as the third chambermaid or something. They're in New York. We're here. Right here, right now. Why are we wasting time?"

Enough conversation; time for some action. She crawled on top of him and swung around so she straddled him. She stroked her hands across his broad chest, marveling at the mighty architecture of his solid form.

He wrapped his huge palms around her wrists. "So you understand what this means. It can only be a fun time. It can't be serious. Not the kind of serious that leads to marriage, anyway."

"Yes, I get it. I will never be the next Mrs. Wareham the Third." The very thought seemed ridiculous and she let out a peal of laughter. "Good thing I never thought of you that way anyway."

His jaw flexed under his beard. "Good thing," he agreed, though a shadow of hurt in his eyes made her wonder. "But there's more. I just turned thirty."

"So?

"My parents promised not to bug me about settling down until I turned thirty. They're about to turn up the heat, hardcore. I'm going back for Christmas and it's bound to be a hell scape of introductions and cocktail parties and..." He released his grip and dug the heel of his hand into his forehead.

"Rollo, it's okay." She cupped his face between her hands. "It'll be okay. That's not until Christmas. That's like, three weeks away."

"But I can't promise anything past that. If my mother picks a good prospect, and the girl is on board with the whole Rollo scene, I might be engaged when I come back to Jupiter Point. Once I'm engaged, that's it."

His tone was so resigned, her heart went out to him. "Maybe you'll like the woman they choose. Maybe you'll love her. Maybe it's not so bleak and hopeless as all that."

His gaze settled on her, a smile growing in his kind eyes. "Oh Brianna. You always look on the bright side, don't you?"

"I don't know. I try to. But I'm not some kind of Pollyanna, you know. Bad things happen. I'm sorry you're in this situation. But it has a bright side, too. You want to have access to your family money and use it for good things. At least that's what your sister says. Was she making that part up?"

"No, she wasn't making that up." He laughed, sounding strained. He curled his hand around her upper thigh. Its warm weight sent a shot of arousal to her lower belly.

"Good," she managed. "That's...good."

"The ball's in your court now," he murmured. "I'm here, I want you, but if this doesn't sit right with you, I get it. You just tell me and we'll stop. We'll go back to being friends. I don't want to lose that."

He moved his thumb gently across her inner thigh, and she had no more desire to talk.

CHAPTER 18

She placed her hands on his shoulders and lowered her mouth to meet his. He tilted his head back to welcome her touch. As soon as her lips brushed his, the sweetest sensation spread through her. His kiss tasted like wine and destiny, like a dream she'd never quite allowed herself to have.

He stroked her back with a kind of slow appreciation. He was so tactile, so reverent. The way he savored the contours of her form made her feel beautiful in a way she wasn't used to. It was a heady experience. Is this what most women felt when men made love to them? Treasured and cherished? There was nothing casual in Rollo's touch. It was intent, focused, sensual.

And it sent deep tremors shuddering through her body.

"Take off your sweater," he whispered.

"Wait." She sniffed the air.

"Wait?" He groaned. "For what?"

"Little green balls. They're burning."

He threw his head back and laughed, then rose from the couch and carried her into the kitchen. He turned off all the burners and covered the pan of Brussels sprouts.

"I'm not about to let any vegetable ruin this moment. Especially that one."

"We really need to talk about your bias against Brussels sprouts." She buried her head in his shoulder as he whisked her down the hall. This was the second time Rollo had carried her somewhere, and she really, really liked it. Even though she was small, she was plenty strong and not one bit fragile. But in his arms, she felt as light as a girl. Or rather, a grown woman about to be ravaged.

Because "ravaging" was written all over his face as he set her onto the king-size mattress on the floor.

He pulled his sweater over his back, his t-shirt riding along with it. As he extracted himself from his tangle of clothing, Brianna devoured the sight of his bare chest. Sweet Lord in heaven, *his muscle tone.* The sheer size of him, the deep ridges of sinew and bone. He was absolutely shredded. She'd always thought of him as a big bear-like man, but that didn't really describe what she was looking at right now. This man was supremely fit, a work of art carved from hard manual labor in the forests of America.

"Wow," she breathed. "Rollo, I knew you were strong, but geez."

She peered at the pendant dangling against his chest. "What is that around your neck?"

"Bear tooth. Found it in Alaska at my very first fire."

"Why do you wear it?"

His pectorals flexed as he tossed his sweater on the floor. "So I don't forget who I am or what's important. Why is your sweater still on?"

She shivered as she sat up and tugged her own sweater off her body. She'd worn her best bra, a lacy little pushup number that Suzanne had given her for her birthday. Only Suzanne could get away with a gift like that.

When Rollo's eyes darkened, she reminded herself to thank Suzanne. She wasn't the bustiest person on the planet, but the bra managed to plump her breasts together enough to disguise that fact.

Based on Rollo's reaction, it worked better than she could have dreamed. He knelt down on the floor before her and skimmed his big hands up the sides of her torso. Such a light, restrained touch, especially compared to the heat in his gaze. When he reached her breasts, he cupped them and slid his thumbs under the edge of her bra. Sharp, sweet sensation sparkled across her skin. She let her head drop back as he played with her breasts, flicking his thumbs across her nipples, lowering the edge of her bra to expose her flesh.

"You're just as perfect as I imagined," he murmured. "Your nipples are the color of rose hips. God, I want to taste them."

She arched her back to encourage that plan. He lowered his head to her breasts. His soft beard brushed against her chest, a teaser for the next onslaught of pleasure. Warm, wet, firm, his tongue swirled around one nipple, tugging blood to the surface.

"Oh God," she whimpered, pushing her chest forward so he could get more of her in his mouth. It felt so incredible, bolts of electric current zipping to her core. She might come just from the way he licked her nipples.

When he was finished arousing the first nipple, he transferred his attention to the other, and this time the pleasure seemed even deeper. It reached all the way between her legs, stirring her arousal into red alert. She wanted him there, inside her, and opened her thighs to show him what she needed.

He got the point.

"Jeans," he growled, undoing his belt. "Get them off before I rip them off."

Her arousal spiked even higher. Rollo the "nice guy" was nowhere to be seen. This was Rollo the "I'm in charge and I want you" guy.

She loved this side of him.

She squirmed out of her jeans and pushed them down her legs. Rollo did the same, bending over to rid himself of his pants. That meant she didn't get a really good look at the full Rollo picture until he stood back up, stark naked. Fully aroused. Breathtaking and stupendous.

His erection jutted from his body. It was built on the same scale as the rest of him, so—a bit intimidating. Thick and solid, its smooth head yearning toward her.

"Do you have..." She swallowed hard. "Protection?"

"In a minute." He fisted himself, drawing his hand down the length of his soaring penis.

Her mouth watered.

He climbed onto the bed and spread her out underneath him. "First, I want to taste you. All the hidden places I've been wondering about. Just lie still, okay?"

She nodded helplessly. His gruff voice sent so many thrills and chills through her, she couldn't control her trembles. And that was before he put his mouth on her. He started in the crook of her neck, inhaling her scent.

"This is where that Brianna fragrance comes from," he murmured. "It's been driving me crazy. Even when we were just friends, I'd get a whiff of this scent and get turned on."

"I'm not wearing anything. I never do."

"I know. This is all you, no one could ever manufacture it. I smell rose petal and moss and oak leaves and a deep lake sparkling in the sunshine."

Brianna, who was more pragmatic than poetic, frowned at that description. "That lake probably has algae."

"Shhh. Don't rain on my parade. You smell amazing, and always exactly like yourself. And it's a fucking turn-on. Like here." He licked his way down her arm to the inside of her elbow. "Here, I smell an extra dash of cinnamon and maybe pear." He swirled his tongue across her skin in slow spirals.

The pleasure was so acute, she pressed her legs together, knowing that moisture was seeping from her.

"You're making that up," she gasped. "How could I possibly smell like pear? That doesn't even make sense."

"The nose knows. Don't ask me how. I'm not a perfume-maker. I'm just a guy who loves how you smell." He shifted away from her arms, back to her body. Placing his hands on her thighs, he gently pushed them apart. She didn't resist, even though he was about to witness the effect his words and touch had on her.

He touched her sex gently. "So wet," he murmured. "Already."

"Already? We've been doing this for hours," she moaned. "Days."

He laughed. "Getting impatient?" He drew his finger along her seam, causing more of her intimate juices to appear. His finger was so long, so skilled, so thick. God, it was like a magic wand casting a spell on her.

With a soft moan, she widened her legs even farther.

"Oh sweetheart," Rollo murmured. "You're so perfect. My God."

Perfect was so far from what she was, but she wasn't even really listening anymore. She was lost in a wild, rich dream world of sensation. It was almost surreal, vivid images accompanying every move he made. The stroke of his tongue along her clit made fireworks explode in a purple sky. The grip of his hands on her thighs, the tickle of his beard against her skin, the brush of his teeth against the soft skin of her inner thigh...it all swirled together into a technicolor kaleidoscope.

She was babbling something, of course. She wasn't sure what and she didn't care. The only thing in the universe that mattered was the feel of his mouth on her sex. The slow drag of tongue on her clit. The clever swirl of fingers, the press of thumb.

And then she flew off the top of the world, soaring through the infinite arching sky, surrounded by the friendly twinkle of every star in the universe. The orgasm blew her apart with a violence she'd never experienced. She thrashed under his mouth, seeking every bit of the incredible sensation. He held her firmly in place and stayed with her through each ecstatic convulsion.

She landed back on the bed with a gasp, just as disoriented as if she'd actually traveled through the ether. Her forehead was damp with sweat, her chest heaving. She felt as limp and boneless as if she'd just run a marathon.

"Oh my God. Jesus, Rollo. What was that?"

"I have a feeling that was months of secret sexual tension building up." He sat back on his heels. She stared at his powerful thighs, the way the muscles bulged next to his erect penis. He unwrapped a condom, but before he could put it on, she reached for him.

"I just want to feel you first," she murmured as she wrapped her hand around the thick shaft. She closed her eyes to soak in the contrast between his soft skin and the hard organ it covered.

"Can you maybe take the tour later?" he asked. "There's that whole stored-up sexual tension thing. I have it too, and I can't take much more."

She withdrew her hand and watched him roll on a condom, an action that seemed to take forever, given the length of his erection.

She swallowed hard. As a relatively petite person, she wondered if he might be a little too much for her. But just because she was short didn't mean other parts of her were equally undersized.

He caught her glance and offered a strained smile. "Don't worry. If it doesn't feel good, we stop. I might die, but I'll stop."

"No dying. I don't need that kind of guilt." She made a teasing face at him.

"Screw guilt. It's a mind-fucker. Take it from me." He positioned himself over her, arms braced on either side of her torso.

She grinned up at him. "I definitely want to take something from you. This will do just fine."

"Smarty-pants." The expression of strain on his face gave her a special thrill. He was just as affected by her as she was by him. "I'm coming inside you now. If it hurts, you tell me right away."

He nudged her opening with the thick head of his shaft. It eased inside her slick channel, creating a sense of expansion that made her see stars.

"Rollo," she breathed, hearing the desperate edge in her own voice. "That feels incredible." She arched up to accommodate him. Everything seemed to move in slow motion. His steady slide, his watchful gaze, his harsh breaths. And then he was all the way inside and she'd never felt anything like it. She'd never felt so close to another person, so filled up and consumed.

"You okay?" he asked her in a low voice, more like growl.

"Oh my God, *so* okay."

He moved inside, long and hard, like an ocean swell breaking over her. And then she couldn't talk anymore. All she knew was him—his hard, warm body surrounding her, his length inside her, his breath in her ear, urgent, rough whispers about how beautiful she was, how amazing it felt, how he wanted to hear her scream in ecstasy, come apart in his arms.

And she did. She shattered under that big body of his. She wasn't an inhibited person in general, never one to hide what she felt. But with him, she didn't have a single drop of restraint. She babbled, she whimpered, she wrapped her legs around his hips, urging him onwards, harder, faster, more. And when he finally tensed in orgasm, his body going rigid above her, the emotion that swept through her triggered something almost like another orgasm. Something soul-shaking and world-changing.

Something slightly terrifying, if she thought too much about it.

Which she didn't, because she was too busy collapsing into a heap of satisfied female.

He lowered himself next to her—still being careful, she noticed—and rolled onto his back. He kept one hand on her hip, his thumb running lightly along her still sensitized skin. It was a soothing, hypnotic touch that lulled her into a sweet state of drowsy contentment.

Thoughts meandered through her head like aimless fish...koi maybe. Right, she was supposed to focus on the koi. But she hadn't. She'd gone to bed with a man she couldn't be with, couldn't marry. They had three weeks until he went back to his own world, where she couldn't follow.

Doesn't matter. She shoved aside the reality check trying to rain on her parade. So what if it was just for a short time? Everything was, if you thought about it.

She'd just enjoy this thing to the max, for as long as it lasted. No regrets.

CHAPTER 19

Rollo couldn't stop petting Brianna, as if she were a cat. The delicate skin just inside her hipbone had an intoxicating effect on him. He couldn't make himself draw his hand away. And that was just for starters. All the sensory impressions from the evening kept overloading his brain. The suppleness of her spine as she arched under his thrusts. The tender whiteness of the skin that didn't get exposed to the sun, contrasting with the golden apricot of the skin that did. The way she abandoned herself to pleasure without hesitation. Her whimpers, her moans, her babbling.

Yup, Brianna babbled during sex. Words of pleasure, of command—do this, touch that—just came pouring out of her, and it was a total turn-on. Especially because he didn't think she even realized it.

"Did you know that you talk a lot during sex?" he teased her when he finally caught his breath enough to speak.

She turned her head to look at him. Her forehead was damp and little tendrils of her hair curled against her skin. "I tend to babble in certain situations. What did I say?"

"You told me that my cock was like a mallet."

"What?" Her look of astonishment made him laugh. "A *mallet*? Sorry. I hope that didn't sound insulting."

He grinned at her, feeling better than he'd felt in a very long time. Sex with Brianna—well, it felt different. He felt more "himself" with her than he ever had with any other woman. He didn't have to hide either part of himself, the wild mountain man side or the wealthy, privileged side. He trusted her, and that translated into a pretty amazing sexual experience. "Yeah, it totally ruined the mood. Couldn't you tell?"

Color swept into her cheeks, but she didn't bother hiding her blush. "I wasn't paying attention. I was too busy having the best orgasm of my life. Just don't get all puffed up about that."

"Oh, I won't. But you don't mind if I put it on my tombstone, do you? 'Here lies Rollo Wareham, he gave Brianna the best orgasm of her life.'"

She burst out laughing. "I dare you."

"It would liven up the Wareham family vault, that's for sure. My black sheep status would be cemented forever." And just like that, his mood dampened. Cripes, couldn't he forget about his doom for a few post-sex moments of afterglow?

She must have sensed the shift, because she rolled onto her side and flung one leg over his. "No brooding. Don't get all Rollo on me now."

"What the hell does that mean?"

"That's when you draw into yourself and I have no idea what you're thinking, except it's probably not good. Your eyes get kind of sad and distant, and you act like you're not really here, you're somewhere else. Like you don't want to get too involved in whatever's going on, because you know it won't last."

He stared at her, struck by that observation. He'd never thought about it consciously, but her description was pretty accurate. He knew he was living on borrowed time and that the bill would come due. He *didn't* want to get too involved. The only time he didn't feel that way, he was cutting line on a wildfire.

Fighting fires took all his attention, which was one reason he loved it so much.

"Look, Bri—" he began. But she put her finger over his mouth before he could finish.

"Don't worry about me. I get it. You know something? Nothing is guaranteed to last anyway. So why let it bother us? Let's just have as much fun as we possibly can until we have to stop."

He tried to speak, but she held his lips closed with her fingers.

"I'm not quite done yet." Her pretty green eyes sparkled at him. "It's not polite to interrupt a lady after hot sex."

He smiled against the soft touch of her fingers, and lifted his hands in a "you win" motion. She lifted her hand so he could speak. "I beg your pardon, madam."

"Pardon granted, since you asked so nicely. Okay, so here's what I'm thinking. First of all, we're friends, no matter what. We were friends before, and I really don't want that to change. Secondly, I had no idea what it would be like to..." Her flush intensified to flamingo pink. "To go to bed with you. It was...amazing."

He grinned at that description. "So far we're on the same page. One hundred percent."

"Good. Then we agree." She rested her elbows on his chest and cupped her chin in her hands. "But here's the thing—I don't want to have to worry about what happens next. I don't want to think about after Christmas, or who your mother will find for you, or whether I can still be friends with you after you get married, or whether you'll even still be here in Jupiter Point. A million different things could happen. There's no point in even thinking about it, let alone worrying about it."

He frowned, and wrapped one of her curls around his index finger. "I'm staying in Jupiter Point. My parents know that. I bought this house and I intend to stay."

"Okay. Good. Fine."

"I hear doubt in your voice. You don't believe me."

She worried at her lower lip with her teeth. "Look, Rollo, I don't know anything about your world, your Manhattan one. But I do know that wives generally have a say in what their life will be like. You're a good guy. You're going to want to make your wife happy, no matter who she is or however you came to marry her."

Thunderstruck, he stared at her, barely seeing her tumbling curls and candid green eyes. He'd never thought of it that way, but she was absolutely right. This hypothetical wife wouldn't be someone abstract, someone he could move around like a chess piece in his future. She would be a real person with desires of her own. And he would want to accommodate those desires.

"What's your point?" he asked hoarsely.

"My point is, let's just face the facts ahead of time. Let's be perfectly clear with each other. That's my specialty—bluntness. Right? Here's the blunt truth. We can only do this until you leave for Christmas. Then we both have to forget about it. It's a limited-time deal. After Christmas, you have to move on to the next phase of your life. We both know it, so let's just make it so. It's less messy that way. Less chance for misunderstandings."

"So...you're talking about a fling."

"Yes, I suppose. A fling. One with a built-in expiration date."

He let his head fall back so he didn't have to look at her innocent, open expression. A fling with an expiration date. On the plus side, he could soak in all the Brianna time he could. But would it work out the way she described? Or would those three weeks make it even harder to walk away? Above all else, he didn't want to hurt Brianna.

But ending this now, after what he'd just experienced in her arms? He wasn't sure he had the strength for that.

"So after Christmas, we go back to being friends? Just like that?" He cupped her face, tracing a pattern of freckles across delicate cheekbones. "You promise things won't be weird?"

"I don't know how things will be," she said honestly. "But we already crossed the line, so why not smash it to bits? You know, with that great big mallet of yours?"

He gave a laugh-snort—the kind of reaction only Brianna ever inspired in him.

"Besides, it's only three weeks until Christmas Eve. I think our friendship can survive three weeks of sex."

His cock stirred again at the sound of the word "sex" in her teasing voice. He shifted under her light weight. "Even fantastic, mind-blowing sex? That sounds like a challenge."

She plopped a kiss onto his chest. "You're always up for a good challenge, right? But I have one other condition."

"Geez, you have more deal points than a corporate takeover. What else?"

"I want to keep this quiet. My friends are already wondering about us. I don't want the whole town thinking we're a couple. When you come back to Jupiter Point with your new wife, I don't want anyone to feel sorry for me, or assume you dumped me for a hot debutante. As far as everyone else knows, we'll still be just friends. Can we do that?"

He gazed at her doubtfully and tucked a stray curl behind her ear. "I don't know. You're Brianna. Blurting things out is kind of your thing. You might want to be telling the whole world about my mallet."

She made a sassy face at him. "You know, I'm starting to think I imagined the whole thing."

"Is that right?"

"Yes, I must have. Silly me." She started to roll off him, but he anchored her right where she was. He slid his hands down her silky skin and gripped the firm globes of her ass.

"Where do you think you're going? We have a deal to seal."

She gave a happy sigh as he positioned his shaft in the still-damp place between her thighs. "Already?"

"No time to waste. Three weeks goes fast. And we still have venison stew and little green balls waiting for us."

*

God, did three weeks go fast. Especially when you spent so much of that time inside a warm, eager body. But the sex was just part of the joy of being with Brianna. Even when they weren't in bed, the time he spent with Brianna sped by, each day like a happy dream.

Then after Sidney was asleep, Rollo would slip away from the property. He'd jog the three miles to Brianna's little one-room cabin. One of her clients had given it to her in exchange for five years' worth of landscaping services. It was made from cedar logs and held a squat little potbellied wood stove, a bed, and not much else.

They didn't need anything else.

The shift from friends to lovers didn't make them awkward with each other. They could still talk about anything, he still laughed at her plant-nerd jokes, she still teased him out of his black moods. Now that she knew about his darker side, he felt like he could tell her anything.

They spent hours telling stories from their childhoods, sometimes until dawn.

They'd drift off, then come awake again. As soon as he became conscious of her sleeping form next to his, he'd run his hands along her curves. He found her silky-smooth body irresistible. He loved to touch the warm nest between her legs, teasing the little nub until it grew plump. Still half asleep, he fondled her breasts, plucking her nipples into hard peaks. He drew her round ass against his cock and palmed her clit until she gasped his name.

And, being Brianna, she got totally wild and demanding. One time she actually ordered him to make her come, like some kind of sexual drill sergeant.

So he made her wait. No matter how much she squirmed and begged, he kept her right on the edge, teasing her swollen sex until it dripped with her juices. Then he drew her onto her elbows and knees and spread her apart. Worked his way into her tight little entrance, felt her body clasp him in a throbbing, mind-blowing embrace. As she buried her head in a pillow and fisted the sheets, he drew out every stroke as long as he could stand it.

Her sweet little body shook and flushes of pink swept over her skin. He stroked her spine, savoring the firm muscles that ran alongside her vertebrae. She was so strong and supple, his Brianna. Perfectly made for his powerful physique. Nothing was ever too much for her. She soaked up every hard plunge of his cock, every passionate thrust into her body.

"Don't you dare stop," she gasped, still ordering him around. "More. Again. Do it." And, eventually. "Fuck me, you big tease. Do it!"

After that, he let off the safety brake and hammered into her, hard. The pleasure her firm body gave him was so intense, it was hard not to come the first time he slid into her. But he made himself wait until he felt the flutter of her orgasm against his shaft.

Then, he let loose, let the blinding detonation wipe his mind clean of everything except pleasure and freedom and *her*.

Always her.

CHAPTER 20

Rollo went around in a sort of daze during those three weeks. Her scent followed him wherever he went. So did the sound of her laughter. He kept hearing it at random moments—at the hardware store buying paint. At the hotshot base cleaning out the crew buggy. At the movies with Sidney.

Brianna, Brianna, Brianna. It felt as if the sunshine of her spirit had infiltrated his blood. He found himself smiling at all kinds of random moments, causing his friends to look at him oddly and ask if he was on something.

Of course, her actual presence was a million times better than the memory of it. Every time he laid eyes on her, a grin spread across his face. He always wanted to touch her right away, no matter who was around. It took incredible willpower to stop himself from feeling her up in front of Evie or Sean or Suzanne or Josh or Finn or Sidney or Merry or any of the other pesky human beings who populated Jupiter Point.

Damn it, didn't they know time was running out? Why couldn't they all just disappear for a few weeks so he and Brianna could be alone?

During the day, Brianna worked at her greenhouse and her flower deliveries to local businesses. She was so busy that when the parts for the koi pond arrived, she was only able to allot a couple hours now and then to that project.

Rollo spread his time between working with the JPFD on fire mitigation and trying to get up to speed on Wareham business dealings. The paperwork drove him nuts. How was he going to handle an entire lifetime of reports and spread-sheets?

"There must be something about it you like," Brianna told him when she found him staring morosely at a quarter-ly report from a fund focused on tech stocks. She peeled off her work gloves and kneaded his shoulders.

"No. These companies are all old-school. They're solid performers but the tech world changes all the time. There are so many new apps and products out there."

"So why don't you invest in some of them? You're in charge. Or you will be, right?"

"That's not what we do. The Wareham Group tends to be risk-averse. We go for the safe bet."

"Oh, like running into wildfires? That's safe?"

"I told you I'm a black sheep. I like risk. God, that feels good." He groaned as her incredibly strong hands worked at his knotted muscles.

"Speaking of risk, where's Sidney?" Brianna asked inno-cently.

"I think she's with Finn getting help with her Spanish." He tilted his head back to look at her. "Feel like getting risky? And frisky?"

She ran her tongue across her lips and that was that. They hurried into his bedroom and locked the door. They got naked in world-record time. He lifted her against the wall and wrapped her legs around his hips. They ground out a quick, fierce, silent orgasm.

He got back to his desk just in time to see Sidney loping across the lawn with her schoolbooks. He could still smell Brianna on his skin, still feel her in every rapid beat of his heart.

But usually, they got together at night. That was when the real joy happened.

After they'd made voracious, hellacious love, they'd spend the rest of the night wrapped in each other's arms, talking, laughing, occasionally sleeping. Then she'd drive him back to his place and drop him off at the end of the driveway. He felt ridiculous sneaking into his own house, but Brianna insisted that she didn't want Finn or Sidney to guess what was going on.

Luckily, Sidney was wrapped up in her finals and didn't notice anything. Thank God for the self-absorption of teenagers. When she wasn't studying, she Snapchatted with her friends. Now and then she hung out with the Filipino kid from Thanksgiving. Brianna made a point of spending time with her. She took her to the movies and to volunteer at the Star Bright Shelter for runaway teenagers.

One evening at sunset, the two of them figured out a way to climb onto the roof of Rollo's house. Sidney fell in love with the view and often stayed up there until the stars were out.

The Jupiter Point passion for stargazing had struck again.

About a week before Christmas, his mother's secretary emailed him the schedule of gatherings he'd be expected to attend over the holiday. Dinner parties, holiday gatherings, three Christmas balls.

"I'm only coming for ten days," he emailed his mother. "Don't you think this is a little much?"

"No whining," she emailed back. "You promised."

The next day, an itinerary arrived in his email. Tickets for him and Sidney. As if he couldn't buy his own plane tickets. He gritted his teeth but decided it wasn't worth the battle. If they could choose his wife, booking his airfare was a minor detail. Nothing compared to the other ways they'd be controlling his life.

Shortly after the email with the tickets arrived, Sidney came storming into the kitchen, where he was making lunch for the two of them. Brianna was meeting with Evie about her wedding, which was scheduled for Valentine's Day. Even though he was happy for Sean and Evie, the thought of weddings depressed him. That would probably be him soon, getting fitted for a tux and choosing grooms from a list of socially advantageous business connections. Getting married to someone "appropriate."

"Mother already bought our *tickets*!" Sidney hoisted herself onto the counter next to the cutting board. "I thought we'd get a chance to talk about this."

"Talk about what? You know you have to go back for Christmas. It's mandatory. Not a single Wareham has ever missed Christmas. And it takes us all of January to recover."

"I know, but I had a really great idea about how to make Christmas marginally less suicidal."

"Suicidal? Is that a threat?"

"No. Unless it would work?" She lowered her horn-rimmed glasses and peered over them. "Hm. I can see it wouldn't."

"And I can see you don't need those ridiculous glasses."

"Who said I did? Haven't you heard of fashion choices? It's not like you need a beard."

"I do need the beard." He needed it to remind him of who he *really* was. The wildfire-fighting mountain man. Without the beard, he looked like any other clean-cut Upper East Sider. With maybe a few more muscles.

"I'm not here to discuss your facial hair. I want to talk about my idea for Christmas. How to make it more fun."

Rollo spread peanut butter on a thick slice of the multi-grain bread he'd baked. Baking was one of his favorite things to do from the list of non-Wareham-approved activities.

"It doesn't involve any banned substances, does it? Or dates with boys who are too old for you? Or piercings or unapproved changes in hair color?"

"Nope, nope, nope, none of the above."

"Then I'm listening."

"I want Brianna to come to New York."

The peanut butter knife slipped and went clattering across the floor. "*What?* Forget it."

He bent down to pick it up, hoping she wouldn't notice how flustered her idea made him. If Brianna came to New York...would that mean an extension of their fling? That would be amazing—no, torture—

"She's never been to New York. How terrible is that? Everyone ought to see New York at some point in their lives. Especially at Christmas. I've been telling her about the tree at Rockefeller Center and the ice skating and all the shop windows. I know she'd love it. They don't even get snow here in the winter!"

"But she'd never leave her family at Christmastime. You saw them at Thanksgiving. Her family actually likes each other. It wouldn't be Christmas without her."

"Shows how much you know." Sidney stuck her finger in the peanut butter and helped herself to a big glob. For once, he didn't swat her hand away from the jar. That proved how rattled he was. "Her parents are going to visit her aunt in Arizona. Brianna is trying to think of a way to get out of it. This could be her escape ticket."

"No. No. You like Brianna, right?"

"Duh. She's like the only grown-up worth spending time with."

She went for the peanut butter jar again but he snatched it away from her. "So why do you want to inflict our family on her?"

"Now that," she pointed her peanut butter finger at him, "is a legitimate objection. But I've been thinking about it and you know what the best thing about Brianna is?"

Rollo was suddenly glad for his beard. Pretty handy when it came to hiding his expressions. The best thing about Brianna...where would he start? Her wild moans when he licked her to orgasm? Or the way she slept naked when she was waiting for him? The way her body curled around him when he slipped into her bed late at night? The passion with which she kissed him, touched him...the passion with which she did everything. Or maybe the open, honest, real way she talked about things.

So many aspects of Brianna competed for the title of "best thing about her."

"You tell me," he finally managed to say.

"The best thing about Brianna is she accepts people exactly the way they are. That's why I like being with her. She doesn't look at me and think, 'oh Sidney, what a rich bitch, or what a spoiled brat, or what a sad example of today's youth.'" She said that last one in a lecturing tone that made it clear someone had used that phrase on her. "When we're hanging out, I feel normal. Good normal. Like I can be my own person."

He knew exactly what she meant. He felt that way too. "Okay, so she accepts people the way they are. What does that have to do with our family?"

"Maybe Mother will like her. The way everyone else does."

"Mother doesn't 'like' people. She just decides if they're useful or not."

"True." Sidney ducked her head, swinging her legs against the counter. Rollo supposed he should tell her to get off, but he didn't have the heart. That sort of thing would never be okay at home, so her window for casual behavior would end soon. "Here's the thing, big brother. I don't want to go home unless Brianna comes. And I'm going to throw a big temper tantrum and make a huge fuss. So you might as well say yes."

For a moment he let himself think about it. More time with Bri. She'd be a bright light during all the tense Wareham family gatherings. It would be...great. But no. It was a bad idea. A terrible idea. It would disrupt their whole careful agreement.

"Kiddo, it's not up to me. Brianna won't want to go," he finally told Sidney.

"So if she says yes, she can come? Because Mother already said I can bring a friend."

"A twenty-eight-year-old friend?" he asked skeptically.

"She didn't mention an age limit. What are you, ageist?"

"Yes, I'm ageist. I say all teenage girls ought to be quarantined," he grumbled.

"Ha ha."

"Look, don't talk to Brianna yet. Let me feel her out first."

Feel her out...or feel her up... Again he gave thanks for his very convenient beard. "She was my friend first, you know."

"Sure. You do that. Feel her out." The innocent tone of her voice had him swinging his head to look more sharply at her. Did she know? Did she suspect? But his sister just blinked at him blandly. "Oh, also? You should pay for her ticket. You owe her for all the work she's putting into that silly pond. And she might need some new clothes if she's going to meet our parents."

"Oh my God." He clutched at his head, which was starting to pound. "Listen, don't say anything about this until I talk to Brianna. I don't want you pressuring her into something she doesn't want to do."

"Dude. What girl wouldn't want an all-expenses-paid trip to New York City?"

"Brianna isn't like other girls," he began, then fell silent. What if he could show her his world, the one he'd walked away from, and the one he'd have to return to? What if it didn't have to end yet? What if they could find a way?

CHAPTER 21

So this was what a "fling" was like.

It sounded so casual, like tossing a Frisbee. Since Brianna had never had a fling before, she didn't know what they were supposed to feel like. Maybe flings were supposed to make your heart fill with joy when you heard a knock on your cabin door at night. Maybe flings always made you want to take care of your lover, to make him grilled peanut-butter-banana sandwiches because he'd never tried them. To rub his shoulders when those shadows passed across his face.

Maybe flings were supposed to be like that—all passion and fire until it burned out. Or got snuffed out by reality.

Brianna considered herself a grounded person. After all, she worked in the dirt for a living. But these days, she felt as if she were walking on air. That phrase "head in the clouds" finally made sense to her. She caught herself dreaming of Rollo at the oddest moments. When she wasn't with him, she was remembering the last time they were together, and fantasizing about the next one.

She refused to look at what day it was or think about how much time they had left. What was the point? The end would come when it came. But for now, this fling thing was amazing. The only problem was that she couldn't talk to

any of her friends about it. Sometimes she wondered if
Sidney suspected, but the girl never said anything. And
Finn had finally gotten into the groove with his screenplay,
so they never saw him.

Nope, it was her and Rollo. Grabbing every opportunity
they could to devour each other.

Once she'd installed the plumbing and the rubber liner,
she ordered gravel to cover the bottom of the pond. When
it arrived, Rollo left his desk work to give her a hand. She
loved it when he helped her out. She got to order around
her own personal super-strong assistant. And sometimes
kiss him.

Rollo manned the wheelbarrow while she directed—just
the way she liked it.

"You are the bossiest boss I've ever seen," he grumbled
as he positioned the wheelbarrow where she told him.

"I'm a perfectionist. That's why you hired me, right?"

"Is it? I don't remember anymore, but I think it had to do
with a crush."

"Ancient history." On her hands and knees, she peered
into the koi pond. "And...go!"

Rollo tipped over the wheelbarrow and poured gravel into the bottom. She hopped into the pond and spread it
around with the back of her rake. Then she climbed out and
accompanied him back to the load of gravel next to the
driveway.

"Why didn't we just plant a flower bed or something?" he grumbled. "Or install a bird feeder. This whole damn pond just to catch someone's eye."

"Worked, didn't it?" Brianna winked at him. "Well, sort of."

He gave her a half-smile. He seemed distracted today. Something was bothering him, and it wasn't the pond or the gravel. Fear speared through her heart. Did he want to end this early? Had something happened? She wasn't ready. They had a few more days. Not that she was counting, because she was trying really hard *not* to count.

By the next wheelbarrow dump, she decided she couldn't take it. It was always better to hear the truth up front.

"What's on your mind, Rollo?"

He started. "Is it that obvious?"

"To me, yes. You'd better just spit it out. That's what I would do."

They reached the pile of gravel and he dropped the handles of the wheelbarrow, folding his arms across his chest. The flex of the muscles in his forearms made her mouth go dry. "Okay, here it is. Sidney wants to invite you to New York for Christmas. She has her heart set on it so she's going to pester you like a frickin' mosquito."

Brianna's jaw fell open. "New *York*?" Excitement surged through her. Her and Rollo together in New York...how romantic that would be!

"I know, it's a terrible idea. We need to figure out how to handle this. I couldn't tell her about us, so I didn't have a good way to head her off."

Brianna felt as if her heart was shriveling up to the size of a walnut. "You...wouldn't want me there?"

"Want—" He stared at her. "*Want* is not the point. We have...you know, an expiration date. And you know what I'll be doing in New York."

Reality slammed into her. He'd be meeting women vetted and preapproved by the Wareham family. He'd be auditioning brides. Every time she thought about it, her insides took a dive. But she'd known this all along. There was no point in pretending it wasn't going to happen. It was always best to face the truth. "Of course I know. I don't have to be part of that. I could stay at a hotel."

"Absolutely not." A scowl drew his eyebrows together. "We have a ten-bedroom fucking apartment. Why would you stay at a hotel? What am I even talking about? You shouldn't even go. This is nuts."

"Why? Why is it so nuts? I've never been to New York. I don't work over Christmas anyway. Sidney wants to show me all the sights. We can do that while you do your...thing." She waved her hand between the two of them. "This is a fling, right? It's just casual. Why shouldn't I go?"

He gripped her by the shoulders. "Because I don't want those people to get their fangs into you."

"Those people? You mean your family?"

He smiled grimly. "Yes. They're ruthless."

"You don't think I can handle your family? Maybe I'm tougher than you think. I once trapped a rabid raccoon in Mrs. Murphy's attic. I built an entire fieldstone wall by hand. What do you think is going to happen?"

He picked up the shovel and thrust it into the gravel. "This is a very bad idea."

"It might be a good idea. I'm a little worried about Sidney going back. She seems so anxious about it. I could be extra support for her."

He didn't answer, but she saw his jaw flex as he shoveled the gravel into the wheelbarrow. She knew he worried about the same thing.

"Rollo. Come on. It would be my first trip anywhere."

"My mother will shred you."

"It's Christmas, why would she do that? Christmas in Manhattan! It'll be just like the movies."

"Yes. Like *Jaws*."

"Come on, Rollo. Don't be mad." She danced around him while he filled the wheelbarrow, scowling the entire time. She knew just what to do when he got this way. Tickle him. She tweaked him in the rib cage, making him start.

"You're playing with fire, Bri," he warned, transferring another shovelful of gravel into the wheelbarrow.

"Well, you're playing with rocks, so I guess we're even."

"This can't change anything. I still have to do what I have to do."

"Yes, but not yet, right? Come on, Rollo. Live for the moment. Seize the day." She tickled him again.

He stuck the shovel into the gravel and snatched her off her feet. He slung her over his back in a fireman carry and strode into his house while hot excitement fizzed through her.

"What have I told you about tickling?" he demanded once they were inside his bedroom with the door closed. As if she weighed nothing, he slid her off his shoulders and planted her on the floor.

"You told me I'd get in big trouble." Her heart was racing, her insides melting into a puddle of goo. Lord, he was sexy when he was fake-mad at her. "Big, *big* trouble."

"That's right. Turn around and put your hands on the wall." His eyes darkened to the color of the gravel in that pile outside.

She swallowed hard, almost too excited to respond. Slowly she turned, wondering if he could see her pulse beating madly in her neck. She put her hands on the cool plaster wall. He came close behind her and ran his hands across her rear. Cutoff cargo pants with ground-in dirt—not exactly the sexiest thing to be wearing at a moment like this.

He didn't seem to mind. With those big, nimble hands, he reached around her and undid the buttons. He slid them down her legs while she tried to remember what underwear she was wearing today. Lately, she'd been paying more attention to such things. Black, she was pretty sure.

Whatever they were, he left them in place and drew the edge away from her sex. She squeezed her eyes shut, knowing he'd find her wet and throbbing. Well, maybe he wouldn't see the throbbing, but she could feel it.

"That's what I like to see," he growled in her ear. "Hot and wet for me."

Oh God. He pushed her panties down her thighs. The cool air felt exquisitely torturous on her overheated sex.

"Widen your legs, sweetheart."

She nearly groaned as he slid his finger up and down the seam of her sex. Tightening her legs would feel so much better than widening them. She craved friction against her clit, his strong finger rubbing it the way he knew so well. In such a short time, he'd learned all about her body and what got her turned on. What got her off. She'd had more orgasms in the past couple of weeks than she had in her entire life. She couldn't get enough.

His knee came between her thighs and nudged them apart.

"You're just asking for it, aren't you?" He pulled on her earlobe with his teeth. She moaned.

"No. Yes. I don't know." Her confusion kind of said it all. He had her completely rattled.

"It's a good thing I know," he said in a tone of complete and utter confidence. It made her melt even more. And then a light swat landed on her bare ass. She squeaked and jumped.

"Too much?" Casually but seriously, he was giving her an out. Did she want it? Warmth spread across her skin, causing a tingling sensation between her legs. And now his big, rough paw of a hand was smoothing the skin, lulling her, arousing her.

She shook her head.

"I want to hear you say it," he murmured.

Of course he would. Rollo would never want to risk crossing any unacceptable lines. He cared too much. He was too good of a person.

"Not too much," she whispered. "Not yet, anyway."

She felt him laugh softly against her hair. She loved the way she always managed to make Rollo smile.

Another little whack landed on her butt. Not harder, not lighter, just enough to enhance the sensation. She found herself hugging the wall, pressing her cheek against it, closing her eyes to soak in the experience. The next swat sent her soaring even higher. With her eyes closed, she felt the restrained force of his big body behind hers, the power contained inside him, the soft brush of his beard against her shoulder, the heat radiating from him. It was all so delirious, so intoxicating.

She was already trembling on the edge of orgasm when he reached between her legs. His palm pressed warm and hard against her. Moaning, she met it with equal force, pushed her hips into him. His index finger dipped inside her. Slick with her juices, it withdrew to find her clit. Rubbing, circling, teasing, pressing, his finger drove her mad with need. She babbled crazily, something about hunting him down and killing him if he didn't make her come.

He let out something between a laugh and a groan as he worked her into a frenzy. When she was practically screaming for relief, he did the meanest thing in the world. He stopped.

"What—"

"Stay right where you are. Don't move a muscle." He stepped away from her and she heard the sound of his zipper.

Oh, thank God. She stood motionless, waiting, waiting, the moment stretching into agonizing suspension. Each passing second ratcheted up her arousal even more, because she pictured what she must look like right now. Pressed against the wall, legs wide, waiting, wanting, wet and eager.

Then he was back, his hot, naked hips pressing against her ass. She nearly came just from the friction of his skin against hers. But she held off because she wanted him inside her. Wanted hard heat against her back, her sex, inside, outside.

And that was what he gave her. With one palm pressed against her clit, he eased his thick shaft all the way to her core. Then he thrust again, deeper and harder, and rubbed her clit with his rough-skinned palm.

Without warning, the pleasure burst inside her, waves after waves of it. Everything exploded into brilliant pieces of shimmering light.

He held her hips still as he plunged into her again and again. As her senses returned to normal, happiness filled her being. Not because of the intense orgasm, but because her body was now giving Rollo pleasure. When he went rigid, his fingers digging into the soft skin of her hips and ass, she nearly came again.

Finally he set her down and she turned, panting, to rest against the wall. He'd only undressed halfway. He still wore his long-sleeved thermal shirt. It didn't cover his powerful thighs and still half-aroused penis. The sight made her heart clutch.

"Wow, Rollo. That was...holy crap."

"I didn't hurt you, did I?" His forehead creased with worry.

"Of course not. Believe me, I would have told you. Or babbled it or something."

Finally, he smiled faintly. "I get carried away sometimes."

She drew her panties back up, then her cutoffs. She was floating, so blissed out. She rested her head against his broad chest and dragged in a long inhale of Rollo scent. "Why do you always smell so good? Better than my greenhouse."

He laughed softly, then snagged her wrist. She looked up at him. The look in his eyes, hot but also achingly tender, made her breath catch. "No matter what happens in New York, let's remember this, okay? Us. Being ourselves."

She swallowed, riveted by all the emotions churning behind the surface of those blue-gray eyes. Then his expression shifted, his gaze travelled down to her mouth, and he cupped her face in his hands. The kiss that came next rocked her all the way to her core. Desperate, urgent, as if she were the most necessary, essential being in the world. As if he couldn't do without her.

And without him saying the words, she knew he was glad she was going to New York.

CHAPTER 22

"First things first," Sidney crowed as soon as the Warehams' chauffeur dropped them off in front of the Park Avenue brownstone. Brianna pulled her light wool coat more tightly around her, shocked by the icy wind whipping down the street. Jupiter Point never got this cold. But here, the long avenues with their towering parades of buildings seemed to act as wind tunnels. She shivered, wondering if frostbite was a real danger on the Upper East Side. "Shopping."

"Now?"

"Yes, now. Mother isn't home yet. That gives us at least two hours to get you presentable."

"What about your father or your brother?"

"No one's home. Right, Rollo?"

Rollo grunted as he grabbed a suitcase in each hand. It was obvious that the doorman wanted that task, but Brianna knew Rollo would never allow someone else to carry stuff while he was around.

"Is it okay if Mace takes us?" Sidney asked her brother. Mace was the driver, Brianna had learned during Sidney's mile-a-minute rundown of the people in the Warehams' orbit.

"Sure, just don't be long. Cocktails at five." Rollo barely looked their way as he and the doorman carried their bags through the highly polished glass and gilt door of the apartment building. He'd ignored her during the flight as well. He'd slipped on sunglasses, tilted his seat back, and folded his arms over his massive chest. She wasn't sure if he'd been sleeping or just tuning out Sidney's chatter.

But she was sure of one thing. They were over.

They hadn't made it official because they didn't have to. They both understood what was happening. The last few times they'd made love, she'd felt the change in him. He was withdrawing, preparing himself for the end.

She had, too. She'd prepared by spending their last night in Jupiter Point in her cabin, crying herself to sleep.

Then had come the flight—first class. Sidney's manic excitement. The fancy Bentley picking them up at the airport. This intimidating tower of an apartment building. And now shopping. Or as Sidney put it, *shopping*!!! With extra exclamation points.

"See you later, Rollo," she called as Mace opened the passenger door of the Bentley again. Without looking back, he gave a gruff wave, then the front door closed behind him.

Brianna swallowed hard. He'd warned her. This was how it had to be. She was here with Sidney. It had nothing to do with Rollo.

"Maybe I should check into my hotel first," she told Sidney as the Bentley pulled away from the curb. She'd insisted on staying at a hotel instead of with the Warehams, no matter what Rollo said. The last thing she needed was a front row seat for the big bride hunt.

"Later. After we shop. You'll have so many packages by then. And we'll pick out the perfect outfit for you for tonight." Sidney practically rubbed her hands together in glee. "This is going to be the most fun Christmas ever."

"You aren't planning to dress me up like an elf, are you?" Brianna asked suspiciously. "Because I'm trying to get away from that look."

"No more elf look. Guaranteed. This look will be history too." The girl waved her hand at Brianna's outfit, which consisted of corduroy pants and a ruffled blouse that she thought of as her fanciest top. She wore it to Sunday dinners at the McGraws and for other special occasions.

"This look? What's wrong with this?"

"Considering I call it 'blind person orders from Lands' End catalogue,' need I say more?"

Brianna's face flamed. Sidney laid her head on Brianna's shoulder.

"Don't be mad. You're my favorite adult, by far. But your fashion sense...it's just a good thing I'm here, that's all."

Brianna hugged one arm around the girl's shoulders. "Just go easy on me, okay? I've never had a makeover before."

"My entire life has been one long attempted makeover," Sidney said in her snarky way. "Attempted, but failed."

For the next few hours, they zipped from boutique to vintage shop to thrift store. It was all a blur to Brianna. Sidney's mood dipped during their shopping spree, as if Manhattan had a gravitational force field she couldn't fight.

"How does it feel to be back?" Brianna asked her while she tried on a cashmere top the color of delphiniums.

"I don't know yet. I'm putting off the fateful moment."

"That's what we're doing here? Procrastinating? It's always better to face things head-on, if you ask me."

Outside the dressing room, Sidney muttered something.

"What was that?" Brianna called.

"I said, some things, maybe."

Brianna slid open the curtain that shielded the dressing room. Sidney was sitting cross-legged on the floor, chewing on her thumbnail. "What do you mean? What is it you don't want to face?"

Sidney looked up and scanned her. "That looks good on you. You should get it."

"Really? It's not too feminine for me? I'm usually such a tomboy." Brianna smoothed her hand down one sleeve. Darn it all, she'd been too blunt with Sidney. She should have asked her question more indirectly. Suzanne would be so much better at drawing out a teenager.

"Of course not. It looks awesome. Let's get it."

Brianna checked the price tag and blanched. "Um...maybe not."

Sidney sprang to her feet. "I'm getting it for you. And don't even argue. It's my thanks to you for coming. You have no idea what it means to me."

"Well, what does it mean...?"

But Sidney was already thrusting another outfit at her. "Cocktail party tonight. This is the perfect thing. Go on. Back in the dressing room with you."

*

Rollo had been back on Park Avenue for less than five hours and already he was twitchy. The collar of his dress shirt was trying to strangle him and the air inside his parents' apartment didn't have enough oxygen. Scented taper candles were set around the "Grand Salon," where the cocktail party was taking place. The candlelight was lovely but the fragrant smoke was driving him nuts. Worst of all, his jaw itched and his face felt naked.

An hour ago, he'd shaved off his beard.

Special request from his mother, and also a symbolic gesture. His time of freedom was over. No more living in the woods and battling wildfires with a chainsaw. "Iron Man" Rollo was gone. Rollington "Money" Wareham III was back.

He kept glancing at the gilt mirror over the mantelpiece. His face looked so strange, with the bottom half so pale and exposed. His beard had given him a gentle-giant look, like Grizzly Adams. Without it, he looked...intimidating. Sort of ruthless. Just like the rest of his family. The Warehams were all tall and blue-eyed and Nordic, with a "masters of the universe" vibe. The beard had softened him. Now he looked just as arrogant as everyone else in the room.

He tuned back into his father and Brent's conversation. They were talking about a business acquaintance who was about to file for bankruptcy. Their gloating tone annoyed him. He tuned back out again and looked desperately around the room, like a parched man hunting for water.

Where were Sidney and Brianna? They were late. Or maybe Sidney was boycotting the party. Maybe Brianna had decided to skip it and hang out at her hotel. Naked in bed.

He rolled his neck, trying to get the tension out. He had to stop thinking about Brianna like that. It was over. Even though it didn't *feel* like it was over—he could still taste her, feel her—it had to be over.

Across the room, his mother caught his eye and gave him an approving smile. Right—the missing beard. He ran his hand self-consciously across his jaw.

She cocked her head, the enhanced blond of her bob gleaming in the light from the many candles. She raised her eyebrows in the direction of a poised young woman chatting with someone on the loveseat in the corner. "Cornelia," she mouthed. Her glance very clearly said, "go talk to her."

Cornelia. Absolutely, he should introduce himself in person. Obviously. They'd exchanged at least twenty emails by now, though only two in the last three weeks. Her emails were intelligent, cheerful. From what he could see, she was attractive. Slim as a ballerina, her hair in a loose knot at the base of her neck. Dressed in a classic little black dress.

Yes. He should go talk to her. Right this minute, if he could ever get his feet to move. *Just go, do it.*

And then...

Brianna walked in.

He felt the floor drop away beneath him.

Brianna...but not Brianna. More like the fairy-princess-wood-nymph-Botticelli version of his friend. She wore a filmy, frothy pink dress the color of strawberry ice cream. It gathered under her breasts and flowed to just above her knees. Her bare shoulders were covered with some kind of glittery body powder. She wore a pretty amber and bronze choker around her neck; he thought it might be Sidney's. Her hair had been blown out into long, loose waves, so different from her usual tumbled ponytail. It was pinned like a crown on top of her head, with long tendrils left to frame her piquant little face. Soft pink lipstick, a light touch with the blush—or maybe that was her natural embarrassment shining through.

Even though Sidney held her by the hand, she looked about ready to turn and flee.

Her gaze landed on him—probably because he was staring—then slid away. Then came back. Recognition flashed across her face, followed by shock. Her mouth fell open and she gasped loud enough to make heads turn.

Pink flooded her cheeks.

Uh oh—maybe he should have warned Brianna about his missing beard. He put his hand to his jaw and pulled a face of apology. Her mouth snapped closed and she shot an embarrassed glance around the room at the guests who had turned to look at her.

Sidney scowled at him. She circled a hand around Brianna's wrist and towed her across the room toward their mother.

Abruptly, he walked away from his brother in mid-sentence and strode after them. No way was he letting his mother meet Brianna without him. He wouldn't be able to live with himself.

He kept devouring Brianna with his gaze as he walked. She wore little crystal-studded high-heeled sandals that showed off the incredible muscle tone of her calves and the cute shape of her feet, with that little toe that curved inwards...

He tripped over the edge of the carpet. His turn to draw everyone's eyeballs.

Straightening up, he cast a general scowl around the room and hurried the last few steps to his mother, Brianna and Sidney. Sidney was in the midst of introductions. She was wearing a garnet velvet dress with long sleeves that came to points at her wrists. Her hair was smoothed over one shoulder. For once in her life she looked like a proper daughter.

"Mother, this is my friend Brianna Gallagher from Jupiter Point. She's been really nice to me. I've been working for her, can you believe it? Me, working. Aren't you proud?"

"You were meant to be working on your schoolwork." Alicia Wareham sniffed, then took Brianna's hand for a cool fingers-only handshake. "Welcome to New York, Brianna. Thank you for joining us tonight. Now may I ask what sort of work you hired my wayward daughter to do?"

Brianna made an awkward motion with her other hand, as if she wasn't sure of the proper etiquette. "Thank you so much for having me, Mrs. Wareham."

Her smile was a more self-conscious version of her usual grin, but even so it felt like a ray of sunshine in this formal environment. Rollo smiled stupidly down at her. Damn it, he didn't have his beard to mask his emotions anymore. His reaction to Brianna was probably written all over her face.

"I'm a landscape designer," Brianna was explaining. "Sidney helped me build a fence around Old Man Turner's garden."

Alicia's eyebrows lifted, as if not a single word of that sentence made sense. "Build?"

"Well, yes, although she actually did the digging."

"Digging?"

"Yes, she dug the post holes. I have a special post-hole digger that I use, and Sidney got the hang of it right away. She earned every bit of that hot fudge sundae."

"And the twenty dollars," added Sidney. "Which actually paid for two more of those babies. You know, I really think they might be the best in the galaxy."

"Right?" Brianna beamed. One of the long tendrils curling against her cheek snagged on her eyelash and she blinked it away. She was so adorable. He couldn't drag his eyes away from her.

Alicia turned to Rollo. "May I speak with you, Rollington?"

Her use of that name set his teeth on edge. With an apologetic glance at Sidney and Brianna, he walked with his mother to the little bar. One of their servants was manning it. Without being asked, he made her another Pimm's Cup. All of the Wareham staff was well-trained; his mother wouldn't stand for anything less.

"What has been going on out there in California? It sounds like obscenely exploitative child labor to me."

"Don't be ridiculous, mother. She dug some holes and got some ice cream. It kept her out of trouble."

"Ice cream sundaes are not on her diet. Sweet Lord, she's grown even bigger in California. She must have put on ten pounds. You should have kept a better eye on her."

He blinked at her. "Sidney isn't overweight. She's a Wareham, we're all that size."

"She's a girl, so she can't let herself get so muscular. Really, Rollington. You've been in the wilderness too long." She accepted the Pimm's Cup with barely a glance at the server. "This time in New York will be just what you need to ease you back into civilized society." She sipped from her glass, Breton brightening her eyes, which were just a shade bluer than his. "I think you'll be very happy with what I have planned this Christmas. Now you must go chat with Cornelia. She came tonight specifically to meet you." She waved to a newly arrived guest.

Rollo clenched his jaw so tight it hurt. "I will when I'm ready."

She fixed him with a stern flash of her blue eyes. "She's perfect, Rollington. Don't ruin your chances with her."

As soon as she left to greet the new guest, he ordered a bottle of beer, only to be told none was stocked. Great. This just got better and better. With a club soda in hand, he went to join Brianna and Sidney, who were now chatting with Brent. Brent was studying Bri with an air of fascination.

"Power tools?" he was saying. "Like what, a nail gun?"

"Sure." Brianna shrugged. "Nail gun, screw gun. Table saw. Jigsaw. I'm no expert, but I can run all those. To tell the truth, I'm a lot better with a nail gun than with a blow dryer."

Brent laughed a little too long and hard. Rollo wondered how many vodka martinis he'd already consumed. His brother would probably be hitting the club scene after the family thing wrapped up. This cocktail party was a warmup for him. "What happens when you use a blow dryer?"

"Oh," Brianna laughed uncomfortably, "I honestly don't know. I don't even own one. DryBar did this." She waved at her lovely, romantic-looking hairstyle. "All they do there is blow dry hair. Can you believe it?"

Brent cocked his head at her. "You're quite the country cousin, aren't you? It's cute. Ish."

An expression of hurt confusion drifted across Brianna's face. Rollo would have given anything to be able to coldcock his younger brother.

"Go have another Grey Goose, you asshat," he said instead. "Or Brianna will use her nail gun on you."

"Fearsome." Brent drained his glass and set it on the mantel. He always did that; at the end of every party there would be a lineup of Brent's empty martini glasses.

Funny how his firefighter crewmates felt much more like brothers than his actual brother.

"Come on, lil sis." Brent slung his arm over Sidney's shoulders. "I'll buy you a Virgin Mary. Right up your alley."

Rollo caught a flash of distress on Sidney's face before she was hauled off in the direction of the bar. Then he forgot all about his siblings and turned back to Brianna. Her arms were folded across her chest. Sparkles of light danced across her skin.

"Why did you shave off your beard, Rollo? I really wish you'd warned me. It's hard enough not to trip in these shoes without a shocker like that."

He made a face and put his hand to his bare chin. "I keep forgetting about it. Then I remember and it's like I cut off a limb. It's a freak show, isn't it?"

Her expression softened. "Of course not. It doesn't look bad. It's just different. When I walked in I didn't recognize you at first. You looked so formal with the suit and the, you know," she waved her hand at him, "face. I thought you were a Danish prince or something."

He tilted his head back and laughed. The sound drew the attention of his mother. He watched her eyebrows draw to-gether, a speculative look passing from him to Brianna. Oh hell. He'd just put poor Bri in the line of fire. He should step away from her right this second. He should cross to that loveseat and introduce himself to Cornelia.

He didn't budge.

Brianna watched him with those wide green eyes of hers, the light from the chandelier striking notes of bronze and fire in her hair. "I'm so tempted to take a picture of you like this and send it to the hotshots back home."

"Is that right? I might have to confiscate your phone, Miss. This is a private gathering. No photos."

She chuckled, the sound traveling into his bloodstream like sunshine. "It's a really good thing I know you're still the same Rollo underneath it all."

"Don't be so sure of that. Six hours with my family and I'm already turning into an asshole."

God, it was true. He'd been rude to his mother, he'd insulted his brother, barely said a word to his father. Blown off Cornelia. This place...he hated the still air, the smell of luxury perfume, the sounds of party chatter. Not even Brianna could completely erase his misery.

"Stop whining, big guy." She gave him a playful swat on the sleeve. "I liked you better when you were the hotshot who rescued Josh. You know, the nice guy who moved to Jupiter Point to support his friend."

"Believe me, I like that guy more too," he muttered, swirling his drink in his glass. "Don't get too attached to him."

"Well, too late. I am attached." He felt her gaze on him, urging him to pay attention. So he forced himself to meet her gaze. "I can tell you hate being back here, but you're still the same person. Think of all the lives you've saved. Think about nearly dying in Big Canyon. You can handle this. Did you ever think that destiny has something in mind for you?"

"Destiny?" He felt as if he was drowning in her green eyes. She didn't know what she was talking about. Destiny? Try doom.

"Yes, destiny." She touched the lump his bear-tooth pendant made under his dress shirt. "Your true self. We all have a destiny, right? Something written in the stars. Something we're meant to do on this Earth."

He snorted. "Written in the stars? Maybe all that stargazing messed with your head. If this is my destiny, why do I fucking hate it so much?"

He shifted his shoulders inside his dinner jacket, dragged the top button of his shirt open. This was torture. Not fucking destiny. The sense of irritation he'd been fighting ever since he walked in overflowed like an explosion of lava.

"Can't wait to hear about *your* destiny," he told her. "Let me guess. Power tools and awkward crushes?"

As soon as the words were out, he hated himself.

She flinched, a quicksilver shift of expression that hit him right in the solar plexus. "That's right. Power tools and awkward crushes, that's me."

He reached for her, wanting to apologize, but she backed away from him. "Brianna. Come on, you know I don't mean that."

She spun away, her flouncy dress twirling around her body. The filmy layers danced through the air. With a sense of horror, he saw the outermost ruffle brush past a tall taper candle set on one of the low decorative tables. The flame leaped from the candle to her dress in a flash of ignition.

Quick as a thought, he flung his club soda at her. The liquid splashed onto her dress and she stumbled. He saw a flicker of flame still licking at her dress. If she kept going, the air might fuel whatever spark remained. He couldn't chance that. He dove after her and tackled her to the polished parquet floor.

She cried out as he rolled her over, smothering the bits of smolder on her dress with his bare hands. The other guests backed away with shocked murmurs. When he was finally satisfied that there was no chance she was on fire, he sat back on his heels. The bottom of her dress was scorched, her hair was tumbling around her shoulders and she looked like she wanted to murder him.

But at least she hadn't gotten burned.

Physically, anyway.

She scrambled to her feet and ran for the door.

CHAPTER 23

Brianna ignored Sidney and Rollo, who both tried to catch up with her during her escape. She ignored the doorman as she flew out the door. She ran half a block down Park Avenue in her wobbly heels, then waved at the first cab she saw. Voice shaking, she gave the cabdriver the name of the little hotel where she was staying, the Parkside. Booked and paid for by the Warehams, but right now she didn't care. She just wanted to be alone, behind closed doors, with no one looking at her funny.

When she reached her suite, which was decorated to simulate a home, if you were the kind of person who liked shades of umber and framed inspirational quotes, she shut herself into the bathroom. And squeezed her eyes shut before the mirror ambushed her.

She had to take this in phases.

She opened one eye halfway, then closed it again with a yelp. Yup, just as bad as she'd imagined. Hair tangled from her mad dash down Park Avenue, dress hanging in damp, charred rags. Grimly, she opened both eyes and stared at her reflection.

This. This was why she couldn't go to nice places or wear nice clothes. Because *this* was what happened. This was who she was. Brianna Gallagher—fashion disaster. Not just fashion disaster. *Guest* disaster. She'd flown all the way to Rich People World to make a fool of herself. She could have done that back home in Jupiter Point. Though not quite as dramatically.

Disconsolate, she stripped off her ruined dress. It was so pretty, too. Best of all, for one magical moment, she'd seen something in Rollo's eyes when he first saw her in it. Not friendship. Not lust. Not affection.

Awe.

She'd never forget that, even though it had gotten ruined so quickly. How long had she lasted at her first fancy cocktail party before nearly catching on fire and getting a club soda thrown at her? Ten minutes? Twenty?

She took a quick shower to wash the residue of humiliation off her body, then wrapped herself in the big, fuzzy robe provided by the hotel. Brianna wasn't one to dwell on things. What was the point? If you tripped on your own shoelace, you didn't stay face down on the sidewalk. You got up and laughed it off. The same principle applied here.

But hearing a friendly voice couldn't hurt. She dialed Evie and told her the whole story. By the end they were both laughing so hard, tears were running down her face.

"Only you, Brianna," Evie gasped. "But please don't feel bad. If anyone laughed because your dress caught fire, they're just a bad person."

"I'm not sure that helps. But thanks."

"Thank God Rollo was there," Evie added more seriously. "He may have quit the hotshots, but he still knows his way around fire."

"That's true. He actually dove right on top of me, into the flames; he put it out with his bare hands, I think. And oh my gosh, Evie, you should see him without his beard! He looks completely different."

"Really? Good different or bad different?"

Brianna chewed on her lower lip. "Well, he no longer looks like a hunter who's been lost in the wilderness for months. You can see his face now. It's a really good face, kind of strong and cheekboney."

"Cheekboney?"

"Yeah. He looks like a tougher version of Justin Bateman. But his eyes are the same."

"I always thought he had the most soulful eyes of anyone I know."

"He really does." Brianna sighed, remembering all the times she'd gazed into those blue depths and felt she was seeing all the way to his core.

"Oh my God," said Evie. "Are you in *love* with Rollo?"

Crap. *Crap.* She scrambled to cover up her error. "Don't be silly. We're friends. Really good friends. And I work for him. I've been putting in that pond at his property, you know. The koi pond. It's coming along pretty well, I have the gravel laid in and I'll order the fish when I get back, and did you know he hired me because I had a crush on Finn?

So I'd have a reason to hang around up there? So, you know, your theory doesn't really hold up..." She trailed off. Lying was *so* not her thing.

Silence on the other end of the phone. "Nope. I'm not buying it. I remember what I saw at Thanksgiving. And I can hear it in your voice. You can't fool your best friend since third grade. You have feelings for him."

Brianna had never been able to hide anything from Evie. She crumpled like an old paper towel. "Yes. Okay. I have feelings. But I miss the old Rollo. I miss his beard. Can you imagine Rollo in a tailored suit?"

"I really can't. Did you take a picture? The hotshots would pay good money for that."

"I said the same thing! I was going to, but then my dress caught on fire and I ended up in a smoky heap on the floor. If I get another chance, I'll take a shot and blow it up to poster size and mount it at the base."

"That would be the perfect wedding present for Sean."

Brianna laughed. She was feeling a million percent better, thanks to Evie. "Thanks for being there for me. You're such a good friend, despite all that annoying gorgeousness."

"Bri, we really need to talk about this attitude of yours. It drives me crazy when you sell yourself short. I wish you could see yourself the way I do. You're beautiful and unique and wonderful."

Unique. That sounded like code for weird. But Brianna decided not to let it bother her. "See? This is why you're such a good friend. You always see the best in people, even when they catch on fire at fancy parties." She broke off when someone knocked on the door. "Gotta go, Evie."

"Say hi to Rollo for me."

"What makes you think—" But Evie had already hung up, laughing.

She was right. It *was* Rollo, his powerful frame still packed into that black dinner jacket and immaculate white dress shirt. A shadow of stubble darkened his firm, unfamiliar jawline, and his blue eyes were on fire with worry as he stepped into the room. His gaze swept across her, taking in her damp hair and bare feet. "Are you okay?"

"Of course." She lifted her chin. "Why wouldn't I be? All I did was catch on fire, nearly drown, and made a fool of myself in front of some Manhattan power brokers. Just another day in the life of Brianna Gallagher."

He didn't smile. "I'm sorry about the power tools comment. It was stupid and asinine. You didn't deserve that. That's how I get when I'm here." He came toward her with focused intensity. "That's why I didn't want you here. I didn't want you to get hurt."

She shivered and pulled her robe tighter around her. "You kept me from getting burned, have you forgotten that?"

"It was a close fucking call, Brianna. It scared the crap out of me."

Her heart did a slow somersault. Things were supposed to be over between them. But the way he was looking at her... "I'm okay, Rollo." Her voice came out about two octaves higher than usual. She took a few steps back, and he followed.

"Well *I'm* not. I'm going crazy. I couldn't take my eyes off you at that damn party. You make everything better and brighter. I can't think about anyone else but you. I look at you and I want you. Over and over and over again."

He stood over her, so close she tilted her head back to gaze up at him. His expression sent hot ripples of excitement through her. The little hairs stood up on her arms.

Slowly, as if he was fighting the urge, he reached for the belt of her hotel bathrobe.

"But Rollo..." she whispered. "We're not doing that anymore. You said me being here couldn't change that. Remember?"

His hand paused. "I know what I said. I know what I ought to do. But I want you. I'm not ready for this to end. I can't stay away, not when you're so close. But it's up to you. I'll leave right now if you want."

She swallowed hard. She'd found Rollo plenty sexy as a bearded mountain man back in Jupiter Point. But this Rollo, with the strong planes of his face exposed, his eyes hot with desire—this Rollo was devastating. She had no defense against him at all.

"But what about your mother...your agreement..."

"I don't know. All I know is I want you. I need you." His desperate tone ripped at her heart.

Why would a wealthy, handsome, eligible catch-of-the-century like Rollo need *her?* But when she looked into his eyes, she saw that he meant it. His vulnerability tore at her. She couldn't say no to that.

And she couldn't say no to herself. Her body was already on fire just from being this close to him. One more chance to make love with Rollo. Maybe her last chance.

She tugged at the belt on her robe and the two ends fell away. The robe itself was so fuzzy that it stuck together, making the gesture much less seductive than she'd pictured.

"In my imagination, that was a lot sexier," she told him.

"It was plenty sexy." With a growl deep in his chest, he parted the two sides of her robe. He spent a long moment scrutinizing her naked body. Brianna wasn't used to thinking of herself as a sex object, but the way he looked at her, she might as well be Marilyn Monroe and Jenna Jameson rolled into one. "You're so gorgeous, Bri."

"Oh come on."

"Shh." He lowered himself to his knees in front of her. "Look, I'm kneeling for you. And I have three pins in my leg, so I wouldn't do that for just anyone." He slid his hands up the backs of her legs, slow and smooth, the rough texture of his palms spreading fire along her skin. "Admit you're gorgeous."

"Ergh..." Her legs trembled. She couldn't admit anything at that moment, because it would involve speaking.

Slowly, deliberately, he glided his palms along the creases between her upper thighs and her ass. He knew perfectly well that it was one of the most sensitive areas of her body. He gripped her lightly, his strong fingers pressing into the tender flesh of her inner thighs, brushing her curls. Wetness gathered between her legs. She grabbed onto his broad shoulders, afraid she might fall over without support.

"Say it. Say it for me." Keeping her legs firmly spread, he licked a path up the inside of her thigh.

"Wha...what?" She'd completely lost track of what he wanted from her.

"Say you know what you do to me. That one look at you in that little fairy dress, with your bare shoulders and your hair all pulled back and..." He slid his tongue across the wet folds of her sex. "And I wanted to throw you down right there on my parents' parquet floor."

"You...you kinda did..." she gasped.

He gave a dark chuckle, which registered as a vibration against her pussy. "Yes, but you still had clothes on. You tried to burn them off, but I still couldn't see your sweet little tits and juicy little—" He used his teeth on her the way a mother lion might lift her cub, pulling her entire mound into his jaws. It was an extraordinary sensation, both vulnerable and electrifying. Her inner thighs trembled with excitement.

"Say it," he murmured. He slid the tip his tongue gently across her clit, which responded with a rush of sparks, like a fountain erupting. "Say you're gorgeous and that you slay me."

"I..." She couldn't do it. She wasn't the gorgeous one. She was the tomboy, the best friend, the lab partner, the... Lab partner?

Seriously?

In the altered state inspired by Rollo's talented tongue, she swam back into a memory she'd shoved deep into the annals of embarrassment. The day she and Singh Dal, her senior-year lab partner, had decided to lose their virginities together.

Naked in his parents' den—supposedly working on their final project—he stared down at her with a perplexed expression. "It looks so red. Is it supposed to be red like that?"

She raised herself on her elbows and peered down her body. She couldn't really see what he was seeing, but she couldn't mistake the worried expression on his face. "Well, I am a redhead."

He scrunched his forehead and looked closer. He definitely didn't look impressed by what he saw down there. "Should we take a photo, do you think?"

"What are you talking about?"

"For diagnosis." She tried to close her legs, but he was still focused hard on her.

"I intend to be a doctor, after all."

"Ugh, there's nothing wrong with me! Do you want to do this or don't you?"

He cocked his head, his horn-rimmed glasses sliding down his nose. "Okay."

It was such an unromantic way to lose your virginity. She'd shrugged it off and the rest of the experience had been a lot better. But maybe that moment had scarred her more than she'd thought. Maybe she'd started to believe there was something ugly about her.

Because at this moment, with Rollo kneeling before her in his expensive tailored jacket, desire screaming from every powerful line of his body, she didn't quite believe her eyes.

So she closed them. Lost herself in the sensation of his thick tongue traveling across her swollen sex. His hands on her thighs, the strength radiating from his grip, the gentle but rough way he handled her. He wanted her so much his body vibrated with it. The tremors of desire traveled between them, bound them together in a golden web.

"Say it," he whispered against her clit. Electricity sizzled across every nerve in her body. Like a bolt of lightning transforming her from one thing to something else. From a tomboy to a siren. From ordinary to spectacular.

And so she said it, because in that moment, under the intoxicating influence of his touch, it was absolutely true. "I'm gorgeous and you want me."

"Yes." His tongue increased its pace and pressure, revving her higher and higher. She was about to fly into the ether, vaporize into ecstasy. "I want you." His lips moved against her sex. Somehow that was even more intimate than just licking. It was licking and vibrating and confessing all rolled into one. "I can't look at you and not want you. Never going to happen. You're beautiful and sexy, especially when you're spread open under my tongue and..."

The rest disappeared into a mumble of words murmured into her curls. He gripped her even tighter and swiped his tongue across her clit. Something hard and rough joined in...oh my God, his thumb...moving just so...and she was gone. Coming against his tongue with shudders and cries and maybe even a few tears.

Because never in her life had she felt so beautiful.

CHAPTER 24

Rollo owed Sidney something big—like a kidney or something. Inviting Brianna for Christmas was a stroke of genius. He'd never enjoyed New York this much. Usually he got antsy as hell, counting the days until he could get out of the city. Now, he counted the hours until he could steal away to Brianna's hotel room.

During the day, either Sidney showed Brianna her favorite spots, or Brianna wandered the city on her own. Rollo did whatever his mother asked of him. That was the deal. He accompanied her to lunches at Barneys, brunches in Soho, coffees on Fifth Avenue. He chatted with Cornelia or other prospects on his mother's list. Cornelia was nice enough, but the others all blended together. The only thing that kept him going was the knowledge that he'd see Brianna at the end of the day.

Being Brianna, she gravitated to places like the Botanical Gardens and the Natural History Museum. She took a million photos and made friends with random groundskeepers and tour guides. At night, she showed him what she'd been up to, while he avoided the topic of how he'd spent his day. They didn't talk about the impossibility of their situation.

But he hated it. It felt so wrong. He kept telling himself he should stop, that it wasn't fair either to Brianna or to any potential future wife. But he couldn't stay away from her. His entire day felt like a boulder sliding off his shoulders the second she opened the door for him.

His family didn't know what to make of Brianna. Luckily, they only saw her in passing, when she stopped in to pick up Sidney. His father barely noticed her, and his mother treated her more or less the way she treated nannies or her social secretary. Someone in the upscale-hired-help category.

Brent alternated between overly attentive and disdainful, probably depending on how hungover he was. Poor Bri looked nervous whenever he swung his attention her way, and no wonder. He asked her things like, "did you find any local flora to chainsaw today" or "how many freckles does it take before you just give in and call it a tan?"

Someone else, someone with a more biting sense of humor or someone better able to fake it, would have no trouble fending off Brent's sporadic jabs. But not Brianna. When Rollo cornered his brother and told him to knock it off, Brent got a knowing, obnoxious look on his face.

"Does Mother know you're freelancing in the lower classes?"

"Don't be such an ass. Just leave her alone."

"I'm not the one you have to worry about. Mother's Spidey senses are going off. You'd better warn your little gardener to watch her back."

Rollo stared at his brother. Was he serious? It was five days until Christmas. Bri would only be in New York another week. How much damage could his mother do? He decided to keep a close eye on things but not to ruin Brianna's vacation.

The next day, something unexpected happened. He and Brianna had stopped at his favorite sidewalk pizza stand. She'd gobbled up three slices already. He was laughing down at her, enjoying the hell out of her always-healthy appetite, when someone tapped on his shoulder.

Turning, he saw a vaguely familiar face.

"Wareham, is that you?"

He squinted at the guy. "Yeah, but I don't..." Recognition slammed into him. "Dougie Berkowitz?"

Dougie grinned. "You got it. I know, I've put on some weight since you creamed me that day."

"Some weight" was an understatement. As a fourteen-year-old kid, Dougie had been wiry. Now he bulged with muscle. He still had that joking, abrasive half-smile that used to get under Rollo's skin. He stammered for a moment, too surprised to say much. The guy was still smiling at him. Didn't Dougie hate him?

He managed to get his wits together enough to introduce him to Brianna. "This is Dougie. We used to go to school together."

"Until he beat me up," said Dougie matter-of-factly. "Have you seen this guy punch? Thing of beauty."

Beauty? Rollo gaped at him.

Dougie's next sentence really threw him for a loop. "How about a rematch?"

"A *what?*" He shook his head, sure he'd misheard.

"A rematch, big guy. Last time, I had no muscle mass or skills. Might be a different story this time."

Rollo glanced at Brianna, who shrugged, her pizza forgotten. "I don't fight people any more. I stick to wildfires."

"Right, I heard about that. What was that, some kind of guilty conscience move? The Doug Berkowitz Fund wasn't enough?" He threw up a hand as if to fend off Rollo's reaction. "Kidding. You know me, I joke a lot."

"Yeah, I remember. So...uh, how've you been?"

"Damn good, as a matter of fact. Wrote a piece of code that's about to make me a millionaire. See, you're not the only bigshot around here. We're equal now, so bring it on, big guy." Dougie raised his fists and play-punched him in the chest. Not hard. But not soft either. "Name the time."

"You seriously want to fight me after all this time?"

"Fuck yes. I always did like to fight. You were the big kahuna back then but I think I could take you now." He landed another blow on his chest.

Rollo squinted at him. The temptation to hit back was so strong. Every muscle tensed and thrummed. He felt Brianna's hand on his arm. Her touch grounded him, made his vision clear.

"Wait a fucking second here. You *wanted* to fight me back then, didn't you?" The whole scene came back to him, Dougie's sidelong sneer, his nasty words. "You goaded me. You knew I'd lose my shit."

"Yup." Dougie tried another jab at Rollo's stomach, but he barely felt it. "It's not working now, though. Guess you *have* changed."

"Guess I have."

"Tell you what, you give me a rematch and I'll pay back all the money you put into that fund."

Rollo couldn't help it; he laughed. "You're a piece of work, Dougie B. How about this? I'll give you a rematch if you tell me more about that code you wrote."

"Done." Dougie clapped him on the shoulder, smiled at Brianna, and took off down the avenue. Rollo watched until he lost sight of him in the crowd of wool coats and shopping bags.

"Whoa," he finally said.

"That was the guy? The one from back then?"

"That was him."

"I don't think he hates you."

He looked down at Brianna. The red neon from the pizza shop sign made her hair even more vibrant. She looked back with her heart in her eyes, pure happiness shining from them. Happiness for *him*.

"I guess not."

*

Things about New York that Brianna loved: snow in Central Park. Cuddling with Rollo. The arch in Washington Square Park. Sex with Rollo. The Chelsea Flower Market. Pizza with Rollo. Really, anything with Rollo.

Things she didn't like as much: cabs that drove right past her, splashing mud in her face. Umbrellas poking her in the face. The way Rollo's mother looked at her. And the way she looked at Sidney.

Every time Mrs. Wareham spoke to Sidney in that critical, nitpicking tone, Brianna wanted to throw herself between them like a shield. Even though Sidney acted so tough and nonchalant, Brianna knew it got to her. Why couldn't Alicia show her a little affection once in a while?

It all came to a head the day before Christmas Eve—the morning of the traditional mother-daughter charity fashion show the Warehams had sponsored the last five years. Usually, Alicia and Sidney walked the runway, along with every other Park Avenue socialite.

This year, Sidney flat-out refused to go. Brianna stumbled into the midst of the controversy when she dropped in to pick up Sidney for a trip to the Botanical Gardens.

"Send me to military school," Sidney was screaming at her mother. "Send me to the North Pole! I don't care! I'm not doing that stupid show!"

"You have to. This isn't optional. We committed, we're part of the schedule, and I will *not* be made a laughingstock. Who's going to wear your outfits?"

"I don't care! Find a fucking crash test dummy! Get a blow-up doll! Hire someone! Don't you always say money solves every problem?"

Rollo strolled into the foyer just then. "What is going on out here?" His gaze shot to meet Brianna's and instantly warmed. Tingles swept from her head to her toes.

"Sidney's being impossible."

Sidney crossed her arms over her chest. "Just because I won't be a fashion zombie? You don't care about me. You just want me to fill an outfit."

"It's Vera Wang..." Alicia sang the name as if it were an irresistible temptation. "A Vera Wang ball gown. It's the highlight of the event. Everyone wanted the Vera Wang, but we got it."

Sidney stuck her finger in her mouth. "A *ball* gown? No. No no no. Let me repeat that—"

"I can fill in," Brianna blurted.

Everyone turned to stare at her.

She shrank under the collective weight of all the Wareham attention. What had she been thinking? Nothing! She hadn't thought. She'd just spoken. Typical Brianna.

Rollo was already shaking his head, but Alicia spoke first.

"You're the right size for the gown, I suppose." She eyed Brianna's form as if even looking at her was granting her a favor. "Sidney's getting too large anyway."

Brianna gritted her teeth at yet another dig about Sidney's size.

"This is ridiculous." Rollo's alarmed tone got Brianna's hackles up. "She's not a family member. It's supposed to be mother-daughter."

"No one would dare object. Not with the amount of our donation." Alicia tilted her head and examined Brianna more closely. "I'll have to book a special session with my stylist. An extensive one."

Brianna bit her lip, determined not to take offense at anything Mrs. Wareham might dish out.

Sidney stomped her foot. "Mother, why do you have to be such a monumental—"

"Excuse us for a minute." Rollo pulled Brianna aside. "Bri, think about this," he told her in a low voice. "Don't do it. You'd be better off visiting the zoo or the art museum or hell...the damn landfill. You'd have more fun."

"I don't need it to be fun. It's for charity, right?"

"Yes, but you don't have to prance down a runway to help people out. You already do that all the time."

"Like how?"

"The Star Bright shelter, Old Man Turner, how about all those pies you and your mom made? I could go on but you'll just start blushing." He lifted his hand to touch her hair, then caught his mother's laser stare and dropped it.

She blushed anyway. "If I do this, maybe your mother will stop glaring at me. I'd like a chance to spend time with her. I'm really hoping to talk to her about Sidney. I wish she weren't so hard on her."

"Brianna, nothing you can say will change Alicia Stockard Wareham's mothering style. That's the way she is. That's how she was with me, with Brent, and now with Sidney. You in a Vera Wang ball gown is not going to make a bit of difference. Do you see that?"

She lifted her chin. "I think you're being too pessimistic. Not only that, I think you should have a little more faith in me."

He drew back, frowning. "Faith?"

"You think I'm a fashion disaster who can't handle a fashion show. You think I'm so tactless I can't handle your mother. Maybe you think I'll make a fool of myself. Light my dress on fire on the runway or something."

"Oh for Chrissake, Brianna. That's not what I'm saying." After a long, hard stare, he shoved his hands deep in his pockets and turned away. " Fine. Do what you want. It's your vacation."

CHAPTER 25

The mother-daughter fashion show took place that evening.

Rollo spent the time working out with the punching bag at his gym. He needed the release. The thought of Brianna willingly putting herself into the clutches of his mother drove him nuts. Why wouldn't she listen to reason? She always thought the best of people. She *counted* on the best of people. Sometimes she was right.

But not this time.

After his workout, Rollo showered, grabbed a quick solo dinner at a noodle shop in Chinatown, and took a cab to the Parkside. Even though he was still pissed at Brianna, he wanted to see her. The fashion show must be over by now. They could put the show and their quarrel behind them and get back to screwing their brains out.

But when he knocked on her door, he got no answer. He checked his watch. Eleven-fifteen and no Brianna. Maybe the show had gone so well that she and his mother were having after-show cocktails and girl talk.

Or maybe not.

He called her cell but got no answer. Like some kind of stalker, he pressed his ear to her door, hoping he might hear her phone ringing. She could be in the shower or already asleep.

Nope.

He jogged down the stairs to the reception desk.

"Can I leave a message for one of your guests?" he asked the concierge as he grabbed a pad and started scrawling a note. "Brianna Gallagher, room twelve."

"Sorry, she checked out this evening."

Rollo's head jerked up. "When?"

"About an hour ago."

Checked *out*? Why? Where was she now? Panic unfurled in his chest. He felt ungrounded without her. At sea. He at least wanted to know where she was.

Heading back to the street, Rollo hit Sidney's button on his phone. Maybe his sister had managed to talk Brianna into staying on Park Avenue with them. But Sidney was at a friend's birthday party and had no clue where Brianna might be.

"Ask Mother," she hollered over the blast of Macklemore. "Fashion show!"

But when he got hold of Alicia, she informed him that she hadn't seen Brianna since the show. "It went perfectly, by the way, not that you care. She was a sensation. Beyond all my expectations."

Around one in the morning, he got a text from Brianna. "I'm at the airport, about to board. Sorry to skip out on

Christmas but I had to get home. Everything's fine, don't worry. No big emergency. I'll see you back in Jupiter Point."

*

The minute Brianna stepped onto the tarmac at the regional airport, a sense of peace descended over her. Maybe her time in Manhattan had been nothing more than a nightmare. It would all fade away as soon as she got back to Jupiter Point and her regular life. She found her truck where she'd left it in the airport parking lot and slid into the driver's seat as if it were a cocoon.

Safe. At last.

She was never going to leave California again. The rest of the world could just go on without her. She was sticking to Jupiter Point from now on. No more elite, upper-class gatherings for her. No more pretending to be someone she wasn't. No more *fashion shows*.

Wincing, she remembered her last conversation with Rollo before the show. She'd flung all her own insecurities in his face, and they all turned out to be true. Fashion disaster, unable to handle his mother, guaranteed to make a fool of herself. Check, check, check.

A bit of memory flashed into her mind as she turned the key in the ignition. Pieces of the disaster had been surfacing like whack-a-moles during the entire flight home. Especially that moment when she took the mic to describe the ball gown she was wearing. They'd given her a script, but she'd misplaced it during the makeup process. Even though she'd mostly memorized it anyway, just in case, every word had vanished from her mind as soon as that microphone hit her hand. She had to say something. Didn't she? So she'd opened her mouth and words had spilled out.

She didn't remember much of what happened after that.

All she remembered was the surprised silence. The scattered giggles. The incredulous expression on Mrs. Wareham's face as she grabbed the mic back.

And of course, she remembered in vivid detail everything Mrs. Wareham had said backstage. After the disaster.

"And I thought Sidney was an embarrassment. How could a grown woman be so utterly awkward? My goodness, how do you get through life at all?"

"I...I..." Brianna was so rattled she wanted to cry. "I couldn't remember the script. I'm so sorry. I had to improvise."

"*Improvise?* Why didn't you simply smile and say 'thank you'? That's not so difficult, is it? There were ten-year-olds reciting their parts just fine."

"I didn't think of that—"

"A gardener, for heaven's sake. I suppose you talk to plants more often than people. This is Sidney's fault, I have no doubt. She'd do anything to embarrass me. She probably snuck into the audience to enjoy every excruciating moment."

"No. No, this has nothing to do with Sidney, and I wish you wouldn't be so harsh with her—"

Alicia gave a cutting laugh that sliced right through her. "Parenting advice, now? Well, you are a bold thing, aren't you? No manners whatsoever." The scornful curl of her upper lip would be branded on Brianna's consciousness *forever.*

Driving her old red truck toward the coast, she wanted to hang her head in shame. The script wasn't even *long.* She remembered it perfectly now. "I'm Brianna, representing the Wareham family, and I'm wearing a silk taffeta ball gown designed by Vera Wang."

How hard was that?

There was more, but even that *one line* would have been enough. Instead she'd said, "I'm Brianna, and I'm wearing a ham and—no, wait, sorry, I'm Brianna and—"

"Agggh!!!" Brianna screamed out loud to chase the memory from her head. Because she hadn't stopped there. No, she'd gone on. And on. So many words had poured out. Too many to remember.

After she'd ripped the ball gown off her body, she'd fled out the back door of the hotel ballroom where the event was being held. It was still early; the show was only halfway over. She'd hurried back to the Parkside, stuffed all her new clothes into her suitcase and called a cab to take her to the airport. She didn't care how much she paid in change fees.

She didn't care about saying goodbye to Sidney or Rollo. They'd be fine without her. *Better off* without her.

She was getting out of New York as fast as she could, before she embarrassed anyone else.

As for Alicia's explanation for why Sidney had invited her to New York, she didn't know what to think. Sidney had a mischievous side. Maybe she'd wanted Brianna to shake things up. It wasn't very nice, but Sidney was acting out in all sorts of ways.

Anyway, she wasn't sticking around to find out. It was one thing to make a fool of herself around people who loved her. In front of the Manhattan elite—not happening again. No way.

It was official; she couldn't handle Rollo's world.

She had to be honest with herself and admit that part of her had *hoped*—hoped against all odds—that Rollo would find a way to choose her. To love her. But never in a hundred million years would the Warehams accept her as a proper mate for their oldest son. Never, ever going to happen.

Her phone dinged with an incoming text. She drew her lower lip between her teeth, knowing it was probably either Rollo or Sidney. Not wanting to face either of them.

But she had to. It was always better to face things head-on, right?

She looked at her phone. The text was from Rollo.

What happened? Why'd you leave?

She texted one-handed, her other hand on the steering wheel. *Homesick.*

Sudden attack of homesickness?

Yes. I Heart Jupiter Point.

It was true, too. The hills ringing her little hometown were rising up ahead, black against the starlight, and she couldn't wait to get home.

All she had to do now was throw Rollo off the scent. She didn't want to tell him what had happened. She didn't want to cause any friction between him and his family. His destiny was set. And it didn't include her.

Have a good Christmas. See ya soon! There, that ought to do it. Casual, carefree, as if nothing was bothering her and her heart wasn't a bleeding mess.

Just like that? WTF, Bri?

Ugh, it figured that she couldn't fool Rollo.

She pulled over to the side of the road so she could talk to him in person without risking her neck. When he answered on the first ring, just the sound of his rumbling voice sent flutters through her belly.

" I'm sorry I left so suddenly. I just...got really homesick. I needed to get back."

He took a long time answering. "What about us?"

She drew in a long breath, trying to figure out the right way to answer that. "What us? We were on bonus time anyway. It'll be better for you if I'm not there. You have a job to do."

"Is that why you left? Because of...the *job* I have to do?"

"Rollo, why does this have to be about you? I wanted to come home. I miss Jupiter Point. It's Christmas. I want to string cranberries on the Christmas tree and make balsam wreaths and paper snowflakes and—" Her breath caught in her throat. Because she did want all those things...and yet more than anything, she wanted *him*. But she couldn't have him.

"Okay. I get that. My family isn't exactly filled with the Christmas spirit."

She pictured him running one hand through his thick brown hair, hurt shadowing his kind blue-gray eyes. "I'll see you back in Jupiter Point, okay?"

"Sure. See you in the New Year. And Bri?"

"Hm?"

"I'm glad you came. It means a lot to me. I'll never forget it."

She didn't answer because tears were clogging her throat. Alicia Wareham would never forget it either. She could guarantee that. "Okay," she finally managed, and ended the call.

She sat for a long moment in her truck, taking in deep breaths, trying to calm the racing of her heart.

This thing with Rollo was so far beyond anything she'd ever felt before. It was elemental, as if Rollo had changed her body chemistry in some way. She loved him. She couldn't imagine *not* loving him ever again.

But she couldn't be with him, even if he felt the same way.

Did he? She had no idea. Sometimes she'd caught an expression on his face...

No. Forget it. *Forget Rollo.* She had to, even if it was the hardest thing she ever had to do in her life.

*

The rest of the holiday season passed in a numbing blur. Since her parents had gone to Arizona, she spent Christmas with Suzanne, Josh, and the six teenagers who were currently staying at the Star Bright Shelter for Teens. The Christmas season was the worst for kids away from home, especially kids in the midst of a crisis.

She got each of the teens a gift, a journal they could pour their emotions into. It made her think of Sidney and the sketchbook she carried everywhere. Would Sidney be okay back in New York? She felt bad about leaving her before she'd really gotten her to open up. Had she done *anything* right at the Warehams? The whole trip had been one big mistake.

She invited Old Man Turner to Christmas dinner, as she did every year. But he declined, as he did every year. As usual, she packed him up a huge basket of leftovers and brought it to him the day after Christmas.

This year, he had a gift for her, too. A savings bond dating from the 1950s.

"Holy mackerel. This thing's probably worth a lot of money by now."

"A-yuh. Haven't paid you a cent in years. Take what I owe you out of that amount. The rest you'll probably need for my sendoff. If my body's ever found after the gang catches up with me." He grimaced as he worked on a can of beef stew with his special adaptive can opener.

"Oh, stop that, Melvin. No one's after you. And why are you eating canned stew when I just brought you all these delicious leftovers? The least you could do is pretend to appreciate them."

"Ho ho ho," he muttered, putting the can aside. "Don't celebrate holidays. Waste of time."

"I know, you're a big old Scrooge." She poked him on his bony shoulder. "But then how do you account for that savings bond you just gave me?"

"Eh. Dementia."

They both laughed. He might be declining fast, but he still had his sense of humor. She took care of a few chores around the place—switched his propane tank, piled his garbage bags into her truck, checked his dog for fleas. When she left, he was tucking into the roast beef she'd included in her gift basket.

She stashed the savings bond in her glove compartment, where most of her invoices and bills ended up until she emptied it once a month. She didn't want his payment. The only reason she'd cash in that savings bond would be if he needed it. She'd read that dementia could make people par-anoid. Old Man Turner seemed like a classic case. Poor old guy.

She spent New Year's Eve at a small party Suzanne threw at the new house she and Josh had just bought. Josh didn't own a stick of furniture, and Suzanne had lived in a small condo before they got married. That left a lot of emp-ty space, which they turned into a temporary dance floor filled with twinkle lights and balloons.

At the stroke of midnight, Sean grabbed Evie and swung her around, covering her face with kisses. Josh gently took hold of the seven-months-pregnant Suzanne and gave her a tender kiss on the lips. Merry sent her a Happy New Year text—she was busy covering the town's official New Year's Eve fireworks celebration.

Kiss any lucky screenwriters? Merry texted.

Good Lord. *Finn.* She'd forgotten all about him.

No. Ixnay on the ush-cray.

She wondered if Finn and Merry would get together. They had a lot more in common than she and Finn ever had. They were both writers, both sort of mysterious and glamorous. Her silly crush seemed so ridiculous now that she looked back at it. Why Finn? The whole dark-and-brooding thing had really sucked her in. But the whole time, Rollo had been right there, in all his slow-burn, sexy glory. Hiding in plain sight.

And now he was all she could think about.

She kept waiting for a New Year's text from him. Or a call. Or something. But midnight came and went with no word from Rollo.

Maybe he was just running late.

She went home and sat on the back deck of her little cabin, arms wrapped around her knees, and gazed up at the vast blanket of stars overhead. Those same stars were showering their light down on Rollo in Manhattan. Was he watching them in the slices of sky visible between those towering buildings? Or was he inside somewhere, drinking champagne and tugging at his collar?

One o'clock came and went. No call. 1:15, 1:30.

At 1:35, she turned off her phone and buried her head under her pillow.

Clearly, her destiny had struck again. Awkward crushes were her doom.

CHAPTER 26

New Year's Eve was probably the worst night of the year for a first date. At Le Bernardin, where reservations had to be booked three months ahead of time, couples filled every table. Romantic, flirting, expensively dressed couples. Rollo and Cornelia, on the other hand...well, they were both expensively dressed. Cornelia was definitely flirting. But romantic? If romantic meant "ball of dread in your stomach"...sure.

"Your mother is amazing," Cornelia was gushing. "She was so thoughtful to book this table for us. Do you know how far in advance she had to do that?"

"Yes. She's very organized."

"She should be running a corporation."

"She does, in a way. Wareham, Inc."

Cornelia smiled, which drew his attention to the deep red shade of her lipstick. He found it unnerving. "The older families like ours are so much responsibility. That's one reason I got both a law degree and a business degree."

Since Cornelia was a compliance officer for a corporation, he didn't really get the connection. But she was definitely smart. His mother hadn't set him up with a flighty social butterfly, and for that he was grateful. Cornelia was focused, poised, ambitious. No one would mess around with her. If anyone could hold their own with Alicia Stockard Wareham, it would be Cornelia.

Best of all, it turned out that her family also had a vacation house in Maine. She'd spent childhood summers about a hundred miles up the coast from him. She even had a firefighting story to tell. "A wildfire came within two miles of our house in Bar Harbor. I'll never forget the men who fought that fire. Very good-looking. Are all firefighters so attractive?"

He laughed, acknowledging the compliment. As they shared memories about tromping through the woods and swimming in the icy-cold Maine water, he finally felt comfortable with her. Even more than the champagne, talking about the outdoors relaxed him.

"I'll always love Maine, but I'm a Pacific Ocean guy these days," he told her. "I just bought a place in California."

A sharp stab of pain shot through him as he pictured his house on the cliffs, with the koi pond ready for fish. What would it be like seeing Brianna around town after all this? He'd always figured they'd stay friends no matter what. In their last phone call, just before Christmas, she'd sounded friendly. But someone like Cornelia might not stand for an unconventional friendship like that.

Cornelia smoothed over his sudden silence. "These days, it's nice to have footholds wherever you can. I'd love to see the spot you've found. Jupiter Point, your mother said? I'm sure it's darling."

"A lot of people think so. I moved there for the fire-fighting and liked the territory."

At the stroke of midnight, he leaned across the table. Candlelight flickered across her smooth skin, giving her even, pretty features a hint of mystery. His gaze dropped to her mouth. Those deep red lips parted, inviting him in. He kissed her, just a quick brush of contact.

And immediately drew back.

The wrongness of it sang through his body. No, no, no. He couldn't kiss anyone else. Not yet, anyway. Not while his heart beat to the sound of Brianna's name and the memory of her burned under his skin.

Cornelia didn't seem to notice his reaction. She smiled warmly at him and wished him a Happy New Year. They ordered after-dinner brandies. They talked about her work. She asked him about his house in California. He wasn't sure how it happened, but by the time he signaled for the bill, Cornelia had made a plan to visit him in Jupiter Point.

*

Only one thing kept Brianna from being able to avoid Rollo. It began with a K, ended with an I, and was filled with Brianna's blood, sweat and tears. The best thing would be if she could fill the damn koi pond with dirt and move on.

But she was a professional, damn it. She wasn't going to run from Rollo. She was going to face him head-on. By now he'd probably heard all about her disastrous fashion show performance. He was probably thanking his lucky stars that things were over between them. If he was a really good friend, he'd never mention that mortifying event.

Of course they were good friends. They'd get through the wrong turn their relationship had taken. They'd get back to their old casual, fun, hangout-buddy status.

In the meantime, she raced to complete the koi pond before Rollo got back. The koi had been ordered, so the only tasks left were to fill the pond with water and plant the water hyacinth, horsetail and lotus that would help filter the water.

And she *almost* made it.

So close. *So close.* She had turned on the hose and was filling the pond when she heard his Jeep drive up. For one crazy moment, she considered hiding in the pond, water and all. But that truly would be a cowardly move, and possibly hypothermic.

So she turned, casual as she could, and waved as he stepped out of his rig.

First thought: his beard was growing back.

Second thought: God, he looked good.

The third thought was more of a physical reaction than an actual thought. It was a full-body flush that swept from her toes, which were tucked under her as she knelt by the pond, to the top of her head, where a bandanna kept her hair out of her eyes.

Rollo waved back and hauled his duffel out of the passenger seat. He slung it onto the walkway and strode across the lawn toward her. All the breath left her body. The glug-glug of the water filling the pond rang in her ears like a bell, blocking out everything else. Her eyes ate him up as if he were Christmas dinner and New Year's champagne all rolled into one. It felt as if her heart sighed. Literally sighed.

He came close, his gray-blue eyes scanning her, the pond, then back to her. "You've been working hard."

"Yeah. I was trying to get it done before..." She trailed off, wincing.

But he caught it right away. A shadow passed across his face. "Before I got back?"

"No, just, you know, I have a lot of other projects going on, and I already ordered the koi and I'm sure you don't want to keep them in the bathtub until the pond is done." Babbling. Totally babbling.

"Homeless koi. Wouldn't be right."

She smiled, then couldn't stop smiling because just the sight of him made her eyes happy. He wore the moss-green cable-knit sweater Sidney had knit for him and his familiar worn jeans and work boots. His beard was about an inch long, which meant he was halfway between clean-cut New York guy and the wild mountain firefighter. She liked both versions, and she liked the in-between version too. She liked all of him.

"So...any luck finding a missus?" She cringed as the words left her mouth. God, what was wrong with her? Why oh why did she have to blurt out *every little thing*?

His eyebrows drew together. "Still single." But from the reserved way he said it, she knew there was more to the story. And she didn't want to hear it. Not yet. Not right away.

"But someone is coming to visit in a few days. Cornelia. I...uh...I hope that's okay."

And there it was. It felt like a hammer right to her heart. "Really? That's awesome. That's perfect timing because the koi should be arriving right around then and I'm sure she'll want to see that."

Really? That was what "Cornelia" would want to see? Koi? What kind of person was named Cornelia, anyway?

"I mean, maybe she doesn't and that's okay too. I'll try to finish up before she arrives. That way you won't have an ex hanging around in your yard. Not that she would know. Or that I am an ex, technically. We were just friends. Still are. Really, really great friends, and I'm very happy you have someone visiting. By the way, did you know that koi can mate with goldfish? Fun fact. I didn't know that. I've really learned a lot on this project, so thank you for the opportunity—" She broke off with a yelp as water touched her knees. The pond was overflowing. She'd been babbling so much she'd forgotten the hose was on.

Rollo bent down and scooped her up, stepping back from the rim of the pond. Water brimmed over the edge, soaking into the lawn on all sides. She gave his chest a hard push.

"Put me down!"

The desperation in her tone must have shocked Rollo. He let her go and she slid to the ground. She ran to the spigot and turned off the hose. She gave herself a moment of fiddling with the hose bib to collect herself.

It was one thing to try to stay friends with Rollo. Being in his arms again—that was a step too far. She couldn't handle that. She had to make it perfectly clear that their relationship would be strictly hands-off from now on.

"Sorry about the overflow," she told him as she stepped gingerly back to the edge of the pond. "The water should soak into the grass. No harm done. We'll just pretend that never happened, right?" Her gaze clung to his, asking him to understand. She meant the overflow, she meant him holding her...all of the above.

A line appeared between his eyebrows and he looked away. He nodded once, stuffed his hands in his pockets. With his wide shoulders hunched over, he surveyed the wet grass and full pond. Then he swung his grave gaze back to her. "You should probably go change. You'll catch a cold out here like that."

She looked down at herself, realizing she'd gotten completely drenched. Her overalls clung to every curve of her hips and legs. Well, it wasn't anything he hadn't seen before.

When she looked up, he was halfway to his house, bending over to pick up the duffel he'd left on the walkway.

"Okay, thanks," she whispered to herself.

*

It could be worse, Rollo kept telling himself. Brianna could be ignoring him. Hating him. Yelling at him. Spreading nasty rumors about him. But then again, she wouldn't be Brianna if she did that sort of thing. That was completely not her style.

Instead, she was acting as if New York had never happened. As if their "fling" had never happened. She gave him friendly smiles every time she saw him. Which would have been fine, but he saw her *everywhere*. Laughing, being adorable, lighting up every nightspot in Jupiter Point.

When he went to grab a beer at Barstow's Brews with Josh and Tim Peavy, there she was, shooting pool with a bunch of guys from the police department. He watched from across the room as she bent over the table, squinting down her pool cue. The overhead lamp lit her hair into a coppery halo of fire. Her cute little rear shifted as she lined up her shot, making him about as hard as her damn cue.

Were those idiot cops checking out her ass too? Fuckers.

He was halfway out of his seat, ready to smash some off-duty heads together, before he remembered that he had no claim on Brianna. That she *should* be looking for someone else. He sank back and signaled for another pitcher of beer.

"Doing your squats?" Josh asked mildly. From the glint in his eye, he knew exactly what Rollo was going through.

"Fuck off."

"Dude, is something bugging you? Want to talk to Uncle Josh about it?"

"Bet it's girl trouble," said Peavy wisely. "If you need advice from a couple of married guys—"

"Then I'll ask those old geezers at the end of the bar," growled Rollo. "I don't need any advice."

"Good. Because no advice will help you, my friend." Josh squeezed his shoulder. "Want to know why? Because you're doomed. Fight it all you want. Won't make a difference. When you find the right girl, it's all over, man." He grinned at Rollo's expression. "In a good way, of course."

"I'm blocking you out right now." Rollo downed his beer just in time for the next pitcher to arrive. As he sipped the foam off his next mugful, his gaze traveled back to Brianna. She was high-fiving one of the cops. Her t-shirt rode up her waist, exposing a flash of skin that went right to Rollo's head.

"Doomed," Josh repeated gleefully.

Rollo also saw Brianna at the hardware store. They chatted long enough for her to explain she was buying bulbs for a hillside of daffodils. He ran into her at Fifth Book from the Sun, where Mrs. Murphy, the town rumormonger, tried to get one or both of them to spill details from Brianna's trip to New York.

"Someone told me you're a secret millionaire and you paid for Brianna's suite at a five-star hotel. But I said, why would a millionaire risk his life putting out wildfires? It just doesn't make sense."

"It really doesn't, does it?" Brianna tossed Rollo a wink as she plopped her pile of books on the counter. "And can you imagine me in a five-star hotel? They'd have to give me one of those Silkwood treatments first. You know, when they put you through the power wash?"

"Don't be silly, Brianna. What are these, westerns? Not your usual choice." Mrs. Murphy rang up the books, barely noting the prices. Most people felt that she ran the business more as a front for gossip than anything else.

"They're for Old Man Turner. He sprained his ankle again."

"Poor man. Speaking of which, someone came in here asking about him."

"Really?" Brianna handed over a twenty for the books. "Someone from out of town?"

"I didn't know him, and I know everyone in Jupiter Point." Mrs. Murphy smiled smugly. "Strange thing, though. He used a different name for Melvin at first. Something foreign. Now I'm wondering if Old Man Turner's been hiding something from us."

"Oh no, I'm sure it's nothing like that...I mean..." Brianna shot Rollo a look of panic. He stepped in and changed the subject to his favorite Louis L'Amour book. Once they made it outside, Brianna let out a whoosh of breath.

"This isn't good. Melvin Turner doesn't want anyone to know that's not his real name. Oops. Not even you." She shook her head, the bright gingery waves gleaming in the afternoon sun. "But if Mrs. Murphy knows, everyone will. I'd better warn him right away. He's been acting so strange lately. I'm really starting to worry. And why was someone asking about him? I don't like this."

"You'd better tell me all about it. Coffee at Evie's?"

"Oh." Her cheeks turned pink and she gave him a flustered smile. "I really can't. Million things to do today. Say hi to Evie, though!" And she hurried down the street. A few minutes later, he saw her Toyota truck rattling down Constellation Way.

She was definitely avoiding him.

Except at night.

Every night, Brianna came to him in his dreams. She danced right up to him, laughing, teasing. Hoisted herself on the kitchen counter, legs dangling. Somehow they were always bare. Sometimes she arrived naked and climbed into his bed. Straddled him, all golden and freckled and mouthwatering. He'd lift his hands to her perky breasts. Joy and peace would flood his being. He'd fill his arms with her sweetness and warmth. And he'd be happy.

Until he woke up and remembered that he and Brianna weren't together anymore. Every morning, he picked up the phone to call Cornelia and cancel her visit. But then remembered his promise to his family. And his commitment to Dougie and the other charitable causes he funded. Except—Dougie was about to become a millionaire. He didn't need that fund anymore.

Maybe Rollo could help his favorite causes in non-financial ways.

Maybe he'd paid enough for his past behavior. Maybe he could walk away from his family responsibilities. Choose a different destiny. Marry someone he...wanted. Needed. Loved?

Was this love, this constant pesky ache?

But Cornelia kept sending him cheerful emails about her trip and he couldn't bring himself to call it off.

And Brianna was treating him like one of her buddies. She'd seen that other side of him—the Park Avenue jackass in a suit. No wonder she was avoiding him. She probably wanted nothing to do with Rollington Wareham III.

CHAPTER 27

Finn finally finished the rough draft of his screenplay and invited everyone over for a "table read." Sean refused, since he was still opposed to the idea of a movie about the burnover they'd survived. But knowing that Brianna would be there, Rollo wouldn't have missed it for anything. Besides, he'd offered up his house since the guesthouse wouldn't hold that many people.

Rollo, Evie, Suzanne, Josh, Brianna and Merry gathered around the coffee table in his living room while Finn handed out copies of the script. Brianna sat cross-legged on the floor, her copy spread open in her lap. She wore one of the new outfits she'd gotten in New York, a baby doll top in star-spangled indigo silk along with rolled up jeans. A length of yarn held back her hair; he overheard her telling Merry that she was getting back into knitting now that the slow season for gardening had begun.

He walked around the room, distributing bottles of root beer, and tried not to stare at the bright-haired firefly perched on his floor. But God, it was so hard. When he handed her the bottle, his arm brushed against her curls; it felt like a bolt of electricity streaking through him. She didn't meet his eyes as she accepted the drink. Instead she aimed a vague smile over her shoulder, as if it were salt tossed for good luck.

He wanted to kick everyone out and haul her into the bedroom and make love to her until that distant look dissolved into one of wild-eyed passion.

Lost in that fantasy, he just stared blankly at Merry when she asked him a question. She smirked and looked back at her copy of the script.

Get ahold of yourself. He passed his root beer bottle across his forehead, hoping the cold glass would keep him on track. He sank into the leather armchair he'd purchased when he realized Cornelia would need a place to sit.

Finn stuck an unlit cigar between his teeth. "All right, listen up, everyone. Your lines are highlighted. Man, woman, doesn't matter. Characterization doesn't matter. Don't worry about your fricking motivation or anything like that. We're firefighters, right? Simple folk. Our motivation is to put out the fire and not get killed."

Merry raised her hand. "Based on my research into hotshots, I have to say that I disagree. What about the motivation for doing such a dangerous job to begin with?"

Finn scowled at her beneath his dark swath of hair. "Why'd I invite you again?"

Merry smirked. "Because of my valuable journalistic skills and sparkling personality."

"She has a point," Evie intervened in that calming way of hers. "Firefighters have all kinds of motivations. Some join because they want to be heroes, some want the adrenaline rush, some just don't want a normal job. Some like being outdoors."

"Then there's Rollo," said Josh. "Rollo, what was your motivation again? You needed help picking up chicks, right?"

Rollo glared at him. "I wanted to hang out with a bunch of idiots."

"Oh right, that was it. Anger management by way of a chainsaw and a forest."

"Don't be silly. It was so he could grow that magnificent beard." Evie smiled at him with gentle affection.

"Nah, you're all wrong," said Finn. "He joined the service to piss off his family. It worked, too."

Merry cocked her head curiously. "Seriously, so what was it? What inspired a guy with a big-ass trust fund to pick a career running into flames? Serious question. I really want to know."

Josh coughed, burying the words "death wish" inside the sound.

Rollo's leg jittered up and down. He wished himself a thousand miles away, in the middle of a forest somewhere. This interrogation was a load of crap. He lifted his bottle of root beer to his mouth.

Brianna caught his eye and made a sympathetic face, as if she knew exactly what he was feeling.

She raised her hand. "I know. Call on me, teacher."

Josh waved his bottle at her. "The redhead in the front row, go ahead."

"Rollo joined so he could save *your* worthless ass from a forest fire." She stuck out her tongue at Josh as the room erupted in laughter and a chorus of "ooh, burn" and "oh, snap." Josh pretended to be struck in the heart with a dagger; he fell back on the couch, where Suzanne plopped a kiss on his nose.

"For which he will forever be my hero," she proclaimed. "Rollo rocks."

"Wait a second," grumbled Josh good-naturedly. "I'm the husband. Don't I rate as your hero?"

"Ask me later." Suzanne kissed him again. "You can be extra heroic tonight."

He grinned and nestled her under his arm, while the rest of them hooted and whistled.

Finn called the table read back to order and they all turned to their screenplays. Rollo focused on the lines marked with yellow highlighter as Finn read the stage directions.

"Exterior. Aerial shot. Big Canyon Wilderness. Miles of untouched forest, a mix of pine and birch. On the horizon, smoke billows. We fly like a bird over the canopy toward the column of smoke. Slowly, sounds are heard. The hum of an airplane engine. The click of a safety harness. The radio spitting out coordinates."

Finn paused and motioned to Evie, who started. "Oops, sorry. Oh my God, it's so good, Finn! I'm totally drawn into it already."

Finn grinned. "Going for the drama. Go ahead, read your line. You're the pilot."

"Approaching the fire lines," Evie read. "Jumpers ready?"

It was Rollo's turn. "Go for jump. Hey, um, just a refresher, we're jumping into those flames, right?" He glanced up at Finn. "Nice. A little humor right off the bat."

"Wouldn't be firefighting without it, right?"

"Roger that," Evie said, reading her next line in a deep voice.

Finn picked up the thread. "The aerial descent begins. The flames come closer. We see nothing but smoke and fire below, as if we're peering into hell. Then the side of the plane opens up. Three firefighters line up at the edge. One by one, they jump toward the flames. The camera follows the last firefighter, but when he heads for an open patch of ground, it veers off in a different direction. Into the flames. Smoke swirls everywhere, the world goes dark.

"Interior bedroom. A man sits bolt upright."

He paused. Everyone sat on the edges of their seats, completely riveted by Finn's dramatic reading.

"Brianna, you're up," he prompted.

"Right. Sorry." Peering at the copy in her lap, she read the next line in a nervous tone. "Fire had invaded my dreams."

"Stand up, if you want," Finn told her impatiently. "I can't hear you down there."

"Sorry, I'm just not much of a public speaker. Someday I'll tell you about the time I ran for class treasurer and had to make a speech in front of the entire assembly."

"You did great." Evie used that hearty tone meant to convince someone they hadn't screwed up. "It was inspiring."

"Yes, *vomit* inspiring." Brianna scrambled to her feet, tugging down her silky top. Rollo watched the way it hugged her little waist. His hands itched to smooth that sweet curve from her ribs to her hips. He clenched them into fists.

Brianna held the script out in front of her. "Fire had invaded my dreams," she read. "Whenever I closed my eyes, it was there. Stalking me. Mocking me." She giggled, then covered her mouth with a dainty cough. "Sorry, got something caught in my throat."

Rollo fixed his gaze on his own copy, knowing that if he caught her eye, he'd be the next to laugh.

"I knew fire, and fire knew me." Her voice sounded strained from the effort of taking her lines seriously. "We were as intimate as lo...lovers." A chuckle burst forth, but she clapped a hand over her mouth with another very obvious fake cough. Rollo glanced up to see crimson flooding her cheeks.

"Sorry, I told you I suck at this," she gasped.

Finn scowled at his screenplay and made a slash with a big black Sharpie.

"Just skip that whole paragraph," he muttered. "Go on to the next part."

"Okay." She swallowed hard. "Next part..." She ran her index finger down the page. "The first time I heard the word 'burnover,' I assumed it came in flavors of apple and blueberry." She snorted, then bit her lip. "Ha! Good one, Finn."

"Keep going. You can skip the commentary."

Brianna lifted the script back up and kept reading. "Think breakfast pastry, maybe a little burnt around the edges. Turned out, I was the dessert." That was it. She burst into a snort of laughter. Once she started, she couldn't stop. She tried to read the next line. "And I was wrapped up in aluminum foil, AKA my emergency shelter." She turned away to hide her convulsions of laughter.

"Finn," she gasped. "I swear it's good, it really is. I'm so sorry. I just completely, totally suck at this."

"No. It's not you."

"It is! I promise. You should have seen me in New York. I did even worse there. Me and scripts just don't get along."

Rollo lifted his head with a frown. What had happened in New York that involved a script? He'd missed that.

Finn tapped his Sharpie on his root beer bottle and rose to his feet. His mouth was set in a grim line. He lifted his copy of the screenplay high in the air.

"Finn? What are you doing?" Rollo asked uneasily.

With his other hand, Finn dug in his pocket and pulled out a lighter. He flicked it, sparking a small flame, then touched it to the screenplay. Flame licked along the edge.

They all watched, paralyzed, as the thick sheaf of pages turned black and flames leapt toward the ceiling.

Then Merry started laughing. "How many damn fire-fighters do we have in this room? And you're all just going to sit there?"

With the silence shattered, everyone sprang into action. Josh stood up and dashed the contents of his root beer at the flaming screenplay. Then he grabbed Suzanne's bottle and did the same with hers, even though she tried to hold on to it. Some of the liquid hit the pages gripped in Finn's fist, but most of it splashed onto Merry, who shrieked in surprise.

Rollo ripped off his overshirt and grabbed the smoldering sheaf of pages with it. He flung them to the floor and stomped out the rest of the sparks.

Finn let out a crazy war whoop. "Yeah! That's the way." He dumped his root beer on top of the script, then stomped on it with one booted foot.

"Finn. What the hell?" Rollo dragged him away from the pile of cinders. "That's my floor. And my shirt."

"And my piece of crap screenplay." He stepped away from the pile of charred cloth and paper. "Thanks, ladies and gentleman, for confirming what I knew all along. I can't write for shit."

"No, Finn, that's not true..." Evie murmured half-heartedly.

"It's fucking true. Sorry, Evie. And everyone. Sorry to drag you all out here to prove I suck. It's actually a relief. Someone else can write their damn screenplay."

An acrid smoke rose from the debris. Rollo coughed and went to open a window to air it out.

Brianna wiped tears off her cheeks. "Finn, I feel terrible about this. Your script wasn't the problem; it was totally me!"

"Nope. You were great. I might even give my dad your number. Next time he wants to know if a script is any good, he should have you read a few lines. It'll be completely obvious. So." He brushed off his hands, looking as if the weight of the world had been lifted off his shoulders. "Who wants a real beer?"

"Count me in. I gotta shower first, though. Josh, your aim sucks." Merry jumped to her feet and headed for the bathroom. Josh helped Suzanne to her feet, and they went into the kitchen to help Finn with the beer.

That left Rollo, Brianna and Evie. Brianna had such a mortified look on her face that Rollo wanted to swoop her off her feet and whisk her into the moonlight, where he could kiss the worry away. He practically vibrated with the need to get her alone.

Evie looked from one to the other of them. "I'll just...help Merry in the bathroom. Because root beer in the hair, ugh, that's just never good. Be right back." She hurried away.

Brianna rubbed a tear away with one thumb, as if she was trying to hide the fact that she was crying. "Why am I such a disaster?"

"Honey, this wasn't your fault. Come on. Let's go outside. It's too smoky in here."

She sniffed, nodding, and he guided her out the door. Finally he had her alone. Starlight shimmered in her eyes, on her hair, on her skin. He ached to take her into his arms and kiss her breathless.

But Cornelia was coming. She was probably on her way to the airport right now. It wasn't right.

"What happened in New York? What were you talking about?" he asked.

Her gaze swooped up to meet his. "No one told—? I mean, nothing. Nothing happened."

A muscle flexed in his jaw. He knew his Brianna and her inability to hide the truth. Obviously *something* had happened, and everyone had decided to keep it secret from him. "Was it why you left so suddenly? Because of whatever happened?"

"I left because I wanted to leave." Furiously, she dashed the tears off her cheeks. "Is that so hard to believe?"

"Not at all. I always want to leave too. But you were having fun. We were—" He broke off. If he could say what he wanted to her, it would be something like "we were having the best sex of my life" or "we were falling in love." But he couldn't say those things because he couldn't be with her. And Cornelia was coming.

"Just let it go, Rollo," Brianna whispered. "Do you think this is easy for me? I—I want the best for you. I care about you. So just leave me alone, okay?"

She stepped away from him, the ocean breeze molding her shirt against her body. He had the sense she was merging with the starlight while she disappeared from his life.

"I don't know if I can, Bri," he said harshly. "I miss you. Come up on the roof with me. We'll watch the stars. Talk the way we used to."

"Sorry, I just can't. We can still be friends, just like tonight. In a big group, it's fine. But none of this sort of thing." She waved her hand back and forth between the two of them.

His control snapped. "You mean none of this?" He stepped closer and snatched her into his arms. Lifting her into the air, he crushed her against him and claimed her mouth. He couldn't tell her how he felt, but he could show her—with his body, with his passion, with his lips and mouth and hands.

She responded with the same raw desperation running through his body. For one perfect moment, everything was exactly how it should be. The stars twinkled, the universe sang, his heart soared.

Then she tore herself away and stepped back. When she stumbled, he reached out for her, but she quickly righted herself and threw up a hand to hold him off.

"Don't *do* that to me! It's not *fair*, Rollo! Do you have any idea how—?" She spun around and headed blindly for her truck. "Tell everyone...tell them I had a gardening emergency. Threat of frost. Plants to protect. Something."

His body one throbbing mass of frustration, he shoved his hand in his pockets and watched her run across his lawn. *Goddamn it.* He'd fucked everything up, for Brianna, for himself, for Cornelia or someone else just like Cornelia.

As soon as she arrived, he'd have to explain that he could offer everything except his heart. Because his heart was Brianna's. And it always would be.

CHAPTER 28

Rollo picked up Cornelia at the regional airport early the next morning. Despite the awkward travel time, she looked fresh and businesslike as she sauntered across the tarmac in white jeans and a lilac blazer with the sleeves rolled up.

White jeans. Who traveled in white jeans? He tried to imagine Brianna taking a risk like that. How many inflight beverage stains would she have by the end of the trip?

They exchanged pecks on the cheek. Rollo helped her into his SUV and they drove into town. He showed her the downtown area with its charming B&Bs and historic cedar-shingled storefronts. "Jupiter Point is kind of a niche market for honeymooners and stargazers," he explained. "They name everything after stars and planets and so forth. There's an observatory just outside of town. Something about the air currents makes the conditions better than average here. We could do a nighttime stargazing sail, or maybe get a tour of the observatory if you're interested."

"That's a possibility. I have some work to catch up on. I estimate I should be able to finish in about two hours and twenty-seven minutes."

He laughed, thinking she must be joking, but she didn't smile back. A sinking feeling settled into his gut. Without all the candlelight and New Year's champagne, things didn't feel nearly as hopeful with Cornelia. "How about some cof-fee? The Venus and Mars makes a mean sticky bun."

But it was hard to impress a New Yorker when it came to coffee or gigantic pastries. They sat in awkward silence as she inspected the mountain of pecans and caramel.

The rumble of a truck engine caught his attention. Good Lord, he was like a tuning fork when it came to Brianna—her vehicle included.

She jerked the truck to a stop at the curb outside. Over-loaded with an armful of fresh-cut flowers in shades of cornflower and lavender, she dashed into the cafe. A gust of fresh, sweet air came with her. "Sorry I'm late," she panted to the cashier. "Engine trouble."

The dreadlocked barista buried his nose in the flowers. "These smell amazing. Did you grow them?"

"In my very own greenhouse."

As she hurried out of the cafe, her gaze swept over him and Cornelia. She stumbled just a bit but then offered a friendly wave and a rushed "good morning."

He smiled at her, trying with all his might to make it look like any other smile. It must not have worked, because Cornelia turned to watch Brianna hop into her truck.

"Oh sweet heavens, I recognize that girl. She's the one from the fashion show. Poor thing, I guess she got as far away from your mother as she could." With a condescend-ing smile, she watched the old red truck cruise down Con-stellation Way.

"What are you talking about?"

"That girl absolutely blew *up* the mother-daughter fashion show. People were talking about it for days. What a scene."

Dread closed like a vise around his throat. "What sort of scene?"

"The sort of scene your mother despises. A public one, very embarrassing. That girl was supposed to recite a little write-up about the dress she was wearing, but instead she went rogue and gave a sort of spontaneous speech. Oh my gosh, what was it she said?" She tapped her finger on her chin.

"You were there?"

"Of course. It's a holiday tradition. Usually it's all the same people, you know, so of course she got attention simply for being new. Then she began her rant about fashion and clothes, and I think she threw something about Cinderella in there, and...hang on. I have the video."

Rollo hauled in a deep breath as she pulled up YouTube on her phone. He didn't really want to see Brianna's moment of fame. But he had to. He had to get the full picture.

And there she was in a puffy ball gown at the end of a runway, standing in a Superman-like pose. The sound was iffy, the video quality sketchy. But he'd know that Brianna nervous babble anywhere.

"Hi, I'm Brianna and I'm wearing a ham. Oops, sorry, that's not right. Okay, trying again. I'm Brianna and I'm not a Wareham. I'm representing the Warehams, which is pretty funny because when it comes to me and clothes, I'm kind of like Pigpen. Or like Cinderella if she just stayed in the fireplace getting all sooty. If there's a speck of dirt *anywhere* nearby, it'll come to me like a magnet. Dirt and me, yup, we're pretty much inseparable. I couldn't even find clean underwear for tonight, so I turned an old pair inside out. Have you ever tried that trick? I swear it's not as gross as it sounds."

His mother, wearing a similar ball gown and a look of absolute horror, tried to take away the mic. Brianna had such a death grip on it that nothing worked. "I'm so sorry, Mrs. Wareham. I told you this might be a disaster. This is a disaster, isn't it? Like a crazy, beyond-awful disaster?"

The shocked silence in the hotel ballroom broke as a wave of laughter swept through the elegant guests. Brianna just kept on going, as if she'd completely lost control of her mouth. "I should just take this ball gown off before I rip it or trample it or wipe my sweaty hands on it...oops, too late...oh, it's Vera Wang! That's what I was supposed to say! And it's taffy. Taffeta. Okay, I think I should go now. Here, Mrs. ...You."

Apparently she'd forgotten his family name by that point. She thrust the microphone at his stunned mother and fled down the runway, past upturned faces and iPhones recording her flight. She stumbled and lost a shoe, but kept going.

Wise choice.

A guest in the front row leaned forward and snatched the shoe off the runway. "Souvenir!" she called. "We'll be auctioning this off later, so save some of your pennies!"

More laughter. His mother's face was somewhere between scarlet and heart-attack purple. She said something into the mic that couldn't be heard over the din of laughter.

And then the video ended.

Cornelia wore an avid look that told Rollo she'd watched the whole thing more than once. "Classic, no? Do you think she'd give me her autograph? I could dine for weeks off that."

Rollo shoved his chair back with a sound like fingernails on a blackboard. "That's a friend of mine. Did my mother mention that?"

"Of course she did." Cornelia offered him a smooth smile. "She said that she'd latched onto Sidney as a way into your family. Your mother wasn't at all surprised by that little meltdown. She thinks she's a terrible influence on your sister. Very relieved she left."

"That's ridiculous. All of it."

"Is it? When you come from families like ours, you have to be careful. People want to be part of our world. But they can't be, can they? There's a reason we need gatekeepers, so to speak."

Rage surfed through Rollo's system, making his blood boil. What a snob she was. He couldn't stand that sort of attitude. Come to think of it, he couldn't stand *her*. She was everything he didn't like about the world he'd grown up in.

"I'm sorry, Cornelia. I have to be honest with you here. This isn't going anywhere between us. I'm sorry you flew all the way out here for nothing. But this just isn't going to happen."

Cornelia smiled coolly and nibbled on a pecan from the sticky bun. "Oh sweetie. Would you relax? Everything will be okay. From what Alicia tells me, she holds the cards. I can't say you're my usual type, since I rarely date lumberjacks. But she swears you're going to clean up your act. So I think you should just get over yourself and drink your coffee and we'll work this out like civilized people."

Rollo put both hands on the table and leaned forward, steam practically coming out of his ears. "What the fuck makes you think I'm civilized?"

Her pupils widened and she drew back. "Oh my. Well, sometimes a little uncivilized behavior makes a nice change. In certain circumstances."

Hell *no*. Was she talking about *in bed*? He didn't want to sleep with her. Or touch her. Or kiss her, or even spend one more minute in her company.

"I'm in love with someone else," he said, enunciating every word. "I won't marry anyone but her. My family is just going to have to deal with it."

"You're going to walk away from your inheritance? Then you're a fool. I don't date fools."

He rose to his feet before things got ugly. Let her think him a fool. What did he care? Maybe he was a fool. A fool for love. "Thanks for coming out, Cornelia. I'll send someone to take you back to the airport. Or if you prefer to do some sightseeing, feel free."

Cornelia busied herself pulling her sunglasses from her purse and sliding them onto her nose. Maybe she was more hurt than she let on. He felt bad about that, but then again, not too bad. "I'll take my sightseeing out the window of my flight back, thank you."

"Fine. Your ride will be here shortly."

Already tugging his phone out of his pocket, Rollo left the cafe. His heart felt light and free—happy. He no longer felt lost in the forest. He'd reached a high ridge and could see everything clearly.

He loved Brianna. He belonged with Brianna. No one else would ever do.

His first text went to Finn. *Pretty blond at the Venus and Mars needs a ride to airport. It's worth a month of rent.*

You don't charge me rent.

I will if you don't pick her up.

His next text went to Bri. *Where r u? Need to see you right away.*

He got no answer from her. Swinging into his SUV, he went old school and dialed her number, but he had no better luck that way. Was she ignoring him? Busy delivering more flowers? Avoiding everyone with the name Wareham?

He started up his rig and set off down Constellation Way. He'd search the entire town and the rest of the galaxy if need be. But he'd find her. And when he did, he'd tell her that she was the opposite of a disaster. She was a miracle. YouTube be damned.

*

After she'd dropped off the Venus and Mars Cafe's weekly flower order, Brianna skipped the rest of her scheduled deliveries. Instead she headed to Old Man Turner's. He was the only person she could handle being around right now. Everyone else would want to chat. She didn't want to chat. She wanted to wallow in her broken heart, and she needed peace and quiet to do so. Old Man Turner was just the guy for that.

He'd been acting more and more strange lately. Every time she showed up, he gave her another one of his possessions. Figuring it was all part of the dementia, she'd been putting his gifts in a big cardboard box in his shed. Hopefully she'd find a way to ease them back into his life without his even noticing.

Just a couple days ago, he'd given her the old rose-printed teapot she'd always admired. This was the perfect chance to sneak into the shed and put the teapot in the box.

She saw no sign of the old man when she pulled into her usual parking spot near the garden. As she stepped across the scrubby winter grass, she drew in a long breath of sweet chilly air, feeling the peace that always came over her anywhere near a garden. With the teapot nested under her arm, she stepped to the shed on the far side of the garden.

Quietly, in case Old Man Turner was behind a shrub somewhere and heard the hinges squeak, she eased open the door. And froze in shock.

A man crouched next to the old red toolbox where Turner kept his important papers. He was rifling through them with black-gloved hands. Come to think of it, he was dressed entirely in black. Something lay on the floor next to him. Something black and ominous and...

She must have made a sound, or maybe just breathed a little too hard, because suddenly the man swung around in one smooth motion and pressed a gun to her throat.

Stars danced at the edge of her vision. She let out a shriek. The teapot crashed to the floor of the shed and shattered.

"Who are you? Where's the old man?"

She shook so violently her teeth chattered. "I...I don't know. I haven't seen him. Probably gone to church."

Gone to *church*? Where had that come from? Turner never attended church, and it wasn't even Sunday.

The man snorted. "Not fucking likely. Never met a Turgenev who was at all religious."

He used Turner's real name. He *knew* him. The man was in his forties, heavy in the jowls, with a dead-fish look around the eyes.

"I...uh...I can give him a message if you want. Are you a friend of his or..." She trailed off, realizing how ridiculous that sounded.

Another snort. "I'll leave my own message, but thanks."

Apparently figuring she wasn't much of a threat, he lowered the gun and kicked at the toolbox. It fell over, spilling papers out. She saw that he'd used a crowbar to wrench it open. A deep fear rose inside her. This man was strong. And he was after something.

She took a step back, toward the door.

"Don't move," the man said almost casually as he crouched next to the box. "Can't have you calling the cops out here."

"No. No. I wouldn't do that. I was...just going to see if I could find Old Man Turner." Total lie. She didn't *want* to find him. She hoped he was a hundred miles away from here.

"Don't bother. I searched the whole place. He ain't here and neither is his money."

"Well, he doesn't really have much of that. He's just a farmer, hardly scrapes by."

"Bullshit. He stole it when he left and he's still got it somewhere." He kicked the lockbox again. "Fuck."

"I'll just...leave you to it, then." She took another step back.

Mistake. The man rose to his feet in one fluid motion and swung the gun against her temple.

Bri dropped to the ground. Pain shafted through her skull. He stepped over her, giving her a little kick in the ribs as he went.

She fought to stay conscious...there was something bad about losing consciousness, right? Focus, focus, ow, ow...

Then another sound sent an entirely different fear through her. A lighter. A spark. The quiet lick of a flame claiming its place in the world.

CHAPTER 29

Where the hell had Brianna disappeared to? Rollo didn't want to waste another second apart from her. But she was nowhere to be found. Her phone wasn't answering, she wasn't at her little cabin. He called her parents, Evie, Suzanne, Merry...no one knew her plans for the day.

In the middle of his frantic search, his mother called. "What is going on out there? I got a call from Cornelia and could barely believe my ears. Have you gone mad?"

"Nope. I told her the truth. I'm in love with Brianna Gallagher. And you know when I realized it for sure? When I watched that YouTube video from the fashion show. So I guess that backfired, didn't it?"

"You certainly can't blame that on me."

"I can and I do. You knew she'd get nervous up there on stage. You wanted to make sure I didn't fall for her."

"I really don't care who you fall for. That's beside the point. You must know that I will never find her acceptable, Rollington. I will not allow that girl into this family."

"That's your choice. I've made mine." If he could just *find* her. And convince her that being connected to the Wareham family wouldn't ruin her life.

He realized his mother hadn't responded. "Mother? Are you there?"

"I won't talk about this now, but I'm furious with you, Rollington. Of all times to make trouble. I already have Sidney to deal with." She whooshed out a long breath. "She's becoming impossible. She refuses to attend the new boarding school I found for her. The term started a week ago and I can't get her out of her room. She's sullen and sulky and an embarrassment. Will you talk to her, Rollington? It's the least you could do for us."

"Yeah, of course." With a stab of guilt, he realized he hadn't talked to Sidney since he'd come back to Jupiter Point. He pulled his SUV to the side of the road. While searching for Bri, he'd wound up outside of town on the road that headed toward the inland farming areas. A smudge of smoke rose from the base of one of the hills. He squinted at it, wondering if he should call it in to fire dispatch. It was probably someone running a burn barrel. Even so, he kept an eye on it as Sidney came on the line.

"Hi Rollo."

"Hi sis. Just calling to say 'hi.' I miss you. Everything going okay back there?"

"I miss Jupiter Point." Over the phone, it was hard to tell if her morose tone was darker than usual. "It was mean of you not to let me come back. No one cares about me here. I thought you were on my side, but you're just a Wareham clone like everyone else."

"Sidney, give me a break. You need to be in school."

"Why? So I can set my curtains on fire again? So I can—" She broke off.

"So you can what?" He held his breath. Was she finally going to talk about what had upset her so much at school?

"Nothing. Anyway, Jupiter Point has schools, too. Brianna would have let me come back. But you drove her away."

"Yeah, well, I guess you're right about that."

"What do you mean? What's going on?"

He rested his elbow on the window frame and ran a hand through his hair. "I can't find her anywhere."

"Why are you looking for her?"

To tell her I love her and want her in my life forever. "I need to tell her something."

"I know exactly what you should say. Tell her you aren't a total loser and that you're going to stand up to Mother and pick your own woman. Not the next Cornelia."

"For Chrissake, Sidney. It's a little more complicated than that. Look, I gotta go. Brianna isn't answering her phone. I've called her about twenty times."

"Then she's probably out at Old Man Turner's. There's like no reception out there. I tried to Snapchat when I was working on the fence and couldn't even get a single bar."

"Sidney, that's genius. I'll drive out there right now." He turned the key in the ignition. Then he remembered the original purpose of the call. "So about this school..."

"Just go. Mother's on my ass to get her stupid phone back. Mother! I'll say 'ass' if I want to. Grrr." The line went dead.

Rollo pulled up a mental map of Jupiter Point, trying to remember exactly where Turner's place was located. It was near the Star Bright Shelter; he'd actually donated the land for the place. But his home was about a mile away, and that was where Brianna had been working lately. A mile to the West, near where... His eyes tracked the column of smoke rising into the still morning air.

Where that fire was coming from.

Holy shit.

He floored the accelerator and called fire dispatch. He gave them the approximate location of the smoke, and told Lou, the dispatcher, that he was on his way to check it out in person. "No cell service out there," he explained. "So I'm calling it in now."

"Ten-four. We're on it. Don't do anything crazy, Rollo. Like run into a wildfire after a buddy."

"Who, me? Nah." He hung up, loving the fact that the people of Jupiter Point knew that much about him. The good stuff, not the trust-fund stuff. Maybe they knew that part too. But they didn't treat him any different.

He gunned the engine and flew down the road. He turned onto the turnoff to Old Man Turner's road so fast he left a rooster tail of gravel behind him. Maybe the fire was nothing. Maybe it was nowhere near Turner or Brianna. But the pit in his stomach told him something was wrong.

*

Someone had turned up the heat. Brianna tried to drag her eyes open to tell whoever was blasting the oven to take it down a notch. It felt like the time she'd fallen asleep in front of the fireplace when she was seven. During the night, wrapped in her favorite Lion King blanket, she'd rolled right up to the edge of the hearth. A stray gust of wind had reignited the coals in the hearth, and she woke up to find herself inches away from becoming cinder. The heat had fanned against her face, making her feel as if she had a sunburn.

Same thing now. Except the sunburn was coming from all sides. And it wasn't cozy and warm, like her parents' hearth. It was absolutely terrifying.

Finally she got her eyes open; the heat made her squint. She was lying on the dirt floor of the shed. The papers in the lockbox were now a small pile of ashes, and the fire had spread to the wall of the shed. Waves of heat radiated from all sides. Flames danced and twisted along the plywood, sending renegade fingers toward neatly stacked garden tools, the workbench, the lawn mower.

Shit. The lawn mower. It had gas in the tank. She'd filled it the last time she was here. She had to get out of this death trap.

She thought about Rollo and all the wildfire stories he'd told. The firefighters always covered their mouths so they didn't get smoke inhalation. And they stayed low to the ground. The air was cleanest next to the earth.

Good thing she loved the earth. And soil. And dirt. Maybe dirt would save her. She pressed her cheek to the floor and filled her lungs with air. The hit of oxygen helped her think more clearly. Don't panic. Panic leads to bad decisions. Stay low. If Rollo and the other hotshots could survive a burnover during a massive wildfire, she could handle one little garden shed, right?

Rollo. She filled her mind with thoughts of him because they calmed her. As if he was guiding her through this. *You got this, Bri. Stay low. Stay calm. Try an elbow crawl. Drag yourself out of there.*

Military style, she crawled toward the door of the shed. Pain raked across her legs. Had the intruder done something to her legs? She remembered the shards of broken pottery from the teapot she'd dropped. She was probably shredding her skin. *Don't worry about that. Just keep going. Before the door catches on fire.*

The asshole had left the door halfway open, probably to create a draw so the fire would burn faster. Wasn't it enough to take the papers? Or burn them or whatever he'd done? Why did he want to kill her?

You saw his face.

Of course. She could identify him, so he wanted her to die. Just to spite the murderous bastard, she fixed an image of his face in her mind's eye. If she got out of this, she'd go right to a sketch artist. Mother-effer.

Crawl, crawl. She reached the door and put her hand on it. And yelped. It was blistering hot, and felt like it might spontaneously burst into flames. She pushed it anyway, causing a billow of hot smoke to rush at her face. She ducked and covered her head with her hands. *Breathe. Breathe. Nice and calm.*

A spark landed on her arm. *Oh God.*

She swiped at it, felt a burn on her palm. A new smell combined with the smoke and old dirt and mustiness of the shed. A scorched smell, like the time she'd tried to flat iron her hair and ended up burning—

Shit.

Her hair was on fire. Fucking *on fire.*

She lost it at that point and let out a bloodcurdling scream. "Help! Help me!"

Her raw and scratchy throat could only handle two "helps" before she fell silent, gasping. She buried her nose back in the dirt. If she was going to die, at least she'd be hugging the earth. Surrounded by garden tools. It could be worse.

Of course, there would be no Rollo, and that was maybe the worst of all. She'd never get the chance to tell him how she really felt about him. Not the friend part. The *everything* part. The heart-and-soul part. The love-him-until-she-died part.

Which might happen sooner than later.

No. Screw this. She wasn't ready to die. Spring planting season was starting soon. Evie's wedding was only a few weeks away. Suzanne's baby was coming next month. And Rollo. *Rollo.* She had to tell him how she felt, because otherwise the truth would die with her in this fire.

A shout sounded from outside. Footsteps running across the ground. She felt the vibration under her face. She lifted her head one more time, for one last "help."

But maybe she said "Rollo" instead, because there he was, kicking aside the blazing door, ripping it off its hinges, storming into the flames.

Rollo.

All her fear fled, because even though she was surrounded by fire, Rollo was here and he'd take care of her. He had something in his hands—blanket? Jacket?—which he tossed over her. The world went temporarily dark as he wrapped her up like a burrito. Then she was being lifted into the air and hurried past heat and flame.

Safe in his embrace, snuggled against his rock-solid chest, a crazy sense of happiness filled her.

She was with Rollo. All was good.

Then she blacked out.

CHAPTER 30

Rollo felt the very moment when Brianna passed out in his arms. She went limp, her legs swinging as he ran with her to his SUV. In the distance, he heard the sirens of the Jupiter Point fire department. Turner's house was burning, too. How the hell had the fire gotten from the shed to the house? It wasn't even windy.

When he reached his vehicle, he laid her out gently on the backseat. He lifted the edge of the old plaid jacket he'd wrapped around her and gave her a quick visual check. Part of her hair was blackened, and a burn festered on her scalp. She had no black around her lips, which would indicate smoke inhalation. He checked her pulse. Fast but even. She was fine. His precious Brianna would be fine.

His hands shook as he remembered the horror of spotting her bright hair just inside a shed entirely engulfed in flames. Never, ever, EVER, did he want to feel such stark terror again. If he'd arrived even a minute later—even thirty seconds later—what would have happened? He rubbed the back of his sooty hand across his eyes to chase the image away.

Brianna's eyes fluttered open. They were bloodshot and teary. She blinked a few times then focused on him. "Rollo," she whispered, her voice hoarse. Smoke really did a number on your vocal cords. "You came for me."

He couldn't answer because so much emotion welled up in his heart. He nodded. He grabbed a bottle of water from his cup holder and held it to her lips. Her eyes half-closing, she took a long swallow. She watched him as she drank, as if she was enjoying him as much as the water.

"There was a man," she said after he withdrew the bottle. "He set the fire. We have to find Old Man Turner."

"Fire department's on its way. I'll let them know."

So that was how the fire had spread. Rollo tamped down his fury. An arsonist had nearly killed Brianna? That fucker better pay, whoever he was.

Just then a ladder truck from the JPFD came cruising into Turner's yard.

"Hang on," Rollo told her. He jogged over to the crew captain and filled him in on what Brianna had told him.

"Have you seen anyone else around?"

"No, just Bri, and I pulled her out of that shed. But Melvin Turner's an odd duck. He could be hiding out somewhere. He has dementia."

The captain gave a signal to the guys on the hose and they hauled it toward the house. The shed was a total loss, but the house could still be saved. "Your girl okay? Need a medic?"

"No, I'll take her in to the clinic. She's in good shape."

When he got back to the SUV, Brianna was sitting up and feeling the charred spot on her head. "Wow, my hair's gone. Am I bald?"

He chuckled and wrapped her back in the jacket. "Nope. Still as beautiful as ever."

She reached up and cupped his face while he still hovered over her. "Thank you, Rollo. You saved my life." Tears shimmered in her bloodshot eyes. "Even before you showed up, you saved me. This is going to sound crazy, but I was thinking about the burnover and how you survived. It helped me stay calm. Otherwise I would have done something stupid like stand up and run into the flames."

He shuddered. "God forbid. That's my job. Only crazy assholes like me are supposed to do that shit."

She stroked his cheek, running her hand across the new growth of his beard. "Are you telling me I'm in love with a crazy asshole?"

He froze, searching her face. Did she mean it? Was Brianna really in love with him? Despite everything...his family...his past?

She smiled tenderly at him. "Need me to repeat that? I love you, Rollo. I was so afraid I'd die before I got a chance to tell you, and now that you're here, I'm telling you. It doesn't mean you have to feel the same way, or say anything, really. I know nothing else has changed. You're still you and I'm still me. The prince and the peasant girl." Another smile flitted across her soot-streaked face. "I just have to say it. That's all."

"Brianna," he breathed. Tidal waves of happiness crashed through him. She loved him! Brianna—his sweet, fiery, beautiful, honest, real, awkward, loyal, generous, kindhearted girl—*loved* him. And she was right here. Alive. Nothing else mattered compared to that.

He pulled his hand away from her face and turned her body so she faced the door. After extracting his upper body from the interior, he straightened to his full height.

Then he dropped to his knees.

"Brianna Gallagher, I love you completely. Every bit of you, inside and out. You're in every beat of my heart. You're a light in my soul. I love you and I need you and I want you. No one but you. When I saw you on the ground in the shed, with fire all around you...my heart just about stopped. I want— I need— Brianna, will you marry me?"

She jumped as if he'd shocked her with something. "*What?*"

He thought back over what he'd said. Granted, it wasn't the most articulate proposal ever. It was spontaneous and right off the top of his head. But was it that shocking? "I love you and I want to marry you."

"No. You can't. I mean, you can love me. I'm glad you love me. I love you too, I think I mentioned that. But Rollo, no. You can't marry me."

His jaw flexed. A pebble pressed into his knee. His stomach dropped like a roller coaster. "See, I think I can. I mean, if you want to. I already told my mother that you're the only woman I'll marry."

She drew in a shocked gasp. "Oh no. No. She's not going to like that. She despises me. I totally embarrassed her in New York. She told me she'd never accept me."

Rollo gave up on the kneeling part of the proposal and rose to his feet. "Let's go somewhere else and talk about this."

"Well, okay, but there's no point. I'm still me. That's never going to change, Rollo."

"I don't want you to change! Damn it." He braced one hand against the frame of his SUV and gazed down at her with a tender scowl. "I want you exactly as you are. Why is that so hard to understand?"

"Because..." Ducking her head, she twisted her hands in her lap. "You know why, Rollington Wareham the Third."

He watched her wring her hands and noticed that her nails were bloody and dirt was ground into her palms. God, he was an asshole. She should be in the clinic by now, and he was trying to browbeat a "yes" out of her.

"Later," he said softly. "We'll talk about it later." He closed the back seat door, then went around to the driver's side and slid into his seat.

Neither of them said anything else as they drove away from Old Man Turner's place. It seemed ridiculous to him.

When two people loved each other, they ought to get married. Why did it matter where his ancestors came from or how much money was in his bank account?

Then a light bulb went off in his head. The solution to everything.

*

"No, Rollo. You're not thinking straight. You're upset because you nearly saw me burn to death." Brianna winced, since that sounded more brutal than she'd planned. "You know what I mean."

"I do, but you're wrong." That set, determined, steel-eyed look on Rollo's face hadn't shifted. The entire drive to the clinic, she'd watched the muscles flex in his jaw, his knuckles tighten on the steering wheel. At the clinic, he'd insisted on carrying her through the door like a child. She didn't mind any of that. It felt good and honestly, her legs were so wobbly she didn't know if she could have walked under her own power.

But now she was back home in her own bed and he was talking about ruining his life.

"You can't just resign from your family. It doesn't work that way."

"No, but I can sign over my trust funds. Tell them to take my name off everything. Hand over all my assets, except the ones I earned myself. The house might have to go." He shrugged. "Sorry about the koi pond. You put a lot of work into it."

That made her laugh, even though laughing scratched her already painful throat. For sure, humans weren't designed to be immersed in flame. "Don't care about the koi. But what about all the other charities you support?"

"Brent can be an ass, but he isn't a bad guy. I'll help all the various groups make their case to my brother and he'll decide. It would reflect badly on the Wareham name if he pulled our support, so I think they're probably safe. The main reason I never considered this before was because of Dougie. But he doesn't need my money. He'll probably be richer than me. Sean will take me back on the crew, no question, but hotshots aren't exactly millionaires, even with the overtime."

"Well, if it comes to that, I can help support you, Rollington Wareham the Third." She widened her eyes innocently. "I actually do pretty well for myself in the gardening biz."

He grinned broadly, light filling his blue eyes. "So is that a yes? You're already putting together the family budget?"

She felt heat rise in her face. She wanted Rollo in her life. And she didn't care about his money. But there was another huge factor to consider. "No, Rollo. It's not a yes. Because there's something you're not considering."

"What?"

"Your family doesn't want me. I know how important family is. You don't want to hurt them. And marrying me—

" She dropped her face into her hands. "There's a YouTube video you should probably see."

He put his hands to her wrists and gently drew them away. "I've seen it. It was adorable. No one could watch that video and not love you with every bone in his body. At least, no one named Rollington Wareham the Third."

She stared at him in astonishment. He'd *seen* it. He knew why she'd run from New York with her tail between her legs. And he still loved her. Still wanted her.

His blue-gray gaze held so much softness, such deep and total acceptance, that she wanted to cry. The air between them seemed to thicken like honey. A smile touched the firm curve of his lips, which were partially covered by his new beard. His wide, wide shoulders hunched protectively over her, as if to fend off any threat, fire or family or otherwise.

"Now when you say 'bone,'" she whispered. "What exactly do you mean?"

Awareness sparked in his eyes. His smile broadened. "I'm open to any interpretation."

The palms of her hands tingled.

"But I need you to know a few things first. I need you to know that when I do this," he kissed her neck, where the pulse fluttered under her skin, "I'm kissing the woman I love."

She sighed as liquid desire spread throughout her body.

"When I do this," he whispered, unzipping her hoodie to reveal the ribbed tank she wore underneath. "I'm undressing the woman I want to marry." He touched one nipple through the fabric, causing it to stiffen into a dark point. "The woman I want to be my bride. My wife."

Her breath came fast, chest rising and falling. "You're crazy, Rollo," she whispered back. "You should find someone who can be what you need. Someone who can handle those parties and those obligations and those people."

"*You* are what I need," he said firmly. "Even when I thought I wanted someone else, the only time I felt right was when I was with you. But Bri..."

He pressed a hand to her lower belly, a warm weight sparking bright streaks of sensation just a little lower down.

"I have the feeling that I'm not the problem here. My family's not the problem. What's going on, really? You said you loved me."

"I do! I love you so much!" She leaned her forehead against his chest and put her hands under his sweater, basking in his heat and the sculpted curves of his torso. If she could touch him like this forever, she'd be perfectly happy. "But can't you understand? I'm not the kind of person who can play a part or fake it till you make it. I just...don't want to let you down."

"You couldn't. It's impossible. Because all I want," he lifted her chin with his finger, "is for you to be you. And to love me. That's it."

"Really?" She scrunched her face in doubt. Those two things couldn't be easier. She didn't know how to be anything but herself. And as for loving him? She couldn't stop that—and she'd tried. "That's all?"

"Well, if you could touch my dick right now, that would be a bonus. Because it's about ready to burst out of my jeans."

Joy bloomed in her heart, as extravagant as a pink peony. She slid her fingers past his waistband down to the hot organ that jumped at her touch. She felt Rollo release a long breath, as if he'd been holding it forever waiting for her answer.

And she hadn't even answered. Her heart wanted to say yes, in a flash. But there was still the Wareham factor hanging over everything. She needed to be sure she wouldn't be doing Rollo more harm than good by saying yes.

"I do love you," she murmured as she enclosed his shaft in her fist. "I want to make you happy, Rollo, so happy. The way you make me."

"You never have to worry about that. No one's ever made me this happy." He nuzzled her neck, his breathing picking up speed. He unzipped his pants and pushed them down his legs. When he'd kicked them aside, he came back to her, tall and broad and strong and fully aroused. He plucked the blanket off her body. She was wearing nothing but pink panties and bandages on her knees from where the teapot shards had cut her. His eyes darkened at the reminder of her wounds.

"It's fine, big guy. Just don't ask me to get on hands and knees. I mean, not now, anyway." She gave him a saucy wink, and that was it.

"Was that a wink? You're asking for it now, wench. Aren't you?"

"Oh yes. I'm not just asking for it. I'm telling you. Get on over here with your bad self."

He settled his big body onto the bed, dragged her panties off of her, and nudged her legs apart. He bent his head between them and offered her a long, luxurious, wet licking that made her nerve endings shriek with pleasure. She dug her fingers into his hair and babbled like a madwoman. She had no idea what came out of her mouth, but whatever it was, Rollo seemed to like it.

When he rose up, eyes full of dark fire, his arms and shoulders vibrating with strain, he looked like a demigod to her. Half man, half god of the forest.

"Make crazy mad love to me," she whispered. "Make me forget everything except you."

And he did. One long, hard stroke at a time. One whispered love word at a time. One intense orgasm at a time. At some point, he brought her a snack and a mug of hot milk with honey. After that short break, he went back to work. He made love to her until she didn't know her own name.

Until he was everything and more. Until she knew there would never be anyone else. That this was it, forevermore.

Figuring out the details, that was another matter.

CHAPTER 31

The buzzing of Rollo's cell phone woke him up out of the sweetest sleep he'd experienced since the last time he was in bed with Brianna. Which would have been New York. Which was where the call came from. Brent was on the line this time. For fuck's sake, why couldn't his family ever learn about time zones?

Then he remembered. Before too long, he'd be free from the family business affairs—maybe even by the end of this phone call. He'd tell Brent first, because ultimately Brent would take over the handling of his share of things. What better time than the present, even if it *was* five in the morning?

He rolled out of bed, treating himself to one last stroke of Brianna's warm skin, right where it curved around her hip. That might be his favorite spot on her body, the slope between her waist and her hipbone. But then, there were so many contenders.

After wrapping a towel around his hips, he took his phone into her kitchen and answered in a low voice. "It's five a.m., Brent. I'm sending you to time-zone school."

"Sorry."

Rollo snapped to attention. An apology from Brent? That wasn't a good sign. Something must be wrong. "What's up?"

"Look, I think you should get back here. Sidney's missing."

"*What?*" Rollo braced his free hand on Brianna's kitchen sink and stared at his reflection in the window. He looked ghostly.

"Yeah, the little brat has been driving everyone nuts. Whining about this and that and everything she can think of. Like she has anything to complain about."

"Think you could skip the part where you insult her and get the fuck to the point?"

"Sorry. Been a long night."

Another apology? This was a first.

"Anyway, there was a big blowout and Mother told her she had to go to some school upstate and Sidney freaked out and went into her room, did the whole slam-and-lock routine. When Mother knocked on the door because Mace was ready to drive her to school, she was gone."

"So she ran away? Did you call the police?"

"No, Mother brought in a private security company. Doesn't want the scandal. Didn't want me to call *you*, either. You're on her black list at the moment."

And that was about to get worse. But he'd save his news for later. Right now, all the mattered was Sidney. "I'll be on the next flight out."

"Fuck that. I sent a Learjet. It's waiting for you at some dinky little regional airport out there."

"Fine. I'll see you soon."

"One more thing. Bring that friend of yours. The red-head."

Rollo squinted past his reflection, out into the predawn sky. A grove of cypresses was silhouetted against the waning moon. Brianna's little cabin in the woods felt a million miles away from Manhattan. "Is this some kind of trick? You want to drag her back to New York and humiliate her again?"

"Man, I wasn't even at that show. Everyone's over it, even Mother."

"*I'm* not over it."

"Look, forget about that. Sidney likes her more than she likes any of us. We need her help."

Rollo gritted his teeth, torn between worry for Sidney and protectiveness toward Brianna. "She doesn't owe us anything. I'll ask her, but I wouldn't blame her if she told us all to fuck off."

After he ended the call, Rollo stepped quietly toward Brianna's bed. She was already sitting up, stretching, naked and glorious.

"I heard you in the kitchen," she mumbled through her yawn. "What's going on?"

"I have to go to New York." He explained the situation as he pulled on his jeans. Dragging a sweater over his head, he cast about for the best way to ask her to come with him.

But he didn't have to. Before his arms were even through the sleeves, Brianna was out of bed and digging in her dresser drawers for something to wear.

"I'm coming with you," she announced. "I don't care what your family says. If your mother doesn't like it, she can just pretend I'm not there."

He stared at her. Warmth dawned at the core of his being then spread from there, filling every inch of his heart. "You'd really go back there? Into all that drama? When my mother's upset, she can get really ugly. No holds barred."

"Rollo." In nothing but panties and bra, Brianna faced him, hands on her hips. "You think I don't know that? I got a pretty good dose of it, up close and personal. This isn't about me. Sidney's missing and I have to be there. We're friends and she might need me. What's a little embarrassment compared to that? Don't worry about me."

He ate up the sight of her, so little and fierce, so luscious in her mismatched underwear, her skin still flushed from sleep. The way she was standing reminded him of when he first spotted her at the Seaview Inn that fateful night. Like a pirate about to dive into the fray. "You're amazing, you know that? Do you know how much I want to haul you right back to bed right now?"

"Forget it, buddy-boy. Come on. Get that hotshot ass of yours in gear."

"What about your injuries?" He brushed a gentle hand across the blackened patch on her scalp. "You need to rest and recover."

"I'll sleep on the plane. Let's go."

*

The entire Park Avenue household was in an uproar. His father, mother, Brent, and all the servants were gathered in the Grand Salon when Rollo and Brianna walked in.

If Rollo didn't know his mother's moods so well, he would never have guessed she was upset. Impeccable as ever in a nubby coral Chanel suit, she barely pulled her phone from her ear to greet them. She raised her eyebrows at the sight of Brianna, then turned her attention to Rollo.

"How could she do this to me? Our security team has gone through everything in her room and found nothing. Not a single clue or lead or anything. I threatened to fire the lot of them so they're looking again now."

"For the millionth time, we should call the fucking police," Brent said wearily. He had big dark circles under his eyes. Rollo figured he'd probably been out clubbing when Sidney's absence was discovered. He probably hadn't slept all night.

Both of their parents shook their heads. "Last resort," his father said. "It would go right to the media and we have a delicate negotiation going on right now. Our people are twice as competent in any case." His phone rang. "I have to take this. Keep me in the loop."

He stepped away to take the call. Something told Rollo that call was more about business than the search for Sidney.

Brianna cleared her throat. "I was wondering if they found her sketchbook when they searched her room."

Alicia turned an icy stare her way. "Excuse me?"

"Her sketchbook. She uses it to express her emotions. We might be able to pick up something from what she's been drawing. That's only if she left it behind, though." Brianna screwed up her face. "She probably has it with her. Never mind."

"Don't raise false hopes," Alicia said sharply. "That's unkind."

"I didn't mean...I'm sorry." Brianna flushed a deep rose. She folded her lips together, as if to keep from blurting anything else out.

Rollo opened his mouth to lash out at his mother, but Brent jumped in.

"I might have seen that thing." Brent shoved his hands in the pockets of his trousers. "I saw her scribbling in something and asked why she was doing homework when she wasn't even going to school. She tried to hit me with it."

"Nice going," said Rollo. "Way to establish good communication."

"Hey, that's our thing. We torture each other. It's a Wareham family bonding ritual."

Rollo couldn't really argue with that. "Did you see what she was drawing? Before she hit you?"

His brother squinted to call up the memory. "It was very dark. Like she'd covered the entire page in charcoal. I figured, Sid being Sid, right? Morose, moody, woe-is-me."

"This is a waste of time," snapped Alicia. "Her therapist was supposed to be dealing with all that emotional nonsense. That woman is fired."

Brent shook his head. "No, it turned out it wasn't like that. She wasn't drawing dark hellscapes, like I thought at first. It was the night sky, with all these constellations. She said she was inspired by the night sky in Jupiter Point."

"Constellations? Well, that's utterly useless. Are you suggesting she's on her way to outer space?" Alicia pressed the back of her hand against her forehead. Rollo's heart twisted at her iron-willed attempts to hide her distress.

"Could you blame her?" Brent quipped. "I guess the West Coast wasn't far enough."

She snapped. "Are you all here to gang up on me? Maybe I should just up and run away like everyone else in this family does! Then who would take care of everything around here?"

Good Lord—she sounded on the edge of tears. *Alicia Wareham*, mother of steel, about to cry? Rollo wouldn't have thought it possible.

He glanced at Brent, who looked just as shocked as he was. Alicia fought to compose herself, the battle visible on her meticulously made-up face. It was like watching slow-motion film of an avalanche getting triggered.

The tense silence was finally broken by Brianna. "I have a question. Just a crazy thought, but is there a roof on this building? I mean, of course there's a roof, that sounds silly. But is it accessible? And if it is, does Sidney know how to get up there? I only ask because back in Jupiter Point, she used to hang out on Rollo's roof sometimes. Remember how she loved watching the stars up there, Rollo?"

"That's true. I know I used to hang out on the roof when I needed a break. Has anyone looked up there?"

"Absurd. The roof? What an idea. Even if she had, she would have come inside by now. It's the middle of winter." Regaining her composure, Alicia smoothed her jacket over her hips.

"Mother, are you rejecting the idea because it came from Brianna? Seriously?"

She glanced at each of her children, then over at Brianna, who was standing a few feet from her. Rollo tried to see Bri through his mother's eyes. She wore her cleanest blue jeans, the ones with only one grass stain. Her forest-green sweatshirt had the lettering, "Got Earth?" arched above a photo of Planet Earth from space. Her curls were a mess, one of her snow boots was coming untied. She looked exactly as if she'd just completed a headlong cross-country trip.

But she met Alicia's harsh gaze without even flinching. Even better, she offered his mother a tiny, rueful smile. Sympathy shone from her eyes. She showed no hint of resentment, anger, or wariness—all things she'd be completely entitled to. Instead, pure concern and compassion poured out of her.

After a long moment, during which Rollo held his breath, Alicia turned away and headed for the door, heels clicking on the parquet. "I suppose it wouldn't hurt to check."

Rollo tugged Brianna close as they followed his mother and Brent out of the Grand Salon. "Have I mentioned that I love you?" he whispered in her ear.

"Have I mentioned that you're crazy?" she whispered back.

"Hey, I'm a hotshot. Goes with the territory."

As in many Manhattan buildings, a cube-like structure sat on top of the flat roof. It housed various electrical and mechanical workings, as well as the access staircase. Some buildings populated their roofs with gardens or lounge chairs or even swimming pools, but not theirs. Rollo had always been grateful for that, since the roof was pretty much guaranteed to be empty when you needed to escape from the people inside.

At the final level, when a steel door was the only barrier between them and the top of the building, Alicia paused. "You'd better go first, Rollo. If she sees me, she might jump."

He raised an eyebrow at his mother. She really was full of surprises today. Maybe Sidney's disappearance had shaken something loose in her. He nodded and brushed past her.

"You too, Brianna," his mother added grudgingly. "She trusts you. Go ahead."

Brianna's eyes went wide, while Rollo nearly stumbled on the last step. This was huge. His mother had spoken Brianna's name. She'd said something nice about her. It was like some kind of miracle.

He pushed the upper door open, allowing a blast of chilly air inside the staircase.

A girl's voice sounded from beyond the door. "Go away!"

Sidney.

Alicia slumped against the wall, so relieved she didn't even object when Brianna squeezed her hand. Rollo stuck his head around the edge of the door. "Hey, sis. What's going on?"

"*You're* here? I thought you went back to Jupiter Point." Her voice floated over the brisk wind cutting across the rooftops.

"I came back. Everyone's been looking for you. Why don't you come inside and you can tell us what's going on? I mean, really going on."

"No. And don't come any closer or I'll do something crazy!"

He looked at the others, worry tightening his throat. She sounded different, not like herself. He heard no snark in her voice, no sass. Just pure sadness. He looked at Brianna and jerked his head toward the door. He trusted her to handle this more than himself.

Bri looked over at Alicia, who nodded her consent. Rollo made room for her at the head of the staircase.

"Sidney, it's Brianna. Don't worry, I won't do anything you don't want. I just want to make sure you're warm. Do you have a jacket out there? Aren't you freezing?"

"*Brianna?* You came back too?"

"Of course I did. I love you, honey. I was really worried. I still am, to tell you the truth. If you've been out here all night you must be half frozen."

"There's a steam vent. It's been keeping me warm. Seriously, you came *back?* After the fashion show and everyone laughing at you on YouTube? And after Rollo invited that witch to visit him?"

Color came and went in Brianna's cheeks. "Well, I wasn't too happy about any of that. But I still care about you. I care about *you* a lot more than YouTube. Are you hungry? You must be starving."

"That's a trick to get me to come inside, isn't it?"

"No," Brianna said quickly. "I can bring something to you. I just want you to be okay."

"No one else does! They just want me to do what they want! No one cares what I want! Not even my therapists. They just want all the money Mother pays them."

"That's not—" Alicia began, but Brianna hushed her. Even though his mother's eyes bulged with surprise, she obeyed and snapped her mouth shut.

Sidney kept going, her voice like a wail. "They all think the only thing that matters is money. Even Rollo. Why else is he giving up firefighting and marrying someone *Mother* picks? It's all pointless. None of us will ever be free. She'll never like anyone *I* want to be with."

Rollo and Brianna exchanged a look of alarm. "Sidney, is there someone you like? Is that what's been bugging you?"

Long silence. "Yes. I think. I don't know."

"Sweetie, how about you come inside and we can talk more about that? We promise to listen."

"No one ever listens."

"I do. We've had some really good conversations, right?"

Another long silence. Rollo fought the urge to just go out there and tackle her. Brute strength wasn't what the situation called for.

"Yes, but you're not part of the family. No one in my *family* listens."

"Well, as a matter of fact, that's going to change," Brianna said. Her gaze flew to his, and the breath stuttered in Rollo's chest.

"How? They'll never change. Why should they? They think everything's perfect the way it is."

"No, I mean the other thing. The part about me not being part of your family. Rollo..."

She paused, her green eyes scanning his face, gauging his reaction.

He jumped in before she could continue. "I proposed to Brianna, Sidney. I want to marry her. I'm going to give up my trust fund and everything else connected to our money."

Brent grinned—probably counting all the money he'd soon be controlling. Rollo risked a glance at his mother. She let out a long, resigned breath. Alicia was many things, but not stupid. She must have seen this coming.

"*What?*" They heard a sound from across the roof, then footfalls coming closer. The next time Sidney spoke, she sounded more alive, more herself. "What did you say, Brianna?"

"Well, I haven't actually answered. I love Rollo, of course. But I wasn't so sure I'd be the right person for him. For the Wareham family. So I had to think hard about it. And I think I'm ready to give my answer. So what do you say, Sidney? Want to come be my witness?"

Alicia gripped her hands together, looking as if she was about to get her teeth drilled.

"Depends," Sidney said. "Is Mother there too?"

Brianna chewed at her bottom lip. But of course she couldn't lie. She was Brianna. "She is, Sidney. So is Brent. We're all here because we care about you, no matter what."

"No matter what? What if..." She paused. They all held their breaths. "What if the person I like...well, what if it's a girl?"

Alicia's jaw dropped. Brent's eyes bugged out. Rollo knew his brother was about to burst out laughing, so he clapped his hand over Brent's mouth. Sidney didn't need a dose of the Wareham family bonding ritual at that moment. He gestured for Brianna to continue.

"Is that why you've been so upset, sweetie? Why you ran away from school?"

"I guess. I was just...confused. I hate having crushes. Crushes are the devil."

"Believe me, I know what you mean. Awkward crushes are my life. But listen, Sidney. You still have a lot of time to figure out who you like. Don't be so hard on yourself. We love you no matter what."

She elbowed Rollo in the side, and he started. "We do, Sid. A hundred percent." He pinned his mother with a hard stare.

"That's right, Sidney," she managed. "Listen to your brother."

"I guess if Rollo can stand up for himself, I can." Suddenly there she was, right outside the door, within arm's reach. She wore a black wool hat with a skull and crossbones pattern, a long wool coat that covered practically her entire body, with a gray scarf wrapped around her neck. Her cheeks were pink from cold, her eyes rimmed red.

Behind him, he heard Alicia draw in a sharp breath. *Good.* Maybe she'd remember this moment and lighten up on her only daughter.

"So," Sidney said impatiently, looking from Rollo to Brianna. "What's the hold-up? It's cold out here. Let's get this proposal on the road."

Rollo grinned, a wide smile that nearly split his face in two. He dropped to one knee, just as he had at Old Man Turner's. "Brianna Gallagher, my one true love, will you marry me despite this crazy-ass family?"

Brianna took his hands in hers, dropping kisses all over them. "Yes, Rollington Wareham the Third, I will marry you. As a matter of fact, the crazy-ass family is starting to grow on me." She aimed a shy smile at Alicia and Brent. Neither of them looked as upset as he'd expected.

Sidney clasped her hands together and squealed with glee—just like any other teenager who'd spent the night on a Manhattan rooftop in the middle of winter. Then she frowned, peering at Brianna. She came closer and stepped inside the stairwell. Rollo closed the door behind her, shutting out the knife-cold wind and city noises.

Sidney didn't seem to notice that her big escape had come to an end. She was busy examining Brianna's head. "What the heck happened to your hair?"

"I've been wondering the same thing," Alicia said. "But with Brianna, you just never know, do you?"

Was that affection in his mother's voice? Rollo wasn't a hundred percent sure, but he figured it was a good start.

CHAPTER 32

Brianna spent two days in New York with Rollo while they got Sidney settled back in with her family. The girl finally spilled the whole story of what had happened at Bridewell. For months she'd had a hopeless crush on another girl, Bella. But then she'd come back from a late-night study session and found Bella kissing her roommate. Furious, she'd set the curtains on fire and run away.

But then in Jupiter Point she'd started to like Eduardo, the Filipino kid from Thanksgiving, and now she didn't know what to think. Was it just a silly crush? Did she really like girls? Was it just a phase? A temporary rebellion?

"I would have told you earlier," she told Brianna, sitting cross-legged on her bed late at night. "I was so afraid of what Mother would say."

"Hey, it's okay. You didn't know me from a hole in the wall."

"Or a hole in the ground." Sidney pulled a snarky face at her. "Filled with fish."

"And...she's back. There's the snarky Sid we know and love."

Alicia dropped the idea of boarding school and enrolled Sidney in one of New York's famous visual arts high schools. Nothing could have made Sidney happier, except for the prospect of spending the summer in Jupiter Point with Rollo and Brianna. Brianna promised there would be lots of work to keep her busy.

Rollo spent most of those two days locked in Mr. Wareham's study with his father and Brent. His decision to back out of his agreement and marry Brianna changed everything.

He was okay with losing his trust fund and being written out of the Wareham empire. But Brianna hated to think she was costing him so much. Even though Rollo kept saying he felt a million times freer and didn't regret a thing, did he really feel that way? Would he still feel that way in ten years, or twenty, when his body couldn't handle firefighting anymore? What if he resented the fact that he'd sacrificed a fortune just to marry her?

Finally, the three Wareham men emerged from Rollington Senior's study. Amazingly, they were all shaking hands as Brent called for champagne.

Rollo's gaze met Brianna's, his fierce expression causing her heart to stutter. "Wha—what happened?"

"Come here." He pulled her into his arms, then dragged her to a private corner of the living room, where he peppered kisses all over her face.

"I created a job for myself. I told them the company was missing out on too many great opportunities. We've been playing it too safe. I suggested using my funds to experiment with some of the cutting-edge new tech companies.

I'll head up a new West Coast branch, working out of Jupiter Point. It's a lot closer to Silicon Valley. My first meeting is going to be with Dougie, as a matter of fact. After I let him whip my ass, of course." He grinned.

"Rollo! That's perfect!"

"Yep. I don't have to deal with the New York crap. I can live where I want, do things my own way. Take all the risks I want. I told them I can always go back to firefighting—just so they know they don't own me."

She flung her arms around him. "I'm so happy for you! I'm happy for me, too, because I won't have to worry about you once the fire season starts."

"Well...about that. I'll probably sign up as a volunteer at the Jupiter Point Fire Department. Just to keep my hand in."

Resting her chin on his broad chest, she gazed up at him. "You're hooked on being a hero, huh? Just can't stop saving lives?"

"Did you just call me a hero? Damn, and I have no witnesses." His tender smile sent shivers through her.

"That's okay. I'll go on YouTube and say it again. I'm not embarrassed."

He chuckled deep in his chest.

This. Just this. Love and laughter and joy. It was all she wanted and would ever want.

*

Back in Jupiter Point, Police Chief Becker filled her in on Old Man Turner's story. After a couple days on the run, he'd turned himself into an FBI office in Sacramento. It turned out that he was a wanted man. He'd tried to leave his old gang in the 1960's, but they wouldn't let him. So he'd fled with the proceeds of a big heist and taken evidence with him as a sort of insurance policy. That was why he lived entirely off the grid, used a different name, and kept the lowest possible profile.

Brianna was stunned by the news. "But he's harmless! He wouldn't hurt anyone. He's just a farmer, he likes growing vegetables and making herb tea."

"I wouldn't call him harmless, but you're right in a way. The Feds are still questioning him, but there's a good chance they'll make a deal with him in exchange for his testimony against some of the others. He's a pretty canny guy, hiding out all these years. Even though his old crew burned the evidence he took, he probably remembers plenty. I'm betting they'll keep him in protective custody. It's too bad he didn't come to us years ago. Paranoid old guy, right?"

Brianna thought of how he'd pushed everyone away, how he only got close to her because she was so persistent and they both loved gardening.

"No, I don't think so," she told the chief. "He wasn't paranoid. I thought he was, but I was wrong. And he wasn't in hiding all that time. I mean, he wasn't *just* in hiding. He was trying to do good. He was trying to make up for the sins of his past. That was why he farmed. Do you know how many vegetables he gave away to the food bank? He loved this town, I know he did. He signed over his farm to the shelter. And he gave me— Oh my God. I think he might have given me...hang on..."

She ran out of the police station to the truck and rummaged around in her glove compartment. Savings bond in hand, she raced back to Chief Becker and handed it over. "He gave this to me as a Christmas gift. Is this evidence? It's *ill-gotten gains*, isn't it?"

He took it with a stern look. "How long have you been hanging on to this?"

She stammered awkwardly until he relaxed into a grin. "We'll check this out. I'll let you know what we find."

As she turned to go, Chief Becker called after her, "One more thing. It's about the assailant you guys disarmed near Breton."

"Rollo did that. I just...threw a thermos."

Becker smiled. "I'd like to talk to all of you about what you heard. We think he was after a woman who volunteered as a Forest Service spotter last summer. We need to interview you, see if you remember anything that might help."

"Of course. Whatever you need, Chief."

That night, Brianna shed real tears for Old Man Turner. Why hadn't he let people in? Why hadn't he told someone? He'd carried that burden of the past all by himself. Rollo held her close in his strong arms and let her cry it out.

"You know, that could have been me," he murmured to her when her tears had faded. "I know what it feels like to live with a guilty secret. I might be a lonely old bugger just like Melvin. I would be, if it weren't for you."

"Me? What do you mean?"

"I got lucky. I found someone willing to take my hand and walk into the flames."

CHAPTER 33

One bright afternoon in late January, Rollo announced that he had a surprise for her. It was the kind of surprise that required a blindfold and a long drive.

"In some ways, this could be considered a kidnapping," she said as they bumped along some kind of gravel back road. "Blindfolds anywhere outside the bedroom are a little sketchy, don't you think?"

"Don't give me any ideas. I might turn this car around and you'll never get your surprise."

"So does this surprise involve us being naked? Just checking."

He made a choking sound. "Uh...that would not be advisable."

"Have I ever cared about what's advisable?"

She teased him for the rest of the drive, until the SUV came to a stop. He opened the passenger-side door and helped her out of the rig. She sniffed fresh mountain air, picking up the scent of pine trees and a hint of snow and earth. They were in a forest somewhere.

"Are we camping?"

"Stop guessing. I guarantee you can't guess this. Save your breath for your shriek of surprise."

"Shriek? I don't shriek."

"Famous last words."

He guided her across hard-packed earth. She heard the squeak of a hinge, and then they were stepping inside a structure of some kind. They climbed a set of stairs, Rollo keeping a careful arm around her as they walked. She sniffed madly at the smells coming at her. Perfume? Some kind of room freshener? And something that smelled like cheese? She hoped there would be cheese. The drive had made her hungry.

Rollo put his hands to her head and untied the blindfold. "You can open your eyes, my love," he whispered in her ear.

Her eyes flew open. She blinked several times in shock. All of her favorite Jupiter Point people were here. Her parents, Evie and Sean, Josh and Suzanne, Merry, Finn, Mrs. Murphy, a few of her best farmer friends. Everyone was smiling and lifting glasses of champagne in her direction.

"Congratulations to Brianna and Rollo!" Finn called out.

A loud chorus of cheers and congratulations followed. "We all knew you were perfect for each other," said Suzanne. "Like, the entire town knew."

"I bet two cases of kitchen tile on it," said Gretchen from the hardware store. She winked at Brianna and tipped her glass back.

A little dazed, Brianna glanced around at the six-sided glass observation deck where she'd spent the night with Rollo, Finn and Merry. The Breton lookout tower. A banner hung over the center island that held the radio and the equipment. Glittery gold letters spelled the words, "Happy Engagement." The airy space was filled with balloons and flowers and champagne bottles and...yes! Cheese platters!

An engagement party. Overwhelmed, she leaned back against Rollo. "How on earth...?"

"I pulled some hotshot strings," he said smugly. "Turns out a lot of the lookout towers can be rented in the off-season. Seemed like the perfect place to celebrate. You like?"

"This is amazing, Rollo." Tears rushed to her eyes. "No one's ever done anything like this for me."

"Well, get used to it. I plan to do all sorts of embarrassing things like this."

She spotted her mother taking a photo of the two of them, and looked down at her outfit, wincing. A mixed bag, really. She was wearing one of her usual overalls along with one of the pretty sweaters Sidney had helped her pick out.

"You look gorgeous," Rollo reassured her with a deep growl into her hair.

"No pirate-elf thing going on?"

"No pirate elves. Not that I would mind. I think you're perfect in all ways. And all overalls."

She smiled up at him, this man she was going to spend forever with. How did an ordinary girl from Jupiter Point get so lucky? In his eyes, she saw the same question, reversed. Her heart expanded with joy. They'd found each other, recognized the soul mate hidden in plain sight, and that was all that mattered.

The door opened and closed behind them. Brianna turned to see what other friend had arrived, only to see a stranger surveying the party with a shocked expression in her huge dark eyes. Her hair fell in inky swaths over her shoulders. One thumb was tucked under the shoulder strap of her backpack. "What's going on here?"

"We rented the tower for an engagement party," Rollo explained. "We're firefighters. Jupiter Point Hotshots."

"But...no one ever comes to this tower."

Brianna suddenly remembered where she'd seen her before. The photo on the bulletin board, the girl with the haunted expression.

Finn came toward them, gaze fastened on the mysterious stranger. "You're welcome to stay," he offered. "We don't mind, right, Rianna? I mean, Brollo? I mean—" He shook his head in confusion.

Brianna exchanged an amused look with Rollo. Maybe Finn was about to find out what an awkward crush felt like.

"Oh no...that's okay," the girl said. "I came out here to...well, to be alone, quite frankly."

Brianna noticed that she had the tiniest trace of some kind of accent. She was so enigmatic. So glamorous, even in a backpack and hiking boots. The kind of woman with fascinating secrets and an air of mystery.

The kind of woman Brianna would never be like.

Brianna felt Rollo's loving embrace come around her again. Who needed mystery when you had a man who loved you just the way you were? She snuggled against him and told the girl cheerfully, "We have cheese. No one can say no to cheese. Please stay."

Her face lit up with a brief, stunning smile. "Maybe for a short while."

Finn tried to help her off with her backpack, but she shot him a "back off" look and did it herself.

Brianna turned her attention back to the rest of the party. Hugs and toasts and champagne and so much happiness, it barely felt real. The afternoon faded into evening as everyone chatted and laughed and ate all the cheese.

Outside their six-sided plate-glass bubble, the fiery sun sank out of sight. When the world had turned the deep blue of almost night, Rollo whispered in her ear, "One more thing."

He turned off the overhead light inside the tower. A hush of anticipation came over the group.

"Everyone please turn your attention to the west-facing windows," Rollo announced. Suzanne caught Brianna's eye and winked. Evie tossed her a kiss. Merry's eyes brimmed with curiosity.

When they were all looking at the western windows and the darkness beyond, Rollo nodded to Sean. He reached for the dangling end of an electric cord Brianna hadn't noticed before. He plugged it in, and three of the windows lit up in a blaze of white twinkle lights. As they glowed against the purple twilight, she realized that they spelled something. Her eyes traced the little bulbs and she read aloud. "Rollo + Bri 4 Ever."

It was so romantic, so silly, so perfect.

Brianna clapped her hands in delight. "That's practically like graffiti!"

"Yes, more or less." Rollo surveyed the lights with an expression of deep satisfaction. All their friends were taking pictures of the lights, smiling and exclaiming at the magical effect. Her mother snapped one photo after another while her father beamed. "This is much better than graffiti, though. This..." He swept her into his arms and kissed her so deeply she forgot they were in a Fire Service lookout tower surrounded by their friends and family.

"This," he gestured with his head toward the brilliant chain of lights in the window, "is written in the stars."

ABOUT THE AUTHOR

Jennifer Bernard is a *USA Today* bestselling author of contemporary romance. Her books have been called "an irresistible reading experience" full of "quick wit and sizzling love scenes." A graduate of Harvard and former news promo producer, she left big city life in Los Angeles for true love in Alaska, where she now lives with her husband and stepdaughters. She still hasn't adjusted to the cold, so most often she can be found cuddling with her laptop and a cup of tea. No stranger to book success, she also writes erotic novellas under a naughty secret name that she's happy to share with the curious. You can learn more about Jennifer and her books at JenniferBernard.net.

ALSO BY JENNIFER BERNARD

Jupiter Point

Set the Night on Fire (Book 1)
Burn So Bright (Book 2)
Seeing Stars (Prequel)

The Bachelor Firemen of San Gabriel

The Fireman Who Loved Me
Hot for Fireman
Sex and the Single Fireman
How to Tame a Wild Fireman
Four Weddings and a Fireman
The Night Belongs to Fireman

One Fine Fireman
Desperately Seeking Fireman
It's a Wonderful Fireman

Love Between the Bases

All of Me
Caught By You
Getting Wound Up
Drive You Wild
Crushing It

Made in the USA
Lexington, KY
16 March 2017